UNBRIDLED VENGEANCE

OF GOLD & BLOOD
BOOK FIVE

Jenny Wheeler

ISBN 978-1-99-117254-9 (Large Print)
ISBN 978-0-473-49310-3 (Paperback)
ISBN 978-0-473-49311-0 (epub)
ISBN 978-0-473-49312-7 (Kindle)
ISBN 978-0-473-49314-1 (iBook)

OF GOLD & BLOOD SERIES

'Very rarely will anyone die for a righteous person, though for a good person someone might possibly dare to die.' Romans 5:7 — New International Version.

If you enjoy Unbridled Vengeance, get a FREE PREVIEW of Hope Redeemed, Book Six in the Of Gold & Blood series.

Details can be found at the end of Unbridled Vengeance.

Prologue

New Year's Eve, December 31 1869

As soon as he stepped into Rancho Del Oro's tiled courtyard, the smells of his childhood assailed him with a force that froze him where he stood. He could hear and smell it; the echo of the vaqueros' laughter as they stood around the oven pits out back; the aroma of old smoke and char-grilled beef. And the strangely comforting yeasty dampness of Fergus Stewart's deerhounds. His fingers twitched to stroke their smooth necks.

Rory Mackinnon had not been in this house since he was ten years old, but the memories still grabbed him by the throat. It had been a house of plenty: abundant food, overflowing laughter, brotherly love. And life after his father's breach with Fergus Stewart had been empty of all those things.

Maybe that was why he'd been dreaming of asking for Josefa's hand in marriage. And why he had such a keen sense of anticipation for this coming meeting with Caleb Stewart. Their fathers were long dead, the feud that erupted between them never reconciled. It was up to the next generation to make peace.

But something isn't right.

There was no sound of echoing footsteps on the tiled hallway. Just the click of restless paws on terracotta — it sounded as though Caleb's dogs were shut inside. He tried the handle and the door opened soundlessly.

He paused at the entry, called. "Caleb? Miguel?"

He halted again as the familiar velvety sense of comfort folded around him. The room looked just the same as it had the last time he'd been here: high-raftered, wood-paneled ceilings, a long communal dining table, empty except for a scattering of eating utensils and a pottle of dark violet flowers. The energy radiating from the red coals in the big fireplace that stretched along one adobe wall reached out to him from across the room. The wrought-iron screens set in place before the glowing coals indicated no one was home.

He strode across the main room to a door in the back corner, and gingerly opened it, hoping the dogs were friendly. Two handsome hounds — nearly as tall as miniature ponies — skittered across the room and stood by the door through which he'd just entered, ears flat against their heads, quivering to be let out. Fergus Stewart's deerhounds used to hunt for venison when elk and antelope were plentiful in the early years. It gave him a warm surge to see Caleb still had their offspring.

"You want to go out? I'm not sure that's such a good idea if no one's home."

He peered into the small study the dogs had vacated. Caleb wasn't sitting at the desk, but the room was not empty. A man lay sprawled face upward, his mouth stretched in painful rictus, a dark purple stain pooling onto the rug under him. The coppery smell of blood — Miguel's blood — rose in his nostrils, filling the room.

In two quick steps he squatted down

beside the old retainer's body, holding his wrist between forefinger and thumb, but he already knew he wouldn't feel the flicker of a pulse.

As he rose unsteadily, the front door opened. A gust of cold air whooshed in and the dogs' paws made a sand papery rustle on the tiles as they rushed out.

"Caleb? Is that you?"

Rory waited, hand on his gun belt. His throat was prickly, his chest so tight he could barely breathe.

He tensed as a shadow fell across the doorway, and a large male form loomed in the gap. It wasn't Caleb, but he knew the face. A second man shadowed the first.

"What the blazes are you doing here?" Rory's question sounded like a bark.

"Me? I'm here for our meeting of course," the man sneered. "What did you think I was here for?"

Rory glanced down. Miguel's blood was inching towards the toe of his right boot. He wrenched his foot away, and remembered he had a gun. *But hold it, man. Not yet . . . Not yet.*

"I understood I was meeting Caleb. No one else. Just Caleb."

"Caleb is otherwise engaged. We don't need him to complete our business anyway. This is all we need." The man pulled out a swatch of paper. "The sales agreement for two thirds of Del Oro."

Despite the heat from the fire, cold beads of sweat broke out on Rory's forehead. "Two thirds of Del Oro? Are you mad? Caleb will never agree to that."

The man eyed him coldly. "Caleb won't have any choice."

"What do you mean he won't have

any choice? He's the recognized owner."

"Ah yes, but your father staked a claim on behalf of his heirs before he died. You know that. And it's not difficult to revitalize that claim. All it takes is your signature."

Rory jerked back. "I'm not doing that. That's tantamount to fraud. It was all lies when my father first made the claim years ago, and nothing's changed since."

The second man, who'd been standing to one side like a silent black vulture, swooped. A cold metallic tube pressed against the side of Rory's head.

"You most certainly will, Mr. Mackinnon. We haven't come all this way to have you play hard to get."

1

"A toast! To our new neighbors, Caleb Martinez Stewart, his mother, the superb Doña Valentina, and all their family — Josefa, the twins, Lucas and Mateo, and all who roam the range at Rancho Del Oro!"

Sir John Russell clinked glasses with his roundly pregnant wife Pania, who'd remained seated beside him when the rest of the party stood to toast in the new year. "To our new partnership in wine."

The long oak table groaned with festive food: turkey pot pie, venison stew, candied sweet potatoes and half a dozen other dishes. The Russells might have an English cook, Caleb thought, but her food tasted as delicious as pretty much anything Rosario cooked at home.

Garrulous chatter ballooned around them again, and Sir John's Australian brother Nathan, who sat on Pania's right, chinked on his glass with a teaspoon to quieten the noise.

"Let me add my congratulations to you on this excellent vintage, dear brother. May the future wines that come from this valley" — he swiveled and dipped his glass in deference to the man standing next to him — "be as good as our New South Wales drop, thanks to this fine fellow." He raised his glass. "To Aristide Laurent, vintner extraordinaire."

Aristide laughed and shook his head. "Cheeky Australian."

Nathan grinned. "And to the Stewart family, whose willing provision of Rancho

Del Oro terroir makes this new venture possible."

The flames on the two silver candlesticks flickered from the expelled breath and movement as everyone sat down again and resumed eating and chattering.

In his straight-backed chair on the corner of the table next to Sir John, Caleb was overcome with a sudden shyness. He was a Johnny Hayseed alongside the international magnate, one of California's richest men, with interests in import and export, mining, railways and now real estate, agriculture and wine.

Granted, the Stewart family still owned five thousand acres of productive grazing land within easy reach of Sacramento's heart in J Street, rolling north to the banks of the smooth-flowing

American River. He was one of the few Californios who'd inherited a Spanish land grant from his father and held onto it. Not just kept it but kept it profitable — just. The golden years of free-roaming rancho beef were gone, and they needed new initiatives if the family was to continue to prosper. Which was why he'd sold part of the estate to Sir John.

He caught his mother's hawk-like gaze as he rose to respond. "Thank you for the very warm welcome, Sir John. We're overwhelmed." He took in Doña Valentina's ram-rod posture, the strongly arched eyebrows over intense dark brown eyes, and his attention moved past her to the rangy forms of his boisterous younger twin brothers, colts still growing into their legs and champing at the bit to get into the race. Across the table from them sat his black-haired, dark-eyed sister Josefa, so like his mother in her aristocratic beauty, but so unlike her in temperament.

"To Vino d'Oro. We all appreciate that the California my father and mother knew when they married is fast disappearing, and if the fifteen years since my father died have taught me anything, it is never to count on past successes. So a toast to the best partners we could wish for. To Sir John and Aristide . . . and Vino d'Oro."

The twins were fidgeting, Josefa's face had that dreamy, faraway light she so often took on these days, but his mother was right there with him. She gave him a barely perceptible nod of approval.

"Thank you for preserving the history of Del Oro by preserving the name."

He sank back into his chair and watched as the easy comfort of loving family life folded around him like a warm blanket. The decibels of gay laughter rose; wives and children, visitors and workers like Laurent and his sister Madeleine, all enveloped in a pleasant glow.

Opposite him an elfin-faced little girl with a mass of dark brown curls wriggled in her chair, set between Nathan and his stunning, singing-star wife Graysie Castellanos. The child gazed from one to the other as she chattered on in a joyful monologue, barely stopping for breath or pausing for answers. She looked to be about six years old.

"Wine is only for grown ups, isn't it, Uncle Nat? Children don't drink wine. And especially not babies, that's right isn't it, Sissy?" She turned her enchanting, freckled face towards Graysie. "My baby brother George definitely can't have wine, can he?" She giggled and helped herself to another ganache chocolate tart.

"What have you been up to, little imp?" Sir John's wife Pania leaned across and tickled her under her chin. "Did you help Mademoiselle Madeleine in the kitchen this afternoon?"

"I did. She let me help fill the tarts with chocolate. And I got to lick the spoon!"

She gave a deep sigh of pure pleasure and gazed adoringly at Madeleine, Aristide's school-teacher sister, a recent arrival from France. Madeleine flashed an answering smile. Pania followed the child's gaze with an amused raised eyebrow, and Madeleine laughed. "Minette did very well, Lady Russell. She spooned the chocolate filling into the pastry shells with hardly a spill. She shows definite promise as a chef."

Russell's striking New Zealand wife laughed. "Pania, please, Mademoiselle. We don't stand on ceremony here."

Caleb felt the stirrings of a deep-down envy, so unlike anything he'd experienced before. He held his breath, waiting for it to pass. It didn't. He shifted uneasily. Had anyone noticed how tense he was? He released his breath slowly and settled more deeply into his chair.

He'd been so consumed with ensuring the ranch's survival, he'd missed out on making a life for himself. His father's sudden death when he was fifteen, the onslaught of droughts and floods and bitter legal battles . . . A wife had been the last thing on his mind. Children? They were something for the future, when the ranch was secure, when his siblings were settled.

It came to him with the crashing of cymbals as he watched the loving, reciprocal interchange around him — Nathan Russell must be about the same age as him. And Aristide? He didn't appear to have a wife, but he radiated a confident intelligence, a man happy in his realm, plainly delighted to have his sister with him.

And the sister? She'd been introduced earlier, taken on as domestic manager for Aristide and the winery when the family weren't here, and as a part-time nanny when they were. She observed the proceedings with sparkling aquamarine eyes that he guessed recorded everything, answering inquiries with carefully crafted but flawless English, her sentences lit unexpectedly now and then by a brilliant smile.

He thought of the fractious Del Oro

household: the twenty-year-old twins in rebellion against him for trying to replace the father they'd never really known, Josefa resenting his attempts to protect her from her own headstrong willfulness because someone had to. He suddenly felt tired, and much older than his thirty years.

He glanced up. Madeleine Laurent was quietly observing him, feathery lines visible around sad eyes, as if the clouds had rolled in and covered the sun. They locked eyes for a long moment, and she gave a slight nod of acknowledgment before turning to answer a query from Josefa, who sat next to her.

"I love being here, Josefa. Just love it. Aristide is my only family left, you see. Mother died last year and my sister several years before that. I can't tell you how glad I was to find him."

She, too, was clearly fatigued. She looked older than she'd appeared moments before. Caleb had the queerest sensation — what did they say? — as if someone had walked over his grave. Like him, she felt that life had passed her by, he would swear it. Either that or he'd had too much wine. He shook his head to clear the crazy thoughts. The legs of his chair shrieked as he pushed back from the table with a decisiveness he hadn't been aware he felt a moment before, and thrust out his hand to start making his round of farewells. The family could stay till midnight and see in the new year. He had a business to attend to.

The waning crescent moon wasn't due to rise until after midnight, so Caleb's ride home was slower than usual. He was maintaining a steady gait on Nero to avoid breaking the black stallion's leg in a gopher hole, but he was a good half mile away from home when two things happened in eerie coincidence.

The moon's silver crescent nudged over the clear black line of the horizon, and two ghostly forms he couldn't fail to recognize came bounding out of the darkness. He didn't need a full moon to know the fluid strides of Jupiter and Venus, the deerhounds he'd left at home in Miguel's safe keeping.

They were benign creatures, but it was a bad breach of animal husbandry to allow them to wander at night. Only something catastrophic would have prevented Miguel from shutting them up in their quarters near the cooking pits before he went to bed.

His heart beat a warning tom-tom as he rode the avenue of evergreen oaks leading to the house. Nero had barely stopped before he slid from his saddle, roughly tethered him by the trough and thundered inside, the dogs hot on his heels.

He drew to a hasty stop on the doorstep, pulling out his revolver, cursing the lack of light. He opened the door a few inches and peered in, weapon raised. The big family room where they did most of their daily living was empty, but it smelled all wrong. The familiar aroma of rising bread and Doña Valentina's spicy perfume were overlaid with a heavy masculine presence: cigar smoke and sweat. And underneath it all, the unmistakable coppery tang of blood.

He pushed the door fully open and the dogs surged ahead of him, leading the way to the office nook where they spent much of the day sleeping. But when they got to the entryway, they pulled up sharply, their muzzles shuddering. Venus was whimpering; Jupiter stared back at him uncertainly. Both were reluctant to enter the room.

Gun raised, Caleb flattened himself along the wall and peered around the door jamb. Miguel lay spread-eagled on the rug, his kind, wrinkled face frozen in a heart-searing howl, the dark stain pooling around him the evidence that he'd bled out in the place which had been his refuge for most of his long life.

Caleb felt exactly like he had as a young teen when he'd been thrown from a horse and badly winded. Gut-punched. He lurched over, clutching his waist, struggling for breath at the same time as he was dry-heaving. His hands were icy, his neck clammy, and for a second or two he thought he might pass out in an intense wave of dizziness.

He clutched at the hard edge of the doorjamb, reminding himself the world was still upright, it was just him that was tilted off center. Slowly, as the big mantel clock ticked laboriously into the first hour of a new decade, he raised himself to his full height and spoke to the dogs.

"You were here, weren't you guys? You saw who did this." He shook his head and wiped away the first tears with the back of his hand. "If only you could talk."

He turned his back on Miguel's supine form and walked out on light feet, as if not to disturb his sleep, though he knew he was being a little batty. "Come on, now. We'll get you bedded down. You've had a nasty fright."

He worked his way to the back of the

house where the estate kitchens were situated. The kennels were out back here too, the dogs familiar with the routine: fed, then bed. The fact that they were still loose in the house when Miguel's attackers came told Caleb the killer or killers must have come early in the evening.

His mind was working overtime as he crossed the yard. Who would have any cause to kill Miguel — and why? The mestizo had been a faithful house manager for more than twenty years, since a bull charge crushed his hip and ended his days as a vaquero. His quiet wisdom and wiry strength had carried them through many a crisis over the years, never more so than after Caleb's father died. He'd lost so much more than a capable man — he'd lost a spiritual connection. Miguel could read nature. He was a man of prophetic voice and stunning premonitions. And yet somehow he'd failed to detect the danger closest to him.

Preoccupied with what he should do next — send a rider for the sheriff, go back to the Russell's to get his mother — he'd got halfway across the courtyard to the kennels when he noticed the dogs were hanging back, acting peculiar again, dragging their tails between their legs, shifty in their movements. It came to him in a rush that he should be more on his guard. Maybe the killer was still in the vicinity. Maybe they were waiting for someone to come home in the hope of better pickings.

He stopped and surveyed his surroundings, moving slowly in a semi-circle, examining every bump and shadow, the yard still poorly lit by the delicate curving moon barely over the horizon. Halfway through the circumference on his search he stopped. What was that thrown across one of the outdoor cooking pits? An unburned log? Some other rubbish? He didn't recall it being there earlier in the day. The men would have eaten here before going out to local grog houses. New Year's Eve was one of the few nights of the year that the ranch was left pretty much deserted.

A rising dizziness, like he'd experienced when he found Miguel, threatened to engulf him again. He turned and ran for the house.

I need a lantern. I might be being ridiculous, but I can't do this without one.

He quickly assembled and lit the lantern, and with the light in one hand and his gun in the other, he stalked across the yard like a man holding a lit fuse.

As he approached the oven pit, he raised the lantern to the full length of his arm to cast a strong, wide circle of light. He squeezed his eyes shut, willing himself to withstand whatever it was he was going to be forced to see.

When he opened them, the dogs began howling. Not just Jupiter and Venus, but all the dogs they had in the kennels alongside, howling as if it was a full moon.

It seemed like just the right response because splayed out before him on his back was the shirtless figure of a man, his bare chest burned with branding irons that carried the mark of Rancho Del Oro — the golden cup that overflowed with good things.

But not tonight. And not ever again for

this poor sod. Caleb wanted to stay rooted where he was, feet distant, but he knew he had to step closer, to see it all. He stepped right up to the edge of the pit and brought the lamp down low over the man's face. It was badly beaten. An eyebrow and lip split open, the lips set in a tortured expression that could have been a cry of pain and could have been a strange half smile.

"Noooo! Oh noooooo!"

He heard a low-pitched keening noise and knew there was no one else here. That noise was coming from him. He didn't need a second view to confirm who was lying there. Rory, his childhood "twin" and the man he suspected Josefa imagined as her *primer amor*, her first love. His gut cramped.

There'd been a bitter estrangement, threats to contest Rancho Del Oro ownership after Dougal Mackinnon's first wife died and he married again. Dougal had died last year, but Caleb and Rory hadn't spoken in more than a decade.

So what on earth had he been doing here? And who would want to kill him?

Caleb pulled himself upright, stiffened his backbone. Right now, he needed to get Rory's body inside, away from the night prowlers, the coyote scavengers. And then he had to get help.

"Are Miguel's people going to be all right for Monday?" Doña Valentina was pale and drawn, but her voice still rang with regal authority even when she was asking a question.

"There's really only Juan, his brother left, so yes. Other than Juan, it's us. Del Oro was Miguel's life, we all know that." Caleb picked at some cold meat slices that sat on the coffee table in front of him.

His eyes flicked to Josefa, who slumped in remote silence, arms folded across her chest, staring at the floor. They were in a small ante room in the Russell house, Josefa distanced in a chair set apart from the sofa where he and his mother sat. Her jaw flexed. She avoided eye contact with both of them.

"As for Rory, the county coroner will have to handle that. I don't know where Consuela is. She'll have to be the one to organize Rory's ending. Meantime the coroner will have him."

From her corner, Josefa jumped to her feet with a noise that could have been a hiss or a stifled sob, and glared at him, her face white and venomous.

Doña Valentina stood in alarm, matching her daughter's stance. She took one step toward her, then stopped. "I know it's been a shock, Josefa, but really, you must hold yourself together, my dear. It's a very long time since any of us had anything to do with that family. And the dreadful time they gave your father . . . It's a tragedy, I know, but it's not *our* tragedy."

Josefa jerked as if she'd been poked in the eye with a hot poker. "You don't know a thing about it!" She glared from her mother to Caleb. "You! You were going to meet him." Her furious control was dissolving into a wail. "How *could* you?"

"Meet him? What are you talking about?" Caleb's hands were blocks of ice. "I haven't seen or heard from him in nearly fifteen years."

"Liar! You're a total liar."

Doña Valentina took another step

forward. "Josefa, you're upset—"

Josefa whirled to face her mother, hands on her hips. "And you! You only care about Caleb. The golden boy who stepped in and saved the family. Well, I'm sick of it. Sick of you all!" She turned and fled from the room.

The muted sounds of teacups clinking on saucers, and snatches of subdued conversation floated in from down the hall, where the rest of the clan was engaged in a restrained New Year's Day brunch. An old clock ticked a loud steady beat on the mantel. The fire hissed.

Doña Valentina faltered. Her skin was gray and lined in the sunless day. "I don't know what's gotten into her, Caleb. What is she talking about?" She stared up at him, her eyes drawn and perplexed. "You meeting Rory? Where could she have got that idea?"

"I don't know. But she knows more than she's letting on, that's for sure. All those visits she's been making to Aunt Bonnie's lately . . ."

Bonaventura was Consuela's mother, and Valentina's cousin. His throat suddenly felt parched, and he took a sip of the tea that had been poured when they first sat down. It was lukewarm.

"I wonder if she's nursing some idea of a romance. You know, she's always had a soft spot for Rory. And she's been so vague and dreamy lately. I guess now we know the answer."

Doña Valentina's face darkened, her brows narrowed. "What? Surely she wouldn't be so disloyal? After the agony Consuela has caused us?"

"Rory didn't have anything to do with it, you know that. It was all Consuela. He can't help it if she's his stepmother."

It still burned. For his mother and, if he was honest, for him too. The spurious claim Dougal Mackinnon had made against Fergus and Del Oro, alleging that Dougal been an equal recipient in the land grant they'd worked together. Claimed he'd not been properly paid out. The discord began within months of Fergus marrying Consuela after the death of his first wife, and they'd always suspected she was the manipulator behind it.

"I accept that Rory had nothing to do with that sad business, but what was he thinking? Coming to our house when we weren't even there. It just doesn't make sense." Doña Valentina frowned and wiped her hands down her face.

Caleb took her by the elbow. "Well, we won't find the answers here. I need to get you home, Mother. We've a lot to do before Monday. Let's collect the boys and get going."

Getting away wasn't easy. The twins, all hollow legs and with no memory of Rory or his family, were wolfing down a hearty breakfast of bacon, eggs, sausages, Welsh rarebit, grilled potatoes and a selection of breads and jams. Even some rolled oats porridge and cream was laid out on the sideboard, in deference, Caleb guessed, to their Scots heritage. His queasy stomach wasn't ready for any of it.

"Doña Valentina, Caleb, do join us. Dreadful business, I know." John Russell guided Valentina to a chair next to Pania's. Graysie and Madeleine sat on the other side of the table, Graysie with her god-daughter Minette nestled in her lap, Madeleine with the baby George on her shoulder. They struggled valiantly at chit-chat about Paris fashion or, Caleb guessed, some other nonsense.

He gravitated to a seat next to Aristide and Nathan, catching Aristide mid-sentence. "They're damned pushy, I have to say." His blue-gray eyes flashed with annoyance. "And they've a very odd way of doing business." He acknowledged Caleb's presence, turning and clapping him on the shoulder. "Sorry to hear the news, mon frère. If there's anything we can do . . ."

Caleb sighed. "I think we've got it under control. I hope so — I've been up half the night getting the sheriff, the coroner, the undertaker involved. It was a huge shock, of course. But don't let me interrupt. We've done all that we can for now. Life must go on."

Nathan nodded. "Suppose so. Aristide was just telling me about these two agents who've been pestering him. They appear to be working for a number of San Francisco high rollers, stiff-arming their way into anything that appears to be making money, aiming at taking a cut. Sanctioned extortion is what I'd call it. Isn't that right, Aristide?"

The winemaker nodded. "Back home in Bordeaux some of the wine districts had cooperatives — all the growers sold to the same agency and the wine was made under a cooperative agreement — and it worked fine if the terms were fair and honest."

"You were part of that?" Caleb's eyes felt as if they had sand in them, but he tried to act interested.

Aristide grimaced. "These guys are pushing to set up the same sort of thing here, but as far as I can judge they're charging ridiculous fees and introducing some very sneaky sub-clauses. I've told Sir John not to touch them with a ten-foot pole. I think they're crooks." The vintner's gray eyes flashed angrily, and then he seemed to make a big effort to let go. He shrugged. "I shouldn't get too wound up about it, I suppose. You just say 'No', don't you? I don't know why I'm getting steamed up." He raised his glass. "To prosperous *sound* business."

Nathan grinned. "I can drink to that."

Caleb had a sudden thought. "Where did you say this pair are based? And who exactly do they represent?"

Aristide's answer was interrupted by a knock at the dining-room door. Madeleine was standing in the entry, her face chalky white. She looked nothing like the sanguine smiling woman at dinner last night. Her eyes searched out the pram, where she'd set down George before going to answer a knock at the door.

"Sir John, excusez-moi. There's two men here to see you. They would not accept you were already engaged."

A handsome man with military bearing strode in, brushing her aside with brusque impatience. He held a hat in one hand; his glossy black hair was echoed by a neatly trimmed black mustache; the cut of his jacket fitted perfectly around broad shoulders. He had the air of a man to be reckoned with.

He was followed in by a second fellow of stringy build. He was a head taller than the first, with a thin ginger fuzz above his top lip that was a poor excuse for a mustache. The leading man was confident and vocal, while the second stood to one side in surly silence.

"Sir John." He thrust his hand forward with assurance. "My word, you're a difficult man to get hold of. Gérard Le Blanc at your service. And this is Roland Durand, my assistant. We're agents for Buffer, Jones and Cottlesloe, a renowned San Francisco law firm, as I'm sure you're aware."

Sir John remained standing with his hands on the back of his chair, ignoring the outthrust hand. His black eyes flashed with irritation, and his jaw set, though he held himself in a controlled neutrality. "That may be, but we are in the middle of a private family gathering here, gentlemen. New Year's Day is not the time for business."

Le Blanc sallied on as though Sir John hadn't spoken. "The information we have at our disposal will be of immense benefit to your business interests, make no mistake, Sir John. And you've been impossible to reach." He emphasized "impossible" with a slightly French lilt and raised one eyebrow theatrically as he did.

The inappropriateness of it all — interrupting a family brunch on New Year's Day, the forced familiarity with a man they'd never met, even though they wouldn't realize the unusual circumstances of last night's deaths . . . Caleb held his breath and watched to see how Sir John would respond.

He's been told the knighthood Sir John inherited had originally been bestowed on a forebear — his father or grandfather, he wasn't sure — a sea captain who'd been honored by a young Queen Victoria when he rescued a British diplomat from certain death at the hands of rioting townsmen during one of the Opium Wars. Watching Sir John's implacable face as he stared down the intruder, Caleb could quite believe the same ice-cold resolve ran in his veins. No wonder behind his back they called him the Black Knight. His hawkish eyes were two points of icy shards.

"Mr. Le Blanc, I am quite certain we have never met before, and nor will we be meeting today. I really wouldn't care if you were an envoy from the Archangel Gabriel. Now is not the time, nor the place."

Le Blanc cast his gaze around the room, hardly discouraged from his original intention by Russell's blunt refusal. "Ah, Mr. Laurent. There you are." He swiveled back to Sir John. "Mr. Laurent and I have had a number of meetings discussing your affairs here at the winery, and I'm confident I have some very attractive proposals to lay before you."

Aristide jumped up, his face dark. "I protest! That's a blatant misrepresentation."

Sir John raised a placating hand, almost as if conferring a benediction. "Don't worry, Aristide, I see how the land lies. Will you be kind enough to show these gentlemen out?" He turned to Le Blanc. "Mr. Le Blanc, I am confident I will not be in the least interested in anything you might have to offer me. Now please, be on your way."

Le Blanc settled a strangely venomous look on Madeleine, who had moved to stand protectively beside George's pram. He then braced his shoulders, bowed to the room and followed Aristide out.

A shocked silence followed. Graysie

had drawn Minette against her chest during the exchange and was stroking her head soothingly. She shot Sir John a grateful smile, and the quiet hum of chatter rose again.

Sir John's shoulders relaxed forward and he gave a wry grin. "Well, that was a bit of a rum old scene, wasn't it? See how these sharks work?"

He turned to Caleb, black brows raised in mock innocence, and Caleb chuckled in response. Aristide returned, carrying with him an anxious nettled air, and the conversation drifted onto other things, but Caleb wasn't really listening. He was watching Madeleine. She had sunk into a chair beside George with a despairing sigh. She caught his eye and lifted her shoulders, smiling. But if she was striving to play her bright animated self, she was failing miserably, Caleb thought.

Deep lines had formed around her eyes. She had the distracted air of someone whose mind was miles away. The tilt of her head was tense, her eyes wary. She shrugged wordlessly as if to mime "What? It's nothing."

He made his way around the table and sank into the empty chair beside her. "Are you all right, Mme. Laurent? You're very pale." *Pale except for the dark rings under your eyes.*

"Perfectly fine, thank you, Mr. Stewart. Just a little tired." Her voice was breathy, clipped, and drained of the joie de vivre that had been so evident earlier. She rose abruptly, gathering her skirts around her. "I am sorry, but I really do need to be excused. I didn't sleep well. I'm afraid I've quite run out of steam."

She gave him an apologetic smile and

moved smoothly toward Graysie. Caleb watched as she offered to take Minette off to amuse her.

"I'll read her a story or she can play with the doll's house."

Graysie shook her head and hugged the child closer to her, saying, "Don't worry, I'd like to keep her with me today. I'll look after it."

She kissed the top of her head as if bestowing protection.

Madeleine moved to the hall, aquamarine eyes flicking in Caleb's direction as she left the room.

He sat, absorbing the charged uncertainty that lingered on from Le Blanc's intrusion. Madeleine Laurent had sustained a shock that had quite knocked her off her perch, and he'd hazard a guess it was related to the French visitors.

He had an uneasy sense of unfinished business. Who was this Le Blanc, and where was he last night? The unwelcome image of Rory's raw branded chest, of Miguel's tortured face, rose before him. If the Frenchman had anything to do with their deaths, then he was the very devil. And if Le Blanc *was* responsible, he, Caleb Stewart, was going to see that he swung for it.

Nathan Russell gazed at his wife's back as she sat at the dressing table brushing her hair in rhythmic strokes, her gaze fixed on the mirror in front of her.

"What do you mean, you've seen Minette's father? When? I thought you said he had no interest in the child."

The lamplight caught the glint of red in her gold hair, and the brush crackled with energy as she drew it across her scalp in a steady rhythm. She was avoiding answering him, even though his breath misted her mirror as he leaned in to kiss the back of her neck.

She still didn't turn to face him when he sat at the end of their bed, but her emerald eyes flickered back at him through the glass. Her voice was low and slow, the intonation flat and bored, but he wasn't fooled.

"This morning. He was one of those dreadful men who disrupted breakfast."

Nathan fell back on his elbows. The bed was soft and welcoming. "You've known this since breakfast, and you're only mentioning it now?" His tone came out sharper that he intended, but it beggared belief that she would have kept something like this from him for even an hour. "Didn't you think I might have liked to have known sooner? Like immediately?"

She turned to him then, her face crumpled in anxious lines, all pretense gone. "Oh, Nathan, I know you adore her. You're the only father she's ever known. Of course you have a right. But I got such a shock. It's taken me all afternoon to get to grips . . ."

She got up from the stool and joined him on the end of the bed, clasping his hand in hers, her arm warm on his thigh. "At first I was so shocked I couldn't believe my eyes. I only met him a few times. He disappeared from Francine's life about the time Minette was born. He was never home, always out gambling. But it was definitely him. I had time to study him while all the other palaver was going on."

"Do you think he remembered you?"

"I'm really not sure. Probably not. He gave no sign of it. Didn't even look at me as far as I could tell."

"And Minette?"

"She'd have no idea. As I say, he disappeared around the time she was born."

Nathan drew his arm consolingly around Graysie's shoulder. "You'll get cold out here. Let's get into bed."

They drew the quilt up around them and sat side by side, knees up, backs braced on the headboard, strangely silent.

They had been married for nearly two years. Their adored baby son George slept peacefully in a bassinet next door, but they were already a family before George made it four. Graysie had given up a rising singing career to fulfil a vow she made to her best friend to care for the tot when her mother died in a gambling hall fire. Nathan had fallen under Minette's spell at their first meeting — certainly long before he fell in love with her feisty guardian.

"She's our darling girl," he mused, stroking Graysie's arm as he thought back over all the precious moments they'd shared, recalled the squirming, surprising solidity of her cuddly little body, smelling of fresh peaches, snuggled up listening to one of Graysie's bedtime lullabies. "I won't let anything happen to her."

Graysie gave him a light kiss on the cheek. "I know, darling. Nor me, either. We just have to work out how we are going to manage this situation."

"If he doesn't know who Minette is already, is it inevitable he will find out?" Nathan asked. "And if he does, how is he likely to try and use that information? Blackmail? Extortion? What?"

The violet-flecked eyes he'd always

found so disconcertingly honest turned on him. "It's clear he doesn't care one whit about his daughter. But he's certain to try and use her to his advantage if — when — he realizes we're vulnerable." She sighed. "I've spent all afternoon trying to think how best we can protect Minette. But I've come to the reluctant conclusion I really don't have a clue what to expect next."

Madeleine Laurent lay in a fetal curl, her knees up to her chest, swallowing down hard on her stomach's churning bilious waves. She squeezed her eyes tight, hoping she could banish the calamity of Philippe Coubert's reappearance. She wanted to make him vanish in the same way Aladdin had conjured something up, in a puff of smoke.

Because that's who he was. Philippe

Coubert. Not Gérard whoever. Philippe Coubert. The man she'd once been married to and who she'd long believed was dead.

She smiled grimly. How did the old proverb go? *"De court plaisir, long repentir."* Short pleasure, long repentance. Clever Englishmen from Shakespeare to Lord Byron had stolen that phrase, turned it into something more colorful: "Marry in haste, repent at leisure." And she was surely going to be counting the cost of those ill-fated nuptials for even longer than she'd thought.

When Coubert ran out on her eight years ago, she never expected to lay eyes on him again. Rumor had it he'd fled to the Americas. North, south, east, or west, she hadn't known where and she didn't care.

In the years since, she'd not heard one word from him and had long imagined — hoped, even — that he'd died of tropical fever or from an infected monkey bite, drowned at sea, or been eaten by alligators. She smiled grimly. There were so many ways he could have died.

She supposed she shouldn't have been surprised he'd lived on under a different name. After all, he was wanted for murder.

She hugged herself for a comfort she failed to find and recalled the day her twice-widowed mother had made her heartfelt appeal, not long after she'd returned home from a teaching job in another town: "Don't be like Francine, please, Madeleine, chasing after love. You're my sensible daughter. You're my only hope."

Her younger sister Francine had eloped at eighteen with the dashing son of a famous circus family and vanished from their lives.

Madeleine had told herself that marriage was a contract, that the idea of romance was a troubadour's fable, that two mature people with good intentions had every chance of creating a civil and stable union. There was evidence for that all around her, wasn't there?

So when Philippe Coubert, the powerful and handsome controller of the local wine cooperative, offered for her hand, she'd considered herself fortunate. He was strong, articulate, attractive . . . So what if they weren't exactly *tombé amoureux*?

What she hadn't anticipated was the sadistic, jealous bully he turned into almost as soon as he put a ring on her finger. She was grateful they'd never conceived a child during the months they were together, although having a prospering family had once been one of her most cherished dreams.

When he brutally murdered a man who was challenging him for the leadership of the wine cooperative and had to flee, she'd refused to accompany him. She wasn't going to be a fugitive for life, tethered to an abusive husband. She'd carried on, the spinster schoolteacher, caring for her aged and ailing mother. Marrying again was out of the question: she wasn't divorced, she had no death certificate to prove widowhood and no money to fund an annulment. She'd reverted to her maiden name of Laurent, but she knew in the eyes of the village she would always be "the murderer's wife."

The faint keening cry of a coyote pierced her misery, and she clenched her jaw to hold back the tears. She didn't deserve the luxury of crying. She'd so hoped this sojourn in California might be a new beginning, and her reunion with Aristide had been so promising. She loved being able to "play house" for him and the Russell clan, even if it was all just temporary. It had been so long since she had any sense of being part of a wider family.

Now she dreaded what the morning would bring. Phillipe would not let any advantage slip away. She'd brought the taint of being "the murderer's wife" into her brother's house, and she was terrified where it was going to end.

Madeleine was standing in the midst of the noisy passion of a Hispanic funeral, but she was a world apart, a reticent figure in a sea of color and movement. Caleb had caught glimpses of her over the afternoon, as the Rancho Del Oro crew and residents from miles around gathered to farewell Miguel. The priest had intoned his last blessing, and Miguel's remains were consigned to a small graveyard on a hill at the back of the house alongside his father and others who'd died in the family's service.

Now they crowded around courtyard tables laden with chargrilled beef — nothing ever happened at Del Oro without beef on the table; trays of *pastelillos*, savory pastries filled with minced beef and cheese; and baskets of sweet *pan dulce* chocolate bread. The smell of roasted beef and chocolate, the zing of marigold petals sprinkled in a fragrant trail along the table, the rattle of castanets and twang of the guitars — it was a carnival of celebration that would have delighted Miguel's heart. Caleb felt a surge of warmth that momentarily swept away his sadness. It was their way — an overflowing of love and anguish at the loss of a loved one — and Caleb had always loved the freedom of expression that came with his mother's Spanish roots. They didn't avoid disaster, they embraced it.

He surveyed the crowd, reluctant to acknowledge he was searching her out. She stood, her back turned away from all the activity, staring out to the mounded grave in the bare brown landscape, her shoulders tense and hunched. He picked up a filled glass from the table and sidled over to her. He spoke in a low voice so as not to startle her. "Your first Californio funeral? It's all a bit much to take in if

you've never experienced one before."
Her eyes fluttered nervously, her
expression guarded.

He thrust the glass he held towards
her. "Here. You look like you need this."

After a moment's hesitation, she
reached out, took it between stiff fingers.
"What is it?"

"Iced cinnamon water. An old favorite
from the friars. They used it as a health
remedy."

"Thank you." She took a cautious sip.
"Very nice."

The guitars were rising in volume and
speed as a popular ballad about bandits
and their darlings drew to a close.
"Come, I want to show you something."
Caleb gently nudged her elbow and led
the way to the temporary altar that had
been erected just outside the cemetery
fence, the hastily constructed wooden

archway garlanded with unhusked corn cobs, oranges and brightly colored paper flags. Small vases held incense and marigolds.

He gestured toward it. "Had to bring those in from out of town. Nothing much grows in the garden at this time of year." The flat shelf below the archway was piled with plates of sweets and steaming drinks infused with the fragrances of coffee, chocolate and cinnamon. A set of brightly colored maracas and a pack of playing cards sat beside them. "We believe sweet smells guide the spirit home, so hopefully old Miguel is in safe hands."

She gazed around her, clutching the cinnamon water in both hands. "The emotion is certainly striking for someone from France — even from the south of France. We aren't that far from Spain, but I'm ashamed to say that even as a schoolteacher I really had no idea."

He could see she was making a valiant attempt to play along, to be convivial, but he sensed despair underlying her forced smile. He thought back to the night when he first met her, and how he'd once before caught a glimpse of the same tired hopelessness.

"We've given him the very best farewell we know how. He'll be delighted to be sharing the same ground as my father. He would have walked over fiery coals for him. And when father died, his sole purpose in life was to serve and protect my mother." He shrugged. "We still don't know what happened here, but I am sure Miguel died trying to protect our home."

Madeleine Laurent shot him a wistful smile. "I'm sure you're right. And you don't see that so much these days — at least not in my experience." She stood for a moment or two as if uncertain what to say next, and then bent again to her drink.

Her finely curved lips lightly brushed the glass, and once again that fleeting sense of promise and possibility he'd experienced the night he first saw her gripped him. This woman had the power to affect him in ways he'd never known in any other, without even being aware she was doing it. A shiver of anticipation ran through him, though he could not say anticipation for what.

"I suppose you're right there. It hurts that we still have no idea who killed him, or why."

She set aside the glass and regarded him steadily. "Yes. I quite understand. It's upsetting not to see justice done.

But the sheriff is still investigating, oui? He may find something."

Caleb shrugged. "I can't help wondering if those men who turned up at Sir John's had something to do with it. I'd like to know a lot more about where they'd been and what they were doing."

Her eyes flickered and she reached for the empty glass. Her long and slender fingers gripped it so hard her knuckles turned white. "Those men?" she whispered. "But they were just knaves and scoundrels, surely?"

"I don't know what they were, Miss Laurent."

Her face had drained of color, highlighting further the dark shadows under her eyes.

"Knaves and scoundrels. But not murderers. Is that what you think?"

She abruptly set the glass down again

and stared at the ground for a few seconds before meeting him with a resolute gaze. "Me? How could I possibly know?" The uncertain echo in her voice did not reflect the staunch expression on her face.

Caleb shrugged. "Forgive me, but maybe because they are your countrymen? Because you know more about them than you're willing to disclose?"

She gasped and jerked her head wildly around the courtyard, as if seeking an escape. "Why would you say that, Mr. Stewart? I've only been in California three months. I know no one!"

"I was watching you when they disturbed us, Miss Laurent. It seemed to me you were upset about something. Perhaps more accurately, in shock. Your reaction seemed to be more extreme than warranted by the intrusion of some inconvenient 'knaves', as you call them."

They stared into each other's eyes for a few moments, neither willing to back down. Then Madeleine took a decisive step back and assumed a regal posture. "I really have no idea what you are talking about, Mr. Stewart. Now if you will excuse me, I must get back to my brother."

As he watched her erect form disappearing into the crowd, the thrumming of the guitars seemed to grow louder, matching a throbbing in his head he'd only just become aware of. So much for any fleeting attraction he might have imagined with Miss Laurent.

He'd struck out there, but he wasn't going to let her stonewalling deflect him from the truth. He had an intuition about those men, and he'd learned to trust himself when it came to that kind of insight. Two men he valued had died, and he was not about to let this go. First thing tomorrow he would see what Aristide could tell him about the French knaves.

2

"We've got to make sure that woman shuts up." Gérard Le Blanc stared moodily out of the American Fork House windows to the busy scene outside. The bustling stagecoach stop and Pony Express station ten miles north of Sacramento, the state capital, was an essential stopping point for miners and visitors on their way to the northern mines.

Roland Durand sat across from him as they mulled over the disastrous encounter two nights ago. He fiddled with the handle of his beer mug and scowled.

"So," Le Blanc resumed. "That means we'll have to make another visit to the

Russell establishment." He tapped stiff fingers in a tense beat on the edge of the bar room table. "It's unfortunate, but it can't be helped."

Roland screwed up his face in distaste. "I've no intention of swinging for her. If you need to get rid of her, then do it. But as far as I'm concerned, it's personal to you, it's not business." He bent his head to the mug of beer in front of him, foam dribbling down the sides of the receptacle onto the table. He slurped at the ceramic edge and wiped away the residue of white froth from his upper lip with the back of his hand. "You're sure she recognized you?"

"She recognized me. And it's business if it affects the deal we have with the San Francisco barons." Le Blanc leaned back in his chair and stared out over the busy highway with unseeing eyes. She knew him. Even with his newly grown mustache, how could she not? She'd been married to him for six — or was it eight? — months.

Madeleine. He'd forgotten what a good-looking woman she was. More than good-looking. A rose in full bloom. She didn't appear to have wasted any time crying over him.

He picked up his beer. Two of the half-dozen stages that made the daily trip from Sacramento up into the Sierra Nevada mining towns were pulled up outside the bar, in the process of refueling passengers and horses. Ten Mile Station did an equally good job of watering the two- and four-legged creatures that passed by. The dining room could feed a hundred diners; extensive corrals catered for a hundred or more horses.

He and Roland had been staying at the hostelry ever since Sir John Russell had tossed them out of the winery two days ago, but they hadn't been idle. They'd already located several more landowners who were up to their ears in debt and wouldn't be able to hold the bailiffs off for much longer. Their debtors would soon be foreclosing. Just the ideal time for Buffer, Jones and Cottlesloe, or their agents, to step in and offer to "rescue" them, promising they'd arrange it so they could stay on the land — with a percentage of the land turned over to the law firm as the fee, of course.

Depending on the circumstances, they presented different offers. A joint venture, perhaps. It wasn't their fault if the landowner wouldn't be able to meet the repayments and would forfeit the land within a few years. And then there was Russell's wine operation. It was imperative he roped Vino d'Oro into the wine collective his San Francisco partners were intent on setting up. Catching a big fish like Russell in his net would make it a lot easier to coerce the smaller fry.

"There's plenty of rich pickings here. We don't need to be moving on just yet," Gérard said. "There's no way they can place us anywhere near Rancho Del Oro last Friday night. None at all."

His neck prickled. He reached up and rubbed at it irritably. In his mind's eye he saw Caleb Stewart as he'd been the other morning, alert and dangerous, his rancher's long-sighted gaze raking the room, missing nothing. Particularly his wife's every move — he'd picked that up as soon as he'd entered the room. Bile burned the back of his throat. He would never forget the humiliation as she betrayed him to the local gendarme, her eyes shimmering in relief. She was glad to have escaped his clutches. He'd been double-crossed, good and proper.

He turned his attention back to Roland. "I knew the woman in France. She knew me all right. However, I don't think she'll want too many people to know about our connection. Particularly not Caleb Stewart." He curled his lip in contempt. "I'm certain she'll be very keen her employers don't know about that little bit of her past. Maybe she hasn't even told her brother."

She might be ashamed to admit what happened. A man can hope.

Roland wiped his mouth clear of froth again. "You're saying she's worth more to us alive than dead?"

Le Blanc allowed himself a slow smile and nodded. "We don't have to kill her.

Come to think of it, wouldn't she just make the sweetest little spy. You never know, she might have already found her way into Stewart's bed."

He'd hazard a guess she'd do anything to save her brother and that rancher honcho. *Anything at all.* Stewart hadn't got a clue what was coming. Once he realized his whole ranch was up for grabs in the Land Claims Court, he'd forget about everything else. Especially finding the killer of the traitor who'd put in the claim.

Another coach was unloading, the staff hustling to serve the new arrivals. He leaned back in his chair with a satisfied grunt. They were in the right place at the right time, and they were going to make their fortunes.

He ignored his sour-faced companion, concentrating on his beer, enjoying the moment. The click of cues hitting balls at the saloon tables, the occasional roar of excitement or despair from men huddled around card games, all punctuated by the yeasty smell of hops and char-grilled meat from the kitchens. Coming to California was the best move he'd ever made.

"We've got a lot of very influential contacts in San Francisco." Durand was still staring down into his mug. "I might be even getting to meet that Senator next time I'm in town."

The place was infused with an electric energy he'd never felt back in France. He cleared his throat. "Are you listening?" It irritated him that he'd been the one to set up all the contacts. Durand was useful as a muscle man who knew his way around the mountains, but he was really just a hanger-on, a drifter down on his luck at the poker tables. *Not like me.*

He nudged him for a response. Durand's surly expression was modified by a raised eyebrow. "If you say so."

"I do. With the bad luck and the high living of the Californios, well, let's just say they're riding their bucking broncos into the gutter. In a few more years they won't have anything left." He rubbed his hands together gleefully, as if he could already feel the wads of cash he would flick between thumb and forefinger.

"A couple more for the road, and then we'll go take care of the woman. She won't be expecting us after dark . . . And there's no moon. Perfect for a midnight call."

Caleb found Aristide in the cool Vino d'Oro cellars, whose walls were lined with oak barrels to twice the height of an average man. It was ten o'clock in the morning, the glass and spittoon at Aristide's elbow evidence he was in the midst of a tasting.

"You're at it early."

The Frenchman set down his glass and greeted him with twinkling blue-gray eyes and a cheerful smile. "Ah, goes with the territory! Just testing the latest Zinfandel." His face sobered. "Wonderful send off for Miguel yesterday. You did him proud. But what brings you out so early?"

"We didn't have a chance to talk yesterday, and there's information I'm keen to find out." The dim hall was deserted, but Caleb knew he was interrupting Aristide's work. "Have you got a minute? Can we talk?"

"Sure." Aristide ushered him to a bare wooden bench at the end of a barrel row and sat down. "Happy to help if I can." He rubbed his hands together as if to warm himself to the task. "I'm not sure I know anything that will be of interest but try me."

Caleb shifted uneasily on the hard, wooden bench. "Those two characters who called here on Saturday — New Year's Day. Who are they, and how long have you known them?"

Aristide cleared his throat and ran a hand through the short dark beard that followed his clean jawline. "They've turned up here twice before, trying to get us interested in joining that cooperative I mentioned the other night. I gathered it was something some *gros bonnets* — you know, bigwigs." Aristide looked up, uncertain if Caleb was following him. "They are pushing it."

Caleb nodded encouragingly. "Yep, I

get it. The San Francisco set. Go on."

"Oui. Similar to what they do in Bordeaux. Except there it was all controlled by locals. Here it's more *les gros fromages* — the big cheeses — muscling in." He stroked his chin again. "In Bordeaux the growers had a big say in the decision-making. But this seems to be run by rich men and lawyers. I'm not keen on the idea and neither is Sir John. It sounds too much like they're trying to corner the market. And also you lose the chance to build your own house, you know, like Cliquot in Champagne."

Caleb grinned. "Wow! You've got big ideas for Vino d'Oro?"

Aristide gave a Gallic shrug. "Bien sûr. Naturellement." He sighed. "But that Le Blanc doesn't like to take no for an answer."

Caleb stood and took a few steps

away from the bench, flexing his hands at his sides as he walked. "What did you make of them?" He fixed his gaze on Aristide's face.

Aristide's brow furrowed. "In what way?"

"Well, did they strike you as capable of murder?"

Aristide's head jerked back. "Murder?" The first syllable with drawn out and emphasized, as if the very idea seemed too shocking to contemplate. His hands widened in a gesture of disbelief. "Really, Caleb? You're serious? They weren't particularly likeable — or honest, I'd wager. But cold-blooded killers? I've no reason to think that."

He gazed out into the cellar, staring at nothing for a long moment. "Rory Mackinnon did a bit of work for us here over the last few months. Did you know that? He appeared on the scene seeking work around harvest time in October. We haven't had much for him lately because of the winter. He seemed *le bon gars* — a good guy. But I gather you've had your problems?"

Caleb's shoulders tightened, and he shrugged to ease the tension. "Our fathers worked Del Oro together in the early days, and Rory and I were like brothers. But that all ended when Rory's mother died and his father, Dougal, took up with Consuela. She's a viper. Much younger than him. She had the old man dancing to her merry tune. My father bought him out to get rid of them. He had no obligation to give him anything, but he was trying to be decent." He pinched the bridge of his nose. "Consuela's never been satisfied, though. Before my father died, Dougal put in a claim of fraud against us. Stated he hadn't been fully paid out, that money was still owing him. The court finally tossed it out last year. Both the old men were dead by then, but it's been an awful business."

Aristide nodded. "I heard the talk." He stood and ambled over to where Caleb stood, still flexing his hands in a tense dance. "Let me give you a bit of a tour while we talk. Now the partnership with Sir John is settled, you'll have a financial interest in it all, won't you?"

They wandered out of the building and into the field next door, where bare-branched vines stretched in long, straight rows. As they strolled, Aristide explained the details of winter pruning and the coming bud burst. "This'll all be fresh green by next month. There's a lot of difference from how we did it in

France, but I love it here. I'm confident we'll make some very good wine." He grinned up at Caleb, who was struck again by his steady good humor. "I'm sure you've heard of the good reviews some local wines have been getting? The whites Charles Krug is making for example? They're 'light, clear, brilliant and very superior indeed', according to *California Farmer* magazine. Of course, Krug is a Prussian. We Frenchmen do it much better." He laughed. "We're very lucky to have Sir John's backing. And the time is right."

Their loop of the new planting completed, they paused on the doorstep. Aristide took Caleb's elbow. "I think it's time for morning coffee. Why don't we go in and get some?"

Madeleine was silent as she served them and disappeared again like a sylph.

Her eyes never met Caleb's.

Aristide and Caleb were standing to say their farewells when the vintner halted halfway to the door, a frown on his face. The sense of warm camaraderie that had developed between them over the last hour momentarily faded. "You know, Caleb, something's been bothering me for the last few days. I didn't think anything of it before, but now I'm not so sure." He ushered him down the hall and into the courtyard where Caleb's horse stood. At the hitching rail he frowned and turned to face him. "On one of the occasions when those agents came, Rory was in the packing shed getting a shipment of table grapes ready for market. I got the distinct impression he'd met them before. It was just something about the way he acted. He seemed ill at ease. He didn't say anything, it was just an impression." Aristide stroked his chin reflectively. "Rory wasn't mixed up in that land claim of yours? I thought you said not. But I definitely got the impression he'd met Le Blanc before."

Caleb's heartbeat accelerated. His fists clenched again, and then he remembered where he was, what he was doing, and shook his head. He wasn't in court now. He opened his palms and let his hands fall. "You know, Aristide, one of my biggest regrets is that I didn't make things up with Rory before he died. I heard he was back in the area. I suspected my sister might have met up with him at our aunt's house, but I couldn't stomach seeing him with the court case still so raw. It cost us a lot of heartache and money to get it thrown out." He shook his head. "I honestly don't think Rory was involved. It was all Consuela's doing. I'm sure of it."

He pulled on his gloves ready for the ride home. "I did have a hunch of my own, though, that I'd like to ask you about." He fiddled with his glove hem, pulling it tighter, suddenly nervous at the thought of broaching the subject of Madeleine's possible involvement. He took a deep breath. "Have you any reason to believe that your sister knows those men? I got the distinct impression the other night that she did."

Aristide's usually open face shut down. His brows drew close, and his jaw tightened. "Madeleine? So help me God, I doubt it. Apart from the fact that they are French, they wouldn't have anything else in common. Why do you think this?"

Caleb shrugged. "I don't know. It might be nothing. But I was watching her

85

that night. She wasn't acting normally. I know it was an upset, the way they barged in, but she was in shock. I'm certain of it. It was more than reacting to an unpleasant interruption. She was frightened of something. I don't mean to cast doubts on her integrity—"

"Her integrity?" Aristide's smile was tight, his eyes wintry. "*Merde*! I don't believe it." He fixed Caleb with eyes that had turned from blue-gray to dark charcoal. "Madeleine is one of the most trustworthy women I know. She's incapable of doing anything underhand. I'm shocked you'd even suggest it. *C'est incroyable*."

The quivering in Caleb's stomach that had been there all morning was replaced by a fiery certainty. "I'm sorry if you don't like it, Aristide, but something is going on there. And if you've got Vino d'Oro's best interests at heart, you'll find out what it is." He turned on his heel and strode out.

Gérard Le Blanc waited under a dark tree canopy, stamping his feet to warm his frozen toes. He'd worn his thickest leather boots, but they didn't offer protection from the freezing night. It was past ten o'clock, an hour past the time he'd insisted they meet, and Madeleine still hadn't shown up. Every time he opened his mouth his front teeth spiked with pain from the cold air.

He'd made certain she received the letter he'd sent her, hand-delivered for a small fee by one of the patent medicine salespeople who circulated the county selling miracle cures and wrinkle creams. So he expected her to show, was surprised that she hadn't, but he had also not forgotten how treacherous she could be. His mind flicked back to a blue-sky spring day in Bordeaux, bees buzzing in the vines, the ancient aphrodisiac grape flower fragrance hanging heavy in the air, and a man lying dead at his feet. That would have been the end of it, if it wasn't for the meddling little bitch.

She set him up good and proper. And then she stayed behind with her damned invalid mother when he'd been forced to flee France. Said she had to look after those she loved. *Plainly I hadn't been one of them.*

He scowled into the scarf wrapped around his neck. She might not care about him, but her avowed love for her family would play right into his hands this time. She wouldn't want anything to happen to her precious brother. He rubbed his gloved hands together.

What a stroke of luck discovering her brother!

He supposed the old duck back in France was dead or Madeleine wouldn't be here. He'd certainly never expected to see her again.

But now that she's here . . .

He recalled the willowy body, the slender, elegant grace of her long stride — and wondered what was to stop him picking up and starting over again. After all, they were still married, weren't they? And she was still an enticing woman.

He kicked at the canvas bag at his feet, the satisfying metallic clunk that came from inside sending a fizz of excitement up his legs and through his body. He would get this business done with Madeleine, and then he'd find himself a decent bed. Staking out the Russell place had been a damned pain.

The combined estate — ranch and vineyard — stretched for miles, with no hotel nearby. He'd been forced to bed down in a stable up the road — the second night in a row he'd be sleeping rough, and he'd had it.

He stamped his feet irritably. *Come on, woman! You might think we're done, but you've no idea.*

When he and Roland returned from Ten Mile Station two nights ago, he'd thought it would be simple to winkle Madeleine out of the place without attracting attention, but it hadn't been easy at all. It soon became evident she and the rest were well-guarded.

He'd had to rethink his tactics and enlisted the snake oil salesman's help. He'd left Roland behind while he made this rendezvous tonight. His sideman didn't need to know any more than he already did about what had gone on between him and Madeleine. *Not yet. anyway.*

The minutes ticked on, and still she didn't show. A hollow uncertainty leaked into his core as he considered what that meant. He'd threatened dire consequences for her brother if she didn't respond and had been sure that would frighten her into submission. Had he got it all wrong? Had she changed that much over the eight years they'd been apart?

Just as he was seriously questioning whether this had been the right approach, he saw the gate that closed off the house courtyard open and a slim figure slip through it and peer up the driveway. Good. At least she'd taken him seriously. He wouldn't have to kill anyone else yet, just to make the point.

Madeleine couldn't believe she was so

stupid as to do this — meet up with her murdering ex-husband! If he and that cold-eyed agent Durand hadn't threatened Aristide, she wouldn't be here.

She shivered as she considered the driveway. It was very dark, and she couldn't make out anything except black tree boles and dark shadows. She moved cautiously forward, keeping close to the tree cover, seeking anonymity in the darkness, her eyes raking the dim light for any sign of Phillipe.

Sorry, "Gérard."

What a farce. And why the new name? She wondered what new misbehavior had required a name change. Maybe he was just being super-cautious about being recognized by someone who might know him from the old days.

There was a man-made pond halfway

down the driveway, set up as part of the vineyard irrigation network. That's where he'd said he'd be waiting, but as she neared the spot, it appeared deserted. She came to a halt, peering into the dark, when a twig cracked behind her and a broad hand reached across her face and wrenched her mouth tight shut. She was enveloped in the smell of the man she'd married, the man she'd wanted to believe in. A familiar aroma, a mix of smoke-filled bars and maleness, but it was overlaid by something new. The smell of horse manure. Le Blanc was fastidious about his personal habits, so that was surprising. He'd slept rough last night; she'd bet on it.

He wrested her roughly against his hard-muscled chest and hissed in her ear, "Well, well. *Ma jolie femme*!" His breath was warm on her neck. "*Ma jolie femme*, here in America," he whispered, with a hint of mockery. "Who would have thought it? Maman died, did she?" He gave a cruel barking laugh. "I guess it had to happen sometime."

He dropped his hand from her mouth and spun her around so she was facing him. An angry heat flushed through her. She took a step back, placed both her hands on his shoulders and shoved him until she held him off at arm's length, her eyes blazing. "I'm not your *jolie* anything. And yes. Maman is dead."

She dropped her hands to her sides and took another step back. "What are you playing at, insisting I come out here in the middle of the night? I'm not doing it again—"

He laughed derisively. "You'll do it as many times as I tell you to."

She shook her head. "I told you,

Philippe. The night you left. I don't want to have anything to do with you or your schemes. Leave me out of it. Whatever it is, I don't want to know."

He tilted his head to one side, a sneer on his lips. "You weren't so reluctant eight years ago. Now it's payback time."

She felt the color draining from her face, and she felt very cold. "What do you mean?"

"We both know I wouldn't even be in California if it wasn't for you. Not that I'm complaining, mind. But I'm collecting on our debt."

"What debt?" Her fingers were stiff twigs. She shook her hands to get the blood flowing.

"Come, come, Madeleine. If there's one thing you are, it's intelligent." He pronounced it in the French way, with a mocking edge. "And look where it's got you. No husband, no children, skivvying for your brother. You'd have done better to stick with me."

"And what? Sleep rough in stables?"

She spoke sharply, and his arm lashed out so fast she had no time to duck. The blow across her cheek sent her reeling; she tasted blood in her mouth. She licked her bottom lip and confirmed a tooth had pierced it. She coughed, spitting out the bloody taste, memories of similar nights assailing her, making her nauseous. She bent over for several minutes, regaining her breath, smoothing the side of her face. He stood over her, silent and threatening. Then she rose to her full height and steadied herself. "You've got three minutes to talk. And then I am leaving."

"You can drop the show, you stupid bitch. You'll do exactly what I want, or you'll be very sorry. Two can play your game." In the dim light of the thin rising moon, his eyes glittered with a venom she knew only too well. It could erupt out of nothing in seconds, and when it did you couldn't be too far away from him.

He leaned over and fumbled in the canvas bag on the ground, pulling out a cloth-wrapped object, nursing it against his chest.

"What's that, Philippe?"

"Firstly, my name isn't Philippe. It's Gérard. Get used to it. And you *will* be meeting me again. And again. I plan for you to be my personal source of information about Vino d'Oro and the pretty boy Scotsman."

He'd been half-leering at her as he spoke, and at the mention of Caleb he stopped abruptly. "What? He reached out and stroked down the cheek he had just slapped, setting up a smarting sensation before she could shy away. "Oh, I see there's some reaction there. Your eyes give you away. Fancy the Scotsman, do you? I wondered the other night if there was anything going on. He seemed to be very aware of you." He laughed derisively. "Forget that one, *ma belle femme*. You know he set up those murders at Rancho Del Oro the other night."

She shoved at him and the object he held was hard as steel against his chest. "No. He never did."

"Oh yes. He's a bad one. Even worse than me. He and his father cheated their friends, and now he's killed the son to shut him up. Too late, though. The papers have already been served."

She stared at him, tutoring her face to

give nothing away, but her thoughts were racing. Caleb? Involved in murder? "You're lying."

"You'll see. You'll just see. Meantime, I've got a little job for you." He thrust the cloth wrapped item toward her. Her feet were frozen to the spot. She would not reach out and take it.

The muslin draping the barrel of a long-cylindered pistol slipped free, the metal glinting briefly before Le Blanc covered it up again.

"What on earth?"

"You're taking this. You're returning it to where it belongs, in Caleb Stewart's stables. You're hiding it in the hayloft, the next time you're there. I don't care how you manage it. Go for a walk, make an excuse you need some air. Pet the horses. You'll think of something."

She backed away, seized with an

impulse to turn and run.

He grabbed her roughly. "No. There's no escape." The words were said in sharp staccato, the planes of his face shadowed and implacable. "Remember Bourreau. If I go down, you go down too, Madeleine. Because he would never have been where he was, a sitting duck, ready for me to kill him, if it wasn't for you. And don't you forget it."

He towered over her, his face screwed up in leering contempt. "You're smart, I give you that, Madeleine. But not smart enough to escape the noose, if it comes to it." He thrust the gun towards her, the canvas bag dangling in his other hand. "Now take it. I want it delivered tomorrow."

When she didn't respond, he dropped both gun and bag at her feet and turned. Madeleine watched his retreat into darkness, shoulders high, arms swinging, a man confident his instructions would be obeyed to the letter.

She knew in her heart she had to make a choice. She had to follow his orders and do what he told her to do. Or she had to run.

3

"Josefa. I've got your breakfast tray here. We need to talk, sis. Please let me in."

The smell of cinnamon coffee and pastries wafted up as he stood and waited for a response to his knock on his sister's closed bedroom door.

Josefa had been locked in her room ever since the scene with his mother on New Year's Day, emerging only for Miguel's funeral, and then disappearing the next day to attend Rory's Requiem Mass in Sacramento's oldest Catholic church, St Rose's, with Bonnie and Consuela. She'd only returned from St Rose's, named after the first American-born saint, Rose of Lima, last night, and she'd then gone straight to bed, ignoring them all.

Valentina and Caleb had decided not to go to Rory's funeral at all, assessing that the circumstances surrounding Rory's death and Consuela's vengeful temperament would make it impossible for them to appear without sparking a dreadful scene.

"They'll be burying him in St Joseph's Cemetery. We'll pay our respects to the boy later," Doña Valentina had said. She gave his hair a motherly tousle. "It's a dreadful business, son, and I know you'd prefer to say your farewells at the proper time and place, but best we don't give Consuela a chance to play up her role as the grieving step-mother."

Caleb had reluctantly agreed, and the household was quietly skirting around

Josefa's torrents of tears. Doña Valentina took food to her and reported that when she wasn't sobbing, she was silent and stony-faced. "I know she was fond of the boy when he lived here, but that's years ago," Doña Valentina said with raised eyebrows. "It leaves you wondering . . ."

Wondering indeed. Caleb thought once more of Aristide's comment of a few days ago and asked himself again whether Rory had any link with the Frenchmen who were buying up land. He made a quick resolution. If his suspicions were correct, and Josefa *had* seen Rory recently, she just might know more about it than he — or even she — realized.

Which was how he came to be standing outside her door with a breakfast tray in hand, waiting.

He was about to give up and slink

away when he heard the key turning in the lock. A bleary-eyed Josefa opened up and then scuttled back to her bed. She sat with her knees tight against her chest, an eiderdown pulled up around her, and regarded him with doleful dark eyes. Her satin-smooth skin was unusually pale, her oval face beautifully framed by dark eyebrows and finely contoured lips, but her eyes were red-rimmed and puffy.

"I don't want food. I never want to eat again." She gave a couple of dry sobs, and he shunted the tea tray to one side of her dressing table.

Hot orange coals glowed in a small iron grate in the corner of the stuffy room, giving it an almost tropical heat. Caleb was surprised her cheeks weren't flushed pink. "It's very warm in here." He stood at her bedside, hands dangling, uncertain what to say or do next.

Her eyes narrowed accusingly. "It's all right for you. Grief is very debilitating. Anyone with a heart knows that."

"Josefa, I know this has been a blow. It's a terrible blow for us all. But we need to talk it through. We need to try and find out who did this awful thing — and why."

A long silence stretched between them before she responded in a halting, cracked voice. "I suppose you and Mother want revenge for Miguel. No one round here cares about Rory."

"Josefa, you know that isn't true. I hadn't seen him for a long time, sure. And his family has given us a dreadful time, also true. But I blame Consuela for that, not Rory. We've got to get to the bottom of it. I want you to tell me everything you know."

Her head shot up. "Know? What do you mean, know?"

"Josefa, I don't think you're just mourning the boy we all knew ten years ago. You've seen him more recently. You've met with him in the last few months, haven't you?" He tried to tamp down the edge of accusation in his voice.

She stared at him with a tight, closed face.

He sank onto the edge of her bed, and she didn't repulse him. "Where did you do that? At Bonaventura's? I think you might know more about what he was doing recently than any of us. And you need to share that."

Inside his hot temper rose at the thought of his Aunt Bonnie allowing his susceptible sister to be meeting with Rory at all. Didn't the old woman know that it was a dangerous thing to do?

What was she thinking? And see where it left Josefa. In this distraught state.

Josefa was staring over her knees, her brow knitted in concentration. She seemed to be considering what he'd said, not dismissing it out of hand, as she usually did.

He settled a bit more confidently onto the bed and reached out for her hand. "Come on, sis. We need to talk. I know it's hard, but you'll feel better for it. And it might help us discover who's responsible."

She choked out a few garbled words, cleared her throat and started again. "We were going to get married. Rory was just waiting for the right time to ask for my hand."

The words gushed forth like a dam that could no longer hold the torrent of water building behind it. The longer she spoke, the more animated she became. Her eyes flashed, and the color flooded back into her cheeks. "I told him that we would make you understand, that you'd see the court case was nothing to do with him. He never wanted it—"

"Married?" Caleb swallowed a knot of shock in his throat. He fought to appear indifferent.

How has this got so far, so fast?

"How many times did you see him? It all seems a bit rushed." He wondered how she had thought she could get around Doña Valentina with this scheme, even if she'd convinced him.

"Just one evening together at Aunt B's," she enthused. "That's all it took. Oh, we saw each other nearly every week right through the spring. Either at Aunt Bonnie's or at my girlfriend's." She gazed at him, intense appeal for understanding in her eyes. "But we knew from that first night we were meant to be."

The eager smile faded, and her hands went to her throat. She fingered the St. Christopher medallion she wore on a thin gold chain. Her voice dropped to a whisper. "That's why it's so hard. I'll never find anyone else like him." She melted into profuse sobbing.

Caleb leaned forward and stroked her head in the same gentle, affectionate way his mother had tousled his hair earlier. "Poor Josefa. I know it's hard." He ran out of consoling platitudes and fell silent, dropping his hand to her shoulders and stroking the back of her neck. Her sobbing gradually subsided.

He took a deep breath and tried another tack. "What plans did you have? I mean, did you discuss where you would live, what job he would do, that kind of thing? How serious was it?"

Josefa's head jerked up from her chest and her passionate dark eyes flashed with fury. "How *serious* was it? Of course we discussed where we were going to live. We wanted to live here. At Rancho Del Oro. Why shouldn't we? It's my home too!"

"Sure, Josefa, sure. There's just the little issue of his stepmother costing us thousands fighting to stop her taking it from us."

"I told you, he had nothing to do with that!"

Caleb cleared his throat. "Did Rory ever talk about the court claim? Did you ever get any idea of what went on there?"

She shook her head. "Not much. It was a painful topic for both of us. He said we couldn't do anything about it, so what was the point of discussing it?"

"Um, the 'not much' bit. What did he say?"

"He blamed his father."

Caleb felt a jolt up his spine. "Dougal? Why?"

"He thinks Dougal lost the cash Father paid him in some bad business deal or gambling and then was too scared to confess it to Consuela. By the time he realized what a venomous snake she was, it was too late. She never let up. Went on and on about it. In the end he just gave in. Gave up and let her create the story she wanted."

She blew a lock of hair that was dangling over her eye out of her line of sight. Her dreamy expression told him she'd momentarily slipped into a Rory memory. Moments later she snapped back and shrugged. "She still does."

"What do you mean? Who? Still does what?"

"Consuela." She sounded exasperated, like she was explaining the obvious to a dumb boy. "Goes on and on about it. Never lets up. How Father cheated Dougal."

Caleb felt a rush of blood to his cheeks. "Still? Even after the court ruled in our favor?"

She nodded. "But Rory never believed her." Her voice held a hint of defensiveness.

Caleb regarded her silently. She was breathing hard, her expression somber. The dark rings under her eyes left her flesh bruised. His hand was still resting lightly on her upper arm. He withdrew it. "Josefa, can I ask you something? Don't get mad at me, but just one more thing?"

She nodded, silent.

"Those Frenchmen who came to Sir John's the other night. Did Rory ever mention meeting them?" He watched her face closely for any tell-tale sign.

"The Frenchmen? No. Why should he?"

"No reason. It's just Aristide Laurent thought he'd acted a bit oddly when they were there once. He got the impression he might have known who they were. That's all." He knew he was sounding lame, apologetic. Quite the wrong tone to take with Josefa when she got mad.

Her eyes flew wide open, her beautiful dark eyebrows arched in indignation. "What are you suggesting? That Rory had some secret deal with those land leeches who are going around cheating Californios? That he was spiteful like his stepmother?"

She thrust her legs violently over the side of the bed, pushing past him to stand clear of him, to escape the room. "And what about you, Caleb Martinez Stewart? Perfect Mummy's boy. He who can do no wrong. I'm tired of you playing the big man of the house, controlling everything. How do I know you weren't the one who killed Rory?" She glowered at him, hands on her hips. "The last time I saw him he told me you'd arranged to meet. That you'd invited him to Del Oro." Her eyes filled with tears, but her gaze was hard and narrow. "He was tremendously excited. He thought maybe you'd heard about our arrangement somehow and wanted to make peace for my sake."

She shook her head and seemed unaware of the tears which had begun to flow. "Yes. Make peace for my sake. And instead you lured him into a trap and had him killed!" She pushed him so hard on the shoulder he slipped off the bed.

"Josefa! What are you talking about?" Caleb stumbled to his feet and stared at her. If she'd had a weapon in her hand — a knife or a bludgeon — he reckoned she'd have used it.

"I hate you!" she cried. "Why should Rory end up dead when all he was doing was accepting your invitation? Even if you didn't actually kill him, it's all your fault." She strode towards the door and stood there, gesturing for him to leave. "Get out. Get out now! I want to get changed. I'm leaving. I can't stand this place another second."

He was there at my invitation? Where on earth did she get that idea? Has she gone mad?

Caleb shambled towards the door.

"Josefa, I have no idea what you're talking about."

"I don't want to hear! Of course you'd say that!" She slammed the door shut the moment he was out of the room.

Where on earth had she got the idea that Rory's death was his fault? And how in heaven's name was he going to explain the last ten minutes to his mother?

Doña Valentina stood in the middle of the kitchen, hands on hips, her dark brows wrinkled in worry, the hair smoothly drawn back from her temples more heavily streaked with gray than Caleb remembered. "What's wrong with Josefa?" she said. "One minute she won't come out of her room, the next she won't stay in the house. What's the matter with her?"

Caleb took his mother gently by the

arm and led her to a chair at the big kitchen table. "We need to talk, Mother. She's got me completely bamboozled. She's dreamed up this crazy idea about the night Miguel died." He licked his lips. "Sorry, I should say Miguel and Rory. Rory's the one she's really concerned about. She thinks it's my fault."

He gazed up into his mother's face. She was running a jerky hand up over the top of her head, tucking loose strands back into place in her well-rounded topknot with a distracted air.

"Are you all right, Mother?"

She bit her lip and nodded. "Tell me. How is it your fault, for goodness sake?"

"She's under the impression that I invited Rory here on New Year's Eve. That I was orchestrating a grand peace gesture, to bury the hatchet after all the feuding."

Valentina's jaw dropped. "Why on earth did she think that?"

"She's been meeting Rory secretly for the last couple of months, using Aunt Bonnie as a cover. She says Rory said I'd asked to meet him."

At the mention of Bonaventura's name the grand dame of Del Oro rose abruptly to her feet. Her hands flew to her cheeks. "No. Bonnie wouldn't!"

She sank back down reluctantly, shaking her head. "Yes, Bonnie would. Anything for peace with Consuela, I suppose. She is her mother. I understand that."

"Josefa says she and Rory were secretly betrothed. The way she sees it, it was only a matter of time before all would be forgiven and she and Rory would come and live here."

Doña Valentina gaped. "Here? With

Rory? Is the girl living in a dream? *Santa Maria Madre de Dios*." She raised her hands to the ceiling in supplication. *"Niña estupida*. Stupid, stupid, girl. My son had to grow up too fast, and now my daughter doesn't want to grow up at all."

She dragged her hands down her face and gave him a hollow-eyed stare. "This is what comes of trying to protect her from the world's evil. As your dear father used to say, 'If wishes were horses, beggars would ride.'" She let out a long deep sigh, a curling whisper of sorrow that seemed to Caleb to circle above their heads, like a silent prayer. "I just pray she hasn't got herself with child."

Caleb shrugged and stood to go. "She won't be homeless. I imagine she'll go to Bonnie's if she doesn't come back home." He embraced his mother gently. "You've had so much to endure, my dear

Mama. I'm sorry it isn't over yet, but we'll survive. Remember father's admonition, his faith talk: 'When you pass through the waters, I will be with you.'" His eyes flickered upwards for a moment. "He hasn't failed us yet."

He kissed the top of her head. "I need to get out there with the boys. We've got the round-up coming, you know that. I can't be sitting around the house."

He went via the kennels to collect Jupiter and Venus, and then to the stables for Nero. The January fiesta was one of the biggest traditional dates on the rancho calendar, and when he was a boy Caleb had loved to hear his mother's accounts of life at Santo Margarita, her uncle's ranch near Los Angeles, when she'd been as a girl. Over three or four days free-ranging cattle were rounded up and sorted out into herds after being mixed up for months with other herds on the open range. New calves were branded, bulls castrated, and hundreds of cattle killed and skinned for their hides.

Things had changed hugely since those days. There had never been the Spanish presence in the Gold Country there'd been in old Mission lands down on the coast, but the anticipation of enjoying fun and games after days of hard slog was just as intense.

Far fewer cattle now free-ranged as the rancho lands had been sub-divided and new settlers moved in, intent on homesteading and grain-growing. The ranchers were being forced to build fences to keep good neighbors, and to breed cattle more suitable for good eating to meet the rising demand for beef created by California's tumultuous growth. But faint traces of the old rodeo times remained. After days of hard work, it was still a welcome excuse for a holiday feast of drinking, singing, eating, and dancing, where everyone mixed in together — the wealthy rancheros with their vaqueros, the common folk with the cowboys. Sometimes they went on all night.

As he tracked through the courtyard to Nero, Caleb had a poignant wish: if only Miguel, Rory and Josefa could all be here for this year's fiesta, and they could all go on as if their deaths hadn't happened.

His left foot was in the stirrup, Jupiter and Venus bounding around him excitedly, when he was interrupted by a call from behind. He dropped back to the ground and turned to see the attorney who'd represented them in their long battle with Consuela striding across the yard.

"Caleb! Hold on a moment!"

Thomas Halliburton was a partner in a prominent law firm with offices in San Francisco and Sacramento. He was a well-built man, with broad shoulders and a military bearing from years as an officer with the Union army. As far as Caleb could ascertain, he was also that rarity, an attorney with integrity. His round, broad face was burnished with wide, gray sideburns and topped by a shiny, bald dome which emphasized his solemn, intelligent eyes.

Halliburton had pulled up in a two-wheeled, open gig drawn by one gray horse, which swished its tail against the flies as the legal eagle strode towards him, waving his right arm urgently to attract his attention.

Caleb strolled across the yard to welcome him, Nero's lead dangling lightly from one hand. "How are you, Mr. Halliburton? Catch the stage to Goldtown and then pick up the gig, did you? Good to see you."

They shook hands and stomped their feet like the horses beside them, uncertain of how to begin.

Caleb jumped in. "What brings you out here in such a rush? You'd normally send word for me to see you in town."

The big man put his paw-like hands on Caleb's shoulders in a paternal embrace. "How are you, son?" His eyes flicked to the lead in Caleb's hand, then to Nero. "You're about to go out."

"We're starting the round-up today. You know what that means. Three or four days of heavy-duty work, and then a night or two of wild celebration." He grinned at the older man. "Our lead rider Santiago will have everything organized, but I like to be there to see what's going on. How can I help you?"

Halliburton's hands were clasped in front of him. "Something's come up." His eyes darted around the yard, prevaricating.

Caleb caught his mood, and an anxious bolt hit him in the gut. *What is it now?*

"I received a copy of another filing in the Land Court yesterday. I thought you needed to know as soon as possible."

Caleb stood stock-still, his hands suddenly freezing at his sides. "What is it? What's happened?"

"Not what, but who. Rory Mackinnon. His lawyers have filed a quit claim deed against Rancho Del Oro. It carries your signature. And it transfers half of Del

Oro's land to the Mackinnon family."

Caleb felt his knees give way, and he reached out to the gray's haunch for support. "A claim deed? With my signature? But that's impossible!" He stared up into Halliburton's worried face. "It's obviously a fake. Surely it won't stand up in court? And Rory's dead now, anyway."

Halliburton bit his lower lip and shook his head. "Sadly, that won't affect the legitimacy of the document. If it's accepted his heirs or estate will be the ones to benefit."

He studied the ground under their feet, suddenly unwilling to meet Caleb's gaze. When he did, his face was grave. "The thing is, if anything, his being dead makes it worse for you. Some might see it as giving you a motive for murder. Do you see? You get word he's trying something tricky, so you get rid of him before he does anything about it." He gave a wry grimace. "Of course I know that's not what happened. But it's fertile territory to work up a hostile audience against you — and you know how easily the court is swayed by public opinion."

Halliburton thrust his hands into the pockets of his finely tailored, woolen overcoat. "We've got a problem here, Caleb. A very big problem."

Three grinding days of roping, branding, castrating, slaughtering and skinning, and the last carcass was loaded onto a San Francisco-bound railway wagon. It had been a good outcome, Caleb thought with a warm inner glow. A good haul of new calves branded and, in the case of the bulls, castrated. And the cattle they'd slaughtered were in good condition. They should fetch good prices and satisfy appetites in The Bay.

From Doña Valentina to the least-experienced field hand, the ranch surrendered itself to a great collective sigh of relief. Their limbs were heavy with fatigue, but they were not so exhausted that they didn't have energy left to party.

Another successful round-up, another boost to the rancho coffers, and they were still holding their own against the vagaries of bad weather and the curse of greedy lawyers.

Caleb parked his butt on an old tree stump and sighed contentedly. The compound was alive with music, people, laughter, and the familiar smell of Doña Valentina's fiesta food: bean soup with chilies and meatballs, and *pozole,* a festive dish made of hominy, chicken, pork, cilantro, onion and radishes served with hand-made corn tortillas.

His mother had been working in the house as hard as he'd been on the land. It was a crying shame Josefa wasn't here to help. He pushed aside the thought and rose reluctantly, fingering the sides of the engraved glass beer tumbler that had been his father's. American glass. It had been his mother's present to Fergus the last Christmas he was alive.

Enough of that.

He gulped a soothing mouthful.

Get back on track.

Josefa couldn't be blamed for having a skewed version of things when Rory had kept his own secrets. He felt a familiar burning sensation in his gut at the thought of what lay ahead.

A signed quit claim deed. It was so fantastic as to be almost believable. His stomach twisted.

Years more of staring down silent accusing faces, of being suspected of taking out his vengeance on Rory for what his father did. But that wasn't the worst of it. He shuddered as he considered the possibility of being charged with Rory's murder. Surely not. It seemed beyond the realm of the reasonable, but he knew that stranger things had happened.

He stepped out to negotiate a path around the merrymakers, a knot of them swaying in a semi-circle, clicking castanets and tapping tambourines, whirling around the fandango band, the gay harmonies of guitar and mandolin following him as he headed to where the children's piñata was set up under the shade of nearby trees.

Before he spotted anything else, he saw Madeleine Laurent, a glowing picture in an apricot dress in a light flowing fabric patterned with darker red and turquoise flowers on a border along the hem. A silky shawl in a matching print was slung carelessly around her sculpted shoulders. She seemed unaware of anyone except Minette, as the child jostled with two or three other small urchins. She was striking at the piñata with a sturdy stick, Madeleine clapping her hands and laughing delightedly in encouragement as the children broke through and were showered with festive tokens and sweets. They chorused squeals of delighted joy, and Madeleine's pleasure in their excitement appeared to equal the children's.

"Glad to see you're having a good time." Her eyes flicked up in surprise. He could see in that instant that she'd been so engaged with the piñata she hadn't sensed his approach.

"Oh, Mr. Stewart. Yes, thank you. We're having a wonderful time." She gave him a radiant smile, her face flushed a flattering pink, her sea-green eyes sparkling with fun. Such a contrast to the clouded face he'd seen when they'd last spoken, the eyes shadowed by hidden secrets.

He arched an eyebrow. "Mr. Stewart?" He laughed. "Caleb, please. Especially on a day like today. The vaqueros see this as a day to forget all divisions of rank."

She bobbed her head in mock compliance. "Caleb, then." She peered around her with an enchanted smile. "I've never seen anything like this before. Of course, we don't have ranches in Bordeaux." She gave him a smile with a hint of self-mockery in it. "And I've never tasted Spanish food like it either!

The *pozole*! Stupendous! And Minette loved the chocolate and vanilla *pan dulce*!" She smiled up at him and made a quick check on the little girl.

"Doña Valentina explained the Mexicans took French pastries as their base and made them into something even more delicious," Caleb said.

She smiled again, but her eyes as she gazed at him had become guarded.

"Come with me and let's search you out a drink. You must be parched." He touched her elbow for a fraction of a second and was immediately aware of a warm current of excitement. She reached out to clasp Minette's outstretched hand. "Come along, *mon ange*, we're going to see some new things."

They found the drinks stand and he got her a sangria made from peach juice his mother had preserved from last summer's harvest. They wandered idly, sipping their drinks, stopping to watch the band, guitars and mandolin rendering a wailing love lament. They moved on to a quieter corner where the men played bochas. He sat Minette on a railed fence, and they leaned in side by side, sipping their drinks, watching the fist-sized wooden bowls land with a soft thud on the impromptu "green," each landing greeted with cheers or groans. He breathed in the fast-cooling evening air, felt the warmth of his restraining arm around the child, and for the first time in days felt his shoulders relax.

Minette wriggled and pointed to a group of children nearby playing marbles. He lifted her down, and she danced over to join them.

The spot where she'd perched was still

warm under his resting arms. He dipped his head towards Madeleine. "I regret my conduct when we last met, and I apologize for my rudeness."

Her eyes widened, plainly startled that he'd addressed the issue so directly. "Oh, no, please. Not necessary. I deserved it."

He raised his eyebrows in inquiry. "Really? Why?"

"I . . ." She hesitated, scanning the surroundings, looking for an escape. "I didn't handle your questions well. And it's quite understandable you were on high alert after the terrible things that happened."

Funny, I still get the feeling she's hiding something.

"I was upset," she said.

He felt the hair on the back of his neck stir. There it was again. That sense she wasn't being strictly honest with him, even though she didn't appear to be a woman given to game-playing.

He nodded in agreement. "It's got even more complicated than when I spoke to you last. Firstly, Rory has made a claim against Del Oro." He lifted his head to take in the scene before them. "He laid a claim to half of the ranch in the days immediately before his death."

Her mouth dropped open.

"Secondly, he told people I'd invited him here for 'discussions.'" He attempted a wry smile. "The old one-two punch routine, don't you think? A crab-claw double-pincer tactic to establish motive and guilt."

She returned his gaze with a fierce strength that took him by surprise and swept away any sense she'd been prevaricating. "How awful for you!" She skimmed the crowd, her eyes landing on where Minette squatted in the dust, one of a ring of urchins playing their version of marbles using the round seed pods scattered underneath a nearby tree. Their sharp little interjections of victory, protest or defeat, the high pitch of their childish voices, was strangely comforting. It denoted just another day of domestic normality; not one of untoward threats or unsettling hidden agendas.

"I have no idea what is going on, Caleb. But I know without a shadow of a doubt that you're not to blame for those deaths. It sounds like an out-and-out case of intimidation — possibly to push you into some completely unconnected result."

He swallowed in surprise. "A what?"

She shrugged, and once again a

shadow of something undisclosed crossed her face. "Aristide has explained a little of the workings of the land sharks around here. The operators with heaps of money and low morals who'll stop at nothing to get their hands on valuable real estate. I'm just thinking it's rather a coincidence they're trying to pressure Sir John in one way, to join a wine cooperative, and you in another. To sell if not all then a good chunk of your estate. It's been happening all over the state, hasn't it? Rancho families who get so deeply in debt because of legal bills fighting to keep their land, that they have to sell it anyway. "Could this be what someone is trying to do to you here? Push you off the land?"

Hearing her spell it out in such a straightforward way gave him goosebumps. He nodded slowly, thoughtfully, and then lost himself in her gorgeous marine eyes. "Yes. Yes, you could be right."

He kept on staring, willing the moment to continue. "You've only been in California a short time. How did you get to be so perceptive about what's going on?"

Her cheeks flushed and he saw from the way she shifted her eyes uneasily away from him that she was embarrassed, rather than complimented, by his statement.

"Ah . . ." She hesitated. "The land might be different, but people anywhere are not so different. A rogue, a murderer, is much the same man whether he makes his bed in Marseilles or Monterey." She gave him a wry smile, and he could see all the joy had drained out of her.

"It sounds like you may have had first-hand experience of this phenomenon," he said.

She shrugged. "Just as an interested observer."

She clutched the canvas bag with its traitorous cargo in one hand and stared across the paving stones that stretched to the open stable doors.

Am I really going to do this again? Act as Philippe's tool?

Sounds of fiesta gaiety — tooting horns, waves of laughter — drifted from the other side of the house, where the round-up merrymaking was reaching its climax. On this side of the ranch, though, all was sleepy contentment in the waning afternoon sun.

Two dogs lay asleep in the dust by the water trough. Through the stable doors, she could see horses leaning out from their stalls, tails flicking as they contentedly chewed hay. The place seemed deserted. The workers had completed their chores and eagerly joined in the amusements at the back of the house.

If she was going to do what Philippe had ordered her to do, now, while Minette was distracted with Graysie, was her best — probably her only — opportunity. But if she had been uncertain before, her conversation with Caleb Stewart had spelled out to her quite clearly the full implications of what "Gérard Le Blanc" was up to. He was intent on defrauding Caleb of his land and framing him for murder. She glanced down at the bag and trembled. She had no doubt she was carrying the gun that had killed two men in this house one week ago. And if she followed instructions, it would be seen as irrefutable evidence that Caleb — or someone in his employ — had pulled the trigger.

She crossed the yard to the water trough and perched on the rough stone edge, dragging her fingers through the water, thinking back to the day of Bourreau's death. Nausea rose from deep inside, and she scooped up some of the cool trough water in her hand and let it run down her face.

Nearly nine years ago, but I remember it as if it were yesterday.

She had risen early that morning, planning to take a stroll in the dawn-light looking for wild mushrooms. Philippe had been out all night and had met her in a furious temper just as she was leaving the house. He grabbed her by the throat, marched her back inside and stood over her in a drunken harangue. Something about Pierre Bourreau, a local vintner and beekeeper, who was challenging him for his position as director of the local wine cooperative. He'd gone too far this time, Philippe ranted. He had to be taught a lesson.

She was barely listening, focusing on wildflowers visible through the kitchen window, waving in the light breeze. She had no idea what Bourreau was supposed to have done, she just wished the tirade would end. She was wondering how much more she would have to endure when Philippe suddenly went quiet. Dangerously so. He stared at her, a conspirator's gleam in his eyes. "And you, *ma jolie femme*, are going to be my honey trap."

She'd seen herself with the same two

options then that she saw now: obey him or escape. She had no money, nowhere to go, and if she refused his demands, she knew she'd pay in other, humiliating ways, in the marital bedroom.

It hadn't been difficult. She knew, and Philippe guessed, that Bourreau had never fully vanquished his teenage infatuation for her. A few hours later she strolled past the café where he always took his morning coffee and engaged him in an animated conversation about the best places to hunt for the special mushrooms that were a gourmand's delight. With a few delicate hints, she wangled an invitation from him to show her the secret spot where he'd seen some prize specimens just last week.

She would never forget the scalding shame she'd felt when they were "surprised" by Philippe, or the sick look of betrayal on Bourreau's face as it dawned on him that he'd been set up.

She dribbled the cooling water down her arms and over her hands, trying, like Lady Macbeth, to wash away the memory. Her hands were, indeed, blood-stained, but Philippe couldn't implicate her in his crime all these years later, could he?

In French law a wife was entirely under their husband's authority. She couldn't appear in court without his permission so he would probably have got off murder for lack of evidence, if he hadn't also been embezzling from the cooperative coffers. When Bourreau's friends came forward to say he'd been investigating Coubert's possible fraud and had, just the day before his death, confirmed his suspicions, Philippe fled rather than face trial.

One of the dogs on the dusty ground beside Madeleine stirred and scratched vigorously. The movement broke her reverie. The powdery smell of dry earth made her nose feel stuffy. She swallowed hard to rid her mouth of a lingering bitterness.

The sweat beading on Pierre Bourreau's brow before the final blow. The anguished screams of his wife Susannah when they brought his body home. The punishing sexual violence she'd had to endure even after she'd done what Philippe wanted, had been the obedient little wife.

She bent double as her stomach heaved at the memories, but all that came forth was a thin stream of bile. She straightened, suddenly anxious she'd been seen.

She would be missed soon. People

would come looking for her. With a sudden sense of resolution, she knew what she had to do. She leaned down and tickled the wakened dog behind the ear. The brindle-haired cur responded with a satisfied yawn and stretched for more.

She wasn't going to play Philippe's patsy a second time round, even if it meant she'd go to jail for being an accessory to murder. Having one man's death on her conscience was more than she could carry. She wouldn't be making it two.

She turned and walked back into the house, hugging the bag to her hip.

4

Caleb and his mother were standing on the Rancho Del Oro path, waving goodbye to the last guests to leave. The gnawing stomach pain Madeleine had suffered all day was easing as she relaxed back in the Russell carriage, ready to drive home.

Minette was tucked in between her and Graysie. The canvas bag with its damning contents was wedged at her feet, partly concealed by the knee rug. Graysie's Nathan was in the driver's seat, the wagon was moving and she could let out a long sigh. Finally. She'd get rid of the bag and its contents as soon as she could, pretend she'd never seen it.

Shouts came from the driveway and the wagon, which had begun to roll under Nathan's steady hand, came to a halt. In a cloud of dust, a six-rider posse headed by a bearded man with a sheriff's star on his chest surrounded them.

The lead man, a full belly hanging over his gun belt, held up his hand. "Hold up there," the big man bawled. "We've got a warrant."

Madeleine's stomach roiled. She stared straight ahead, avoiding eye contact with anyone.

Caleb crossed to the riders, his demeanor relaxed. "What's the problem, Sheriff? We're just finishing a private family party here. We've had no problems."

"You might not have. That doesn't mean I don't."

Doña Valentina strolled to her son's

side. "How can we help you?"

"Sheriff Wayne Arkwright at your service, ma'am. Investigating the deaths here last weekend. I'm looking into a report you have weapons — illicit weapons — hidden here. In pursuance of that report, I've a warrant to search the premises." He waved to the men who rode with him. "In you go, boys and get started." He gestured toward the stables. "Start there."

"Illicit weapons?" Doña Valentina spoke with aristocratic iciness. "What a nonsense, Sheriff. Utter nonsense. I warn you, if one plate is left damaged, one cushion left out of place, you'll be hearing from me."

The sheriff's men hovered in a nervous cluster, unsure about continuing. Arkwright waved an airy hand to them. "Get on with it, boys. I'm thinking this isn't going to take long. The stables."

Again he pointed.

Doña Valentina stuck to Arkwright's side. "This is plainly ridiculous, Sheriff, but I see no reason why our guests should be detained. The child needs to get home to bed."

Arkwright cast an assessing eye towards the wagon. Minette had dropped off to sleep, half-sprawled across Madeleine's lap. He eyed them suspiciously then gave a resigned shrug. "Very well." He turned to Nathan. "Be on your way. Just don't interfere with our operations here."

As Madeleine watched the sheriff's men fan out to the stables, the bitter taste she'd experienced earlier flooded her mouth, more acid than ever. That sheriff knew what he was expecting to find, and where. She stared straight out over the field, silently praying.

Please, Nathan. Hurry up. Get driving.

As if he'd heard her unspoken plea, Nathan turned toward the wagon. "If we can't be of any use here, Caleb, I think it's best we get the girls home. Is that okay?"

Caleb's face was white, the furrows around his mouth settled in darker lines. "No problem, Nathan. Best go while you can."

As the wagon started moving, Madeleine felt none of the relief she'd registered the first time they headed homewards. Arkwright was going to be furious when he didn't find what he was expecting. And that meant Phillipe would come looking for revenge. There was nothing surer.

Long after the workers had gathered to sing popular folk songs around a bonfire and he'd retired to his office with a brandy, Caleb reflected on the night. Well, not the night so much. Everything had gone swimmingly, as he could have anticipated. Rather, he reflected on the magnetic, the mysterious Madeleine Laurent. She was a beautiful woman in every sense. So why was she unmarried? Why was she hacking out a life as her brother's housekeeper and his employer's part-time nanny? And why, despite her very shrewd and clear-eyed reading of the situation he faced, did he feel she was still holding something back?

He couldn't ignore the attraction he felt for her, the impulse he had every moment he got within a few steps of her to pull her into his arms and pepper her with light kisses. He'd never felt so giddy and light-headed about a woman before, but he couldn't afford to give into this weakness now.

She was a distraction, that was all. He had life-and-death stuff to face. He'd spent fifteen years fighting to ensure the family's future on the land, preserving his father's legacy. Just as it seemed he'd won fair and square in court, he was having to contest that battle all over again.

But to do that, he needed to go digging, he realized with a jolt. Madeleine was right. Something stank about the whole Rory thing. He needed to find out who and what was behind it.

If he found out some unsavory truths about Madeleine Laurent in the process, then so be it. He just hoped his usually reliable intuition that the French dame knew more than she was letting on was wrong. Just this one time, he would really prefer not to be proved right.

"Josefa, things are going crazy at home. I need your help."

She stared up at him from Aunt Bonnie's bulky old armchair, her beautiful face shadowed with suspicion.

They were in their aunt's living room, and he, God help him, was standing over his sister like some desperado. He hated that his voice had taken a high-pitched, querulous edge, but he couldn't let that stop him now. After Arkwright's raid last night, he was close to his wit's end. Whatever the sheriff had been expecting to find hadn't turned up, that was obvious, but could he be confident there wouldn't be a next time?

Who were these invisible enemies? Could he trust anyone?

Josefa poked him in the side. "What's wrong? You're miles away." She sighed and rolled her eyes at him, just as she had when she was eight and he was fourteen and they were arguing over the last piece of cake.

He plopped down alongside her and took her hand gently in his. "A posse of lawmen spent two hours searching the ranch last night. Looking for 'illegal weapons.' They were obviously looking for the gun that killed Rory. And I don't have a clue why they didn't find it. They seemed so sure they were onto something at the start. As if they had inside information."

Josefa yelped and put her hand up to cover her mouth. "Really? How did mother take that?"

"She was furious, as you can imagine." Caleb got up and paced to the window, hands behind his back. "Josefa, I am sorry about Rory's death. You know I am. And just in case you're wondering, I had absolutely nothing to do with it. Nothing at all. That's why I don't get all the stuff that's happening."

"Stuff? What stuff?" She sniffed belligerently. "Apart from the raid. I agree that's weird."

"Well, like the claim against the ranch. Rory never agreed with Dougal making the claim first time round. And in the end, they lost the case. Why would he start it all over again?" He bit his lip. "Don't you see? If this goes through, we're ruined. Mother, the twins, and you. We'll have nothing left. Even if — when — we win."

Her mouth was grim. "I don't have anything now, so I don't see why I should care."

He saw the bitter curl of her lip, the downcast set of her eyes. She was hurting even more than she was embittered. "Josefa, you know that's not true. You have a comfortable home for life at Rancho Del Oro, whatever happens. Quite different from here."

. His aunt's home had an unloved air. The stuffing poked through sofas and chairs; amateurish oils hung lopsided on the walls. Everything was permeated by the lingering stink of burnt fat and blocked drains that stuck in your hair for days after you'd visited. It spoke of a family well and truly down on its luck.

Like Doña Valentina, Bonaventura was the granddaughter of a prominent landowner, a former Governor when California was still part of Mexico. Even after the Americans took over, the family lived a life modeled on the indulgences of

Spanish gentry. They'd had a girlhood of expensive clothes and extensive leisure, the grunt work in household and ranch done by Mexicans and Native Americans.

But Bonnie had not adjusted to the changes of the last two decades, and Caleb's canny parents had. While Fergus and Doña Valentina simplified their lifestyle and cut back on expenses, Bonaventura sailed on as if a world where she spent $200 on one dress was never going to end.

After her heavily indebted husband lost the ranch, she'd settled in a corner of Sacramento where sinking fortunes were the general rule. She'd resigned herself to her fate, but her daughter had not. Consuela was eaten up with bitterness that while the Stewarts had retained their land, Consuela's father had not been so canny.

Caleb tapped Josefa's shoulder affectionately, re-establishing the link between them. "You'll always have a home, Jo, as long as I have one. But don't you see? You're a smart woman. Someone is trying to set me up. That ridiculous raid last night was the last straw. They were expecting to find the murder weapon there, I'm sure of it. Which means someone is feeding them lies. And I think Rory might have been sucked in by the same people. I don't blame him, honestly. But for his sake as well as ours, we have to get to the bottom of it."

Josefa's eyes were feverish and over-bright. For the first time since Rory's death he felt he might be close to a breakthrough. Hope kicked in his chest. "Think really carefully. Did Rory ever mention meeting someone to talk about the land? Did anyone ever hint or promise they might be able to do something for him? If he was planning to marry, he'd have one thing on his mind, and that's finding somewhere for you both to live. Did he ever hint he might have a good solution just around the corner? That everything was going to turn out right?"

He saw a spark in her bright eyes. "Yes. Yes, that's exactly what he said." She was excited now, her voice rising, the words falling in an eager cascade. "A few days before he died. He said he'd met someone who had the answer. That it was all going to turn out fine. That's when he also said he was meeting you. That you'd suggested a meeting . . . It was the same evening."

Caleb shook his head. He ran his hand affectionately down Josefa's right cheek, brushing back a lock of dark brown hair that had fallen across her face. "Sis, I never suggested a meeting. I wouldn't have exactly been against the idea, but I never suggested one. Whoever told him that was playing him like a fish."

Tears welled in her eyes, and she put her hands to her mouth, as if suppressing any sound. He gently peeled away one hand and squeezed it reassuringly. "Jo, take it really slowly and think hard. Did he ever mention any names, or give you any idea of who this person or persons might be? Do you know how he came to meet them?"

She shook her head, her eyes narrowed. "No, I can't think of anyone." She flexed her fingers. "He didn't even have time to buy me a ring." She stared down at her hand, and then back at him. "You know, there was one time. One night when he came home from the winery. He said he'd met this guy from France who knew all about wine — and no, it wasn't Aristide. This guy was a bit mean about Aristide and Rory didn't like that. The man had said Aristide didn't know where the big money was. That there was no point in piddling around in wine barrels. That the money was in land."

She stared into the middle distance, recollecting. "Yes. I think Rory said he was a Frenchman who had been a winemaker once, but now he was onto bigger and better things. He didn't mention him after that first meeting, I guess because he felt disloyal talking about Aristide that way. But that's the only time I remember."

Her eyes had the uncertainty of a seven-year-old seeking big brother's support. "Do you think it could have been him?"

"The more I get to know about this, the more likely I think it was."

"Rory was staying at Barney's at Ten Mile. There might be something in his room that could explain things. But I still don't really understand it. What did he have to gain? I mean, why bother? He'd be almost certain to lose again." Josefa peered up at him, her classic features screwed up into a frown.

Caleb cleared his throat. "Let's say someone wanted to drive Del Oro to the wall. Push us into so much debt we'd be forced to sell up and walk off. One way would be to persuade someone like Rory to bring a claim against us. Doesn't matter how outrageous, as long as it causes us years of legal bills and harassment. They convince him it will all work out fine for everyone. They con him just long enough to get his signature on a document. Or they even forge his signature, like they did mine. And then they kill him, so he won't be able to recant."

"But what about Miguel?" said Josefa. "Why kill him too?"

"I think poor old Miguel was just in the wrong place at the wrong time. Maybe they didn't realize he lived in the house with us. Maybe they thought he was going to be out with the rest of the work gang. Whatever happened, he interrupted them at an inconvenient moment, and it cost him his life."

Just then a commotion erupted on the other side of the room. Consuela burst in, hands on hips, eyes glittering. She turned on Caleb. "What are you doing here? Get out! Get out now." She pointed to the door, her face contorted in ugly rage.

Then she rounded on Josefa. "I thought you would have known better than this, Josefa."

Josefa's eyes flickered from Consuela to Caleb. "Better than what? He's my brother. Aren't I allowed to talk to him?"

Consuela roared, "Better than to trust a murdering coward! Better than to sit drinking with a killer!"

Josefa protested. "He didn't! We weren't—"

"Oh, so he's got you conned too, has he? When is the world going to wake up to the fact that the Stewarts are all liars and cheats?" She forced a smile. "Except you, of course, Josefa. You're so lucky you got away from them while you could."

Her arm was paralyzed with pain.

His hot breath steamed on her cheek.

Sunlight flashed at the end of the alley, but here in the narrow depths it was cold, dark and muddy.

Another wrench of her arm up her back, and she cried out.

"Shut up!" Warm spittle spattered her face, and the hold on her throat tightened.

White flashes danced before her eyes. Another half an inch and he'd snap her elbow.

"What did you think you were doing?" His voice was rasping, venomous. "What?"

Madeleine knew the man who called himself Gérard Le Blanc was not expecting an answer. Her knees buckled, and she pitched towards the ground, retching as she collapsed. She was going to die in a miserable alley, a rubbish-strewn, boggy corridor between a brothel and a gambling parlor. And she deserved to.

When she came to, she was lying on hard, cold ground. Icy ground, in fact. Her eyes bolted open and she lifted her head gingerly. The end of the alley was still in bright sunlight. She probably hadn't been unconscious for long.

As dizziness threatened to engulf her again, Gérard's voice came back: "I am going to teach you a lesson you will nev-air forget."

After nearly eight years in California, his English was almost perfect, but he'd lapsed into accent, beside himself in his fury. "You little be-etch. You'll pay for what you've done. And so will your precious brother." Another wrench on her arm. "You'll see."

The smell of rotting vegetation filled her nose, and she shifted to get away from the stench. If she could just roll away . . . The pain that flooded through her threatened to send her under again, back to darkness. She flopped face-down, nostrils filled with the pungent decaying odor, and waited for the dizziness to pass.

She had taken the horse and trap, driven herself to Ten Mile Station on the excuse of doing a few errands for Graysie. And then without warning Gérard had grabbed her by her hair and dragged her into the alley. One minute she was on the way to pick up some shoes that were being mended, the next she was paralyzed by pain. She hadn't had a chance to protest. She could only remember screaming once.

She snorted as the memories flooded back. The sharp intake of breath choked her nostrils with alley debris but she hardly cared. The residual pain was flooded over by a surge of warm triumph as she recalled how she'd tossed Gérard's gun, still tied up, canvas bag and all, off a bridge on the way here. How she'd jumped up and down, beside herself with excitement, as it bobbed downstream. By now it was lodged under a boulder on some forsaken river arm, or it was on its way to burial in Sacramento Delta sludge.

She remembered Gérard's mad raving before she passed out. How he was going to get even with her for this second betrayal. She'd never seen him in such a rage, and that was saying something. She'd fully expected to die. Had been prepared for it.

So why didn't he kill me?

Pushing up with her sound right arm, she lifted her face from the muck.

Why hasn't he killed me?

As if in answer, she heard footsteps, saw the black tips of a man's boots. She braced herself for the next assault.

"Ma'am?" The voice was male, tentative. Not Gérard, then.

"Ma'am? Are you awake? Help is on the way."

She attempted to push herself up further, but once again the pain overwhelmed her.

"No, no, don't do that. Just wait. We have a stretcher coming."

She groaned and, ignoring the man, rolled onto her side and drew her legs up. An older man in a gray suit, face grooved in kindly concern, peered down at her. A stethoscope dangled from his neck. "You were lucky, ma'am. Some fellows heard the noise and chased off the scoundrel, but I'm sorry, he got away. I'm Dr. Rosen. Let me help you."

5

Barney's Camp House was situated right next door to Ten Mile Station, and the whistles and shouts of the wagon drivers as they negotiated the highway traffic penetrated the thin walls of Rory Mackinnon's sparse room.

Caleb's chest ached with sadness. This was where his childhood friend had spent his last nights on earth. A narrow single bed with a lumpy mattress; a bedside table that listed to the right, one leg dangerously at an angle; a wrinkled newspaper lying on top alongside a comb and a box of matches. Rory had always been a gentle dreamer, with a tender heart for animals. Dougal was always trying to toughen him up, Caleb recalled. He was an intuitive horseman, but not a natural-born rancher.

He'd come to Barney's seeking clues as to Rory's comings and goings in the days before his death. Who he'd talked with, who he'd met. Desperation, really, as he had so little else to go on.

He'd offered the excuse that he was here on behalf of the family to collect his belongings, and a surly manager had shown him to Rory's room. A shaving kit, its instruments spilling out of a leather pouch, lay half under the bed. His clothes — a couple of cotton shirts, two pairs of work trousers — hung over the single hard-backed chair in the corner. Under the chair a pair of dust-worn, toe-stubbed working boots lay discarded.

It was clear that no one else had come for his personal effects, and Caleb wondered if he should collect what was here and return it to Josefa. His meagre belongings felt so cast aside and uncared for, as if Rory's departure from this earth was of no consequence to anyone.

On impulse he swept up the newspaper under his arm, then stepped across to the chair. He checked through the trouser pockets, searching for anything that might indicate where Rory had been, who he'd been visiting. The stub of a San Francisco steamer ticket from ten days ago. Strange. He wondered what business Rory had in the big smoke, but in itself it meant nothing. Maybe he'd been seeking work.

He took in the rumpled sheets, half-pulled off the bed as if the occupant had left in a hurry, late for an appointment maybe, and noted a sheaf of papers on the floor, showing from under one corner of the hanging sheet. He reached down and retrieved them.

The flowery, scripted letterhead announced it as a communication from the law firm of Buffer, Jones and Cottlesloe, advising Rory that he had been identified by their agents as someone who may be eligible to make a claim against the estate of "Fergus Septimus Mackinnon, being the lawful husband of Doña Consuela Valaquez Alvarado, grand-daughter of the former Californian governor . . ."

Caleb had heard rumors of a flood of false claims being orchestrated by dishonest law firms, but this was the first time he'd eyed possible evidence. The letter gave no further details but invited the recipient to make an appointment with one of the partners to further discuss the matter and be apprised of his rights.

The firm tread of a male boot echoed in the hallway outside and on impulse Caleb folded and stuffed the letter into the inside pocket of his jacket. No one need know he'd even seen it, and it wasn't going to be any use to Rory now.

He turned as the door opened. The bushy beard, the belly hanging over the gun belt, a sheriff's star on his right shoulder. The same lawman who carried out yesterday's raid. He'd gone away empty-handed after turning the place over for two hours. The scowling, tanned face of the sorely disappointed Sheriff Wayne Arkwright glared at him from the doorway.

A bitter man who believes his best years are gone forever.

The lawman regarded Caleb through narrowed, gimlet eyes. He'd entered with his gun drawn, and waved Caleb away from the bed with the gun still in hand. "Well, well, I do believe we've met before, Mr. Stewart." He raised an eyebrow questioningly. "Now why would Caleb Stewart be in the murder victim's room? What is your business here?"

"I was just checking on behalf of my sister. Josefa was betrothed to Rory. I wondered if anyone had taken care of his personal effects . . . She's very upset and I thought it might help."

Even to his own ears, it sounded a weak excuse, and the sheriff raised a cynical eyebrow. Caleb felt the back of his neck heat up as the realization dawned that this might not have been his smartest move. He was a suspect, and he was casing the victim's room.

Arkwright sucked in a gulp of the stuffy air with a wheezing noise that sat oddly with the tanned face. "Looking for what exactly?" His stare was cold and calculating. "Making sure there's nothing here to compromise you, I suppose. Seeing as I understand you were meant to meet him on the night he was killed."

Caleb gave a vehement shake of his head. "That is simply not true. I haven't seen Rory Mackinnon for a long time, more than a decade — since his father left my father's ranch. I'd heard he was back in the area, but I never met up with him."

The sheriff continued to regard him coolly. "Is that so?" He abruptly put his gun back in his belt and stepped closer to the bed. Caleb backed away, putting more distance between himself and the lawman's hostile presence. "You understand it's incriminating to be found going through the victim's room when you are one of the suspects in his murder? Or didn't that occur to you?"

Arkwright's jaw worked in slow rotation, releasing a sweet sugary smell of fruit gum as he chewed. Caleb was momentarily mesmerized by the regular, rhythmic movement. He cleared his throat to get Arkwright's attention.

"There are witnesses who can swear I was nowhere near the scene when Rory and my house man died. Because I wasn't. As I have told you already, I was at a New Year's Eve dinner at Sir John Russell's. I imagine his word would hold some credibility."

When the sheriff had entered, Caleb had been momentarily taken aback, but now his anger was stirring. He felt the blood pounding at his temples, and he took a deep breath to calm himself. "I don't know where this information that I invited him for a meeting came from, but it is false." He took another step towards the door. "However, having spoken to my sister who was close to Rory, I've got the idea that he may have genuinely believed it — that possibly someone was feeding him false information. Setting him up, for reasons I am unable to fathom. It's the only thing I can think of." He spread his hands wide, palms open, to indicate he had nothing to hide. "So I came here, wanting to talk to anyone who might be able to tell me something about Rory's movements in the last few weeks."

It sounded perfectly reasonable to him, until he saw the cold smirk on Arkwright's face. His feet were planted hip width apart, his arms were folded across his chest, and he was rocking back and forth in a stance of contempt. "There's more than one way to skin a cat," he said.

"What if I was to tell you I've got witnesses who saw you meeting Rory?"

The pulse that pounded at Caleb's temples turned into a rushing noise in his ears. "You what?"

The sheriff smirked. "I've got a witness who saw you with Rory Mackinnon and overheard you making an arrangement to meet him on New Year's Eve. What do you say to that?"

"I'd say they've got the wrong man. Either they're lying, or it's a case of mistaken identity."

The sheriff rolled his eyes. "Now don't they all say that? Don't go anywhere, Mr. Stewart. Let me rephrase that. Get out of here right now, and don't come back. But don't go far from home. You've got a lot of questions to answer before I'll be satisfied this one's over."

"Guns?" The grizzled, gray-haired shop assistant at Herb's Hardware shifted nervously behind the counter. "You want to buy a gun, ma'am? For yourself?"

Madeleine gave him her best soothing smile and took a step toward the gun cabinet in the back corner of the shop. The cobalt-blue alpaca and silk dress she'd bought ten minutes ago at the haberdashery next door brushed her legs. Her smile deepened. "It is indeed. I'm sure I can rely on you for the best advice, Mr.?"

"Haber. Herb Haber at your service."

"Well, thank you, Mr. Haber. I am Mrs. Laurent. My husband thinks it's a very good idea for me to carry protection. You know, for those rare occasions when a woman might require it." She flicked her long dark lashes. "Better to be safe than sorry, as they say."

Twenty minutes later she emerged from Herb's Hardware with a New Model Remington wrapped in plain brown paper. It was bigger than the Muff pistol that she knew Graysie carried in her bag. But she wanted to be certain she could defend herself. With its eight-inch barrel and two pounds of weight, she hoped it wouldn't let her down if Gérard came after her again.

She had a new dress, a new gun, and a sorely bruised body which reminded her with every step why it was needed. Dr. Rosen had done his best to patch her up, told her she was lucky to escape with cuts and bruises and a severely wrenched arm, but she'd suffered no permanent damage. She gave a silent prayer of thanks that the attack had been interrupted. Goodness knows what he'd planned to demand next, but he hadn't had the opportunity.

She paused to pull the scarf around her, covering as best she could the bruise marks Gérard had left on her face and throat, and stepped toward the Russell trap. She couldn't wait to get home.

6

Caleb reeled out of the Camp House, his hands clammy, a dull thud hammering over his eyes. He muttered a quiet curse at the lawman who thought he'd already solved the case — and found Caleb guilty. He needed a drink. He stomped across to the American Fork House, oblivious to the hustle and bustle of teamsters and horses, tourists and miners as they surged in and out of the popular watering hole.

Clutching a cold ale, he scanned the pulsating beer hall, searching for the quietest corner to hide, somewhere he wouldn't attract attention and could collect his thoughts. He edged across the room to the wing furthest from the billiard tables, where the noise levels were more moderate and family groups and lady travelers gathered. Somewhere he could bury himself behind Rory's old newspaper and try and calm the pounding in his head.

He sank gratefully into a tight corner, his back to the room, and took a long draft of his cold ale.

Unbelievable. I might be staring at the prospect of a murder charge. All on the basis of false evidence.

He had a sinking feeling that there was a lot more to this than he'd realized. This wasn't a random attack; it was a conspiracy. And he was being set up just as much as Rory had been.

He opened the newspaper and skimmed its contents with a desultory eye. His mind was still back in Rory's spartan room, staring at the lawman's sneering face. He put his ceramic mug down on the newspaper and pressed chilled hands against his eyes. He moved to take up the tankard handle again and noticed some columns at the bottom of an inside page had been ringed in black ink. He leaned forward to see what it was that had caught Rory's attention.

Buffer, Jones and Cottlesloe, respected attorneys and advisers on all land claims, announce they will be holding claim clinics for all interested parties still seeking justice for historic land disputes. If you or your family have legitimate grievance against the state of California and the Land Claims Court, make an appointment for free advice from one of our highly experienced attorneys.

He had to conclude that Rory had

made the marks. Had he also taken steps to make an appointment with Buffer and Co.? He pulled the letter he'd retrieved from Rory's room out of his jacket and spread it out on the table before him. It was dated late October, and it was January now, so there would have been plenty of time for Rory to act on it if he'd had the inclination. He put his head in his hands and massaged his forehead with his thumb and forefinger.

Rory had been meeting with lawyers? He could only assume they'd been discussing Rancho Del Oro. He fingered the letter, idly turning it over in his hands as he sat lost in thought. More scribbling on the back of the paper caught his eye: "New Year's Eve. Meeting with agents. Caleb there."

A vise-like pain grabbed him. He bent double with its intensity, groaning into his handkerchief. For several minutes he sat hunched, his face buried in his handkerchief until it eased. Then he glanced around almost guiltily, checking if anyone had noticed him. No one. No one at all was bothered about a man drinking alone. There was nothing unusual about it. He folded the letter into a tiny square, then tucked it back into his jacket pocket. He'd put a match to it as soon as he got home.

He was sitting in dumb shock trying to process what he'd found when he heard a familiar voice behind him. Glancing over his shoulder he glimpsed Gérard Le Blanc and Roland Durand settling down half a dozen tables away. They thumped their beers down and started a subdued conversation in their native language. A very subdued conversation. Caleb hid behind his newspaper, his back to the room, and focused all of his attention on them, straining his ears to pick up any word. The bar was pumping, and the noise levels gradually rose to drown out the Frenchmen's words. But before the noise completely submerged the voices, he made out a few scattered phrases. *"Le sheriff . . . Le pistolet . . . La viande morte . . . Cette Laurent salope."* And *"Ce connard Stewart."* From which he concluded that Sheriff Arkwright was hopping mad about a gun, someone was dead meat, a person called Laurent was a female dog, while he, Caleb Stewart, was worse than dead meat or a female dog. He smiled grimly. He didn't need a translation. And everything was still as clear as mud.

He waited for the Frenchmen to leave before stowing Rory's newspaper inside his jacket and sauntering out after them.

The snatches of conversation he'd heard were enough to confirm that Le Blanc and Durand were involved in Rory's death, and it wasn't jumping too far to conclude they were behind the plan to plant the gun.

But that was as far as he wanted to let his mind go. The unthinkable — that Madeleine Laurent was one of the conspirators, had perhaps even been charged with planting the murder weapon — he just didn't want to believe. What was she? Some sort of black widow? He wasn't sure he wanted to have that question answered.

Down the road from Ten Mile Station, the street scene was one of peaceful industry. Outside the haberdashery a woman was holding a bolt of fabric up to the bright sunlight, checking on the material's see-through factor. A couple of small boys played at the water trough, keeping an eye on tethered horses while their owners had a quiet drink.

And coming out of Herb's Hardware next to the haberdashery, walking with a tentative gait, as if she was in pain, carrying a big brown paper parcel, was Madeleine Laurent. Madeleine Laurent as he'd never seen her, with a blue-black bruise down her face and pieces of straw in her tousled hair.

He was certain those were fingermark-bruises on her throat. As if suddenly aware of her vulnerability, she pulled the scarf closer, and tucked it into the standup collar of her dress. She stepped awkwardly forward, seeming to favor one side over the other. Caleb headed her off. In a couple of big strides he was standing in front of her, doffing his riding hat. "Mademoiselle Laurent. What brings you out on this lovely winter's day? Is Aristide with you?"

She stopped abruptly, and in the seconds before she regained control, he saw panic flit across her lovely features. Panic, and fear.

She swung around nervously, as if checking the street for further ambush, and let out a long breath. "Oh, my goodness, I was miles away. You did startle me. How are you, Mr. Stewart? Doing some chores?"

Caleb pursed his lips in a mischievous grin. "I asked first."

"Oh." She took a deep breath. "Just doing some errands for Graysie." Her eyes flicked to the brown paper parcel.

"So I see. Something from the hardware store?"

He waited for her to comment, but her

mouth tightened into a straight line. "Yes. And from the shoe-mender's." She half-heartedly lifted the shopping basket up to reveal more packages. "Quite the little delivery woman."

"So what takes you into Herb's Hardware? Buying something for Aristide?"

He knew he was being cheeky, too nosy by half. But he watched her like a hawk as the comment landed. Saw the involuntary start as the query hit home. The quick little gasp of surprise at his brazenness. The rapid paling in her face as she struggled to maintain appearances. Her hand came up to her throat and dropped away just as suddenly.

The woman is frightened. Frightened for her life.

She glanced around again, as if

expecting attack from an unknown quarter.

He stepped closer, lowered his voice, the fake jollity gone. "Is everything all right, Madeleine? You're not full of your usual bonhomie. What's happened?"

She pulled back, stiffened her spine, though she winced as she did. "Thank you for your concern, Caleb, but I am perfectly fine, thank you. I just took a little tumble on an icy step. Now I must be getting home. Aristide will be expecting me."

She knew he didn't believe a word of it, and nor should he. She headed for the Russell trap, holding herself as carefully, as resolutely as she could, against her body's tenderness, already stiffening into a soreness that protested with every movement.

As the steady brown mare headed homewards, the momentary euphoria she'd felt at having survived Gérard's assault evaporated, replaced by a yawning pit that opened inside. How much was she going to tell Aristide and the others? What if Caleb told him he'd suspected her of buying a gun? And even with the gun in her bag, how was she going to keep Gérard at bay without being arrested for murder?

Caleb had barely slept, and he'd been up since dawn, breakfasting on the lightest of rations — sweet *pan dulce* washed down with coffee — before getting out on the range to check on the young bulls castrated during the round-up. He couldn't afford to lose any animals to insect infestation or infection.

But he was aware that he was moving

among the herd with the robotic stare of one of the clockwork toys he'd treasured as a boy. He was looking, but not really seeing. His mind was somewhere else.

Wind me up and let me go.

His life had broken in two, and, like a melon split with a cleaver, he didn't think it could ever be restored to wholeness.

He was further away than ever from securing his family's fortunes. He wasn't even sure he could guarantee his mother's safety. He'd conceived a painful attraction for a woman who was completely untrustworthy. Who was probably a black widow. A woman who would feed off a man — mentally and materially — and then leave him for dead.

And any day now, he could be arrested for murder. That still seemed too fantastical to contemplate. But the thing that had kicked his faith in a virtuous world out of the arena was the looming sense that the threats he faced were more personal, and the stakes much higher, than he'd ever envisaged.

He moved in an unconscious rhythm, flowing with his stallion's rolling stride. As the day brightened to dazzling light on the open plain, he contemplated the likelihood that he was fighting a conspiracy aimed at nothing less than stripping the Stewarts of their entire domain.

Twenty-four hours ago that would have seemed so far-fetched he would have been embarrassed to admit to thinking it. But now he felt compelled to examine it as a definite possibility. He considered the cast of players.

The city lawyers — he felt certain they'd be found to be sharp and scurrilous — who had been wooing Rory with promises on which they couldn't deliver.

The persons unknown who'd set Rory up with the hope of reconciliation.

And the so-called "witnesses" the sheriff claimed were ready to testify that he — or she — had seen them together.

None of it true. All of it lies. And yet with the aggregation of a mountain of circumstantial evidence, maybe even his closest allies would start to doubt. And that might make him someone with whom Sir John Russell wouldn't want to do business. Would he want his reputation sullied by partnering with an accused murderer?

An image of Madeleine Laurent, as she'd been at the round-up festivities, a lock of hair falling over her sparkling eyes, flashed across his mind. It had taken all his self-control to not reach out and gently slide it back into place behind her ear, to run his hand down her bright cheek. Now that cheek was turning black and blue, and it wasn't because she'd taken a tumble in the street.

He raised his eyes to scan the sky overhead. Far off, downwind, vultures circled high in the sky, riding thermal flows from the nearby mountains.

Carrion feeders like vultures were not good birds to see hovering. He kicked Nero into action and galloped to the copse of trees where they circled. The carcasses of several powerful bulls lay, freshly bleeding. The smell of meat in the early stages of decay grew stronger as he drew nearer.

He drew parallel to the first carcass. A red hole pierced the white blaze on the beast's head. One of his valuable breeding bulls, the gateway to his hopes to improve the quality of stock Del Oro was producing, deliberately slain.

He didn't need to go any closer to see that every one of them had been shot, executed at close range. From the tracks in the grass, it appeared they'd been rounded up by more than one rider, and then picked off with a hunting rifle as they turned and stood, backs to the trees that blocked their escape.

The air collapsed out of him as he rested on the horn of his saddle and contemplated the bloody details. Whoever did this knew their animals. They'd targeted the most valuable, the least easily replaced blood lines.

He'd been right the first time round. His world was being upended, and there'd be no going back to what had been.

"What do you mean, they've been shot? *Que pasa*? What's going on?"

Doña Valentina's hands held out a cast-iron brunch pan of huevos rancheros, the fragrant egg and salsa dish she served with crispy strips of fried tortillas that usually had his digestive juices gushing at the first scenting. But not today. His stomach was as hard as lead, the muscles tight as a drum, his gut churning. The last thing on his mind was food.

"One or two had wounds in the flanks, but most had been shot straight through the head." He threw his mother an anguished glance. "I can't eat today, Mother, I really can't."

He pushed away the plate she'd placed in front of him before she had a chance to pile it up with the warm egg mixture. "This isn't just a case of malicious mischief. Nor is there anything random about it. We're being targeted in a coordinated campaign. Everything Father stood for is threatened. I'm even worried about keeping you safe."

Doña Valentina set the pan down on an iron trivet with a thud. "You're not serious!" She sank into a chair at the opposite side of the kitchen table from where he stood facing her.

"Unfortunately, Mother, I'm completely serious."

"And what do you mean, 'campaign.' That's nonsense talk, son. Surely?"

"A couple of days ago I would have agreed with you. Now, I'm not so sure. Someone is out to get us."

"But why? And why now?"

He shrugged. "Maybe someone's got greedy. Maybe they fear they are running out of time to get their hands on

land in Sacramento County. You've seen
how fast the best land is being sub-
divided and sold off." He sat down and
poured himself some coffee. He mightn't
be able to eat, but he wouldn't go
without his morning cup. "Those French
agents who were at the Russell place.
I'm sure they're involved. Rory was just
another pawn."

Doña Valentina's brow furrowed. "Is
Josefa going to be all right?"

He shrugged. "Honestly? Who knows if
any of us are going to be 'all right' by
the time this is over? I surely hope so."
He searched his mother's face for a
flicker of understanding. "We've faced
horrendous floods, drought, locusts,
plagues of almost Biblical magnitude in
the last ten years, but I've never felt in
as much danger as I do right now. I just
don't know any longer who I can trust."

Doña Valentina reached over and topped up his coffee, as if offering the only comfort she could at that moment.

He grasped the cup with both hands and looked down into the dark brew. "The woman who's working at the Russell's, Madeleine Laurent. Aristide's sister." He glanced up at his mother, blinking rapidly.

"What of her?" Doña Valentina had sat back down and was resting her head in her hands, elbows on the table.

"She's involved somehow. Or at the very least, she knows something she's not telling. I saw her at the American Fork House yesterday and she was very on edge."

He related the events of the previous day — searching Rory's room, the confrontation with the sheriff, slinking away to the coach house to gather his wits, finding the marked newspaper before stumbling across first the bullying agents, and then Madeleine.

"She looked terrible. Like someone had beaten her up. Is it a coincidence they seemed to all be there at the same time?"

Doña Valentina reached across and took his hands in her own, gently squeezing them in solidarity. "I hear what you're saying, Caleb. We're all going to have to be especially watchful. As Fergus used to often say, 'A lie is halfway roon Scotland afore the truth has its boots oan.'"

She gave him an encouraging smile. "News travels fast, dear boy so be careful what you say — and who you say it to."

7

"Aristide, have you got a minute?"

Madeleine stepped quickly inside the small office her brother used in the winery and shut the door behind her.

"*Parbleu*!" He looked up with a surprised grin as she entered, and his eyes widened. He jumped up from his seat. "What on earth has happened? Your face—"

Madeleine held up her hand, palm flat toward him. "It's nothing. I don't want any fuss." She slipped onto the stool and nodded to the seat he'd just vacated. "Please, Aristide. No fuss."

"*Sacré bleu*, tell me!"

"I'm getting to it. Give me a chance."

She'd got back to the house yesterday afternoon and gone straight to bed with the excuse she wasn't feeling well and needed to rest. When Graysie popped in to check on her in the early evening she made vague excuses of having fallen in the street to explain her injuries. But she'd barely slept, and when morning came, she knew she was going to have to tell Aristide about the gun. Gérard's threats had to be taken seriously, and the whole family had a right to know.

Aristide poured her a glass of water from the carafe that sat on his desk. "Drink this and then tell me. What happened to your face?"

She sipped the cool water, willing her racing heartbeat to settle. The gun she'd bought yesterday, still wrapped in brown paper, was stuffed into a bag at her feet.

Where to start?

She reached down and pulled out the package, placed it on the desk in front of her. "Aristide, I want you to teach me how to use this." She opened the wrapping and lay the New Model Remington before him.

His eyes bulged. "Where did you get that?"

As simply as she could, she explained how Gérard Le Blanc had attacked her when she was out yesterday, and how she'd bought the gun because she felt unsafe. "He made threats, Aristide. I had to get it."

His lips flattened into a grim line. "There's something you're not telling me, Madeleine. Why would that man attack you at random, even if he is a scoundrel?"

She didn't respond immediately. She didn't know how.

"Come on, Madeleine. Out with it."

"I knew him in France. More than knew him." She buried her head in her hands. Steeled herself to spit it out. "He's my husband. My ex-husband."

It came up like vomit. Something so sickening she couldn't keep it down any longer.

Aristide gave her an incredulous stare and then said with careful deliberation, "He's what?"

"The man I was married to, who deserted me. I haven't heard a word from him for eight years. I thought he was dead."

"Gérard Le Blanc?" Aristide's tone was disbelieving.

She nodded. "Except that wasn't his name then. He's changed it."

Aristide ran a hand down his jaw and sat back. "So let me get this straight.

This scoundrel who we've considered capable of God-knows-what-humbug is your living husband? And you've known this, since when?" He fixed her with a steely gaze.

Her composure faltered. A bilious wave rose in her throat and she feared she really was going to vomit, all over his desk. She grasped the water glass and gulped. Began stuttering. "I-I-I recognized him that night they came here. I didn't know the second man. Just Philippe. I didn't know what to do. I was just too shocked to think."

Aristide waved a hand. "Slow down, Madeleine. You're not in trouble. I'm just stunned."

"Oh, but that's where you're wrong. I *am* in trouble. Deep trouble. We all are. Because he's come back. Twice."

Aristide stared, and a long silence

stretched between them. Finally he echoed, "Come back?" He took a deep breath. "You need to tell me the whole story. Not just bits and pieces."

"So who are these witnesses? Haven't I got a right to know who's accusing me of murder?"

Sheriff Wayne Arkwright hoiked a gob of phlegm past his mount's right front leg and jammed a fresh tab of gum in his mouth. "What, so you can go and frighten them off? Do you think I was born stupid?"

Caleb and the lawman were mounted side by side, watching as Santiago and his men roped and dragged the stiffened carcasses he'd found earlier into a heap, ready for torching. The day was fast drawing in, and they wanted to get the pyre lit before night fell.

The older man's attitude had changed from the cold skepticism he'd displayed in Rory's room the day before. Tonight, the curl of his lip betrayed smug satisfaction. He'd gone straight for the jugular. "I'm putting the picture together, Stewart. I've talked to more witnesses, and it's not a pretty picture for you. They confirm you set up a meeting with Rory Mackinnon the night he died." Arkwright leaned forward in the saddle, flesh testing the buttons of his plaid shirt.

Caleb's jaw clenched. "You know as well as I do, I was at Sir John Russell's that night. He can vouch for that."

"Ah yes, but who knows? Maybe we got the timeline wrong first up. Maybe you did it later. Or maybe you got someone else to do your dirty work."

Caleb stared out over the brown

pasture. Santiago and the boys had just about finished the job, were about to torch the woodpile and set the animals alight. He gestured resignedly. "Half a dozen prime bulls. Shot between the eyes. Someone is determined to make life very difficult."

The Sheriff's jaw rotated slowly, the expression in his eyes tight and unyielding. "You're being over dramatic. And who's to say you haven't staged this yourself?"

Caleb ground his back teeth.

Foul black smoke billowed from the pyre, and Arkwright wheeled his horse to leave. "I'm closing in. You'd be surprised the stories I hear out there, Mr. Stewart."

He spat out his gum in a practiced spume and settled back into his saddle with a satisfied wiggle.

"You're just a pretty boy who inherited his father's hard work." His eyes held a malevolent glitter. "But don't think you fool me. I'd say with what I know already you'll be locked up by this time next week. Six days more freedom, Stewart. Enjoy them."

Sir John's thick-walled manor house usually had an enveloping warmth in winter, but tonight Madeleine could not feel it. She rubbed her icy hands down the sides of her skirt to rid herself of the numbness, but the homely coziness of fires from several rooms brought her no sense of comfort. She was frozen on the inside, locked up in an overwhelming sense of failure and impending doom.

She'd done her best to explain everything to Aristide. She really had. But there were some things so deeply shaming she couldn't bring herself to talk about them. He'd had a hard enough job assimilating what she'd told him.

He'd greeted her account of Le Blanc's attempt to get her to plant the gun in the Stewart stables with shocked disbelief, tugging at his beard as if to convince himself that he was in the real world. "I don't believe it . . . I can't . . . You kept that from me?" When she'd then confided she'd thrown the gun into the river, he'd paced the floor in jerky agitated steps.

She couldn't stay sitting when he was so overwrought. She'd jumped up too. "Don't you see? I had to. What if they decided to search the Russell house and blame one of us? Even arrest *you*? What if Le Blanc got his hands on it again somehow and planted it at Caleb's anyway? I couldn't risk it!"

Aristide had regarded her with blank-faced amazement. And now she had to go over the whole thing again.

Vino d'Oro was an original — an old family home built before the Gold Rush on a Spanish land claim — and it had that consoling, rooted sense of durability that came with its adobe walls and unpretentious design. The apricot tint of old Spanish walls reminded Madeleine of the pink of the well-used French corsets her mother wore. Remembering that again as she sat in the parlor with the assembled Russell family members made her feel even more alone.

I don't belong here, and they have every right to tell me to go.

The original ranchos had built spacious rooms to cater for the typically extended Californio family, so the house was ideally suited to Sir John's tribe, embracing as it did his two brothers, their wives, and the wider circle of cousins and relatives by marriage.

Sebastian and Isabella were busy with their Sacramento lives — Isabella with her stage career, Sebastian with looking after Basil Stockton's California interests. Madeleine had met them only once. Sir John's wife Pania, in the late stages of her first pregnancy, was resting. But the remainder of the family — Graysie, Nathan and Sir John — were gathered in the cozy room they used for intimate family time like playing cards after dinner or sharing a quiet morning coffee. Freshly loaded pine logs resting on a bed of red-hot coals hissed reassuringly in the grate; no other sound penetrated the thick walls.

You could sit here and feel safe and

secure from anything. And you'd be so wrong.

Aristide had gone ahead of her and warned Sir John they needed to talk. She could tell that from the sense of curious anticipation that reached out to her as soon as she entered the room. The tycoon and clan senior raised his powerful shoulders and gazed at her with his penetrating black eyes for a second or two before gesturing to a chair by the fire. "Do take a seat, Mademoiselle. It's a cold night."

He took a seat on the opposite side of the fireplace, and Gracie and Nathan and Aristide completed an accepting semi-circle around them.

They're friendly now, but wait till they hear what I've got to tell them.

Sir John nodded to Aristide. "I understand your sister has come to you with something you believe we all need to hear. Can I leave it to you to explain what this is all about?"

Aristide stepped to the back of her chair, his hands resting lightly on her shoulders, demonstrating to the whole room his support for his sister. "I've learned more today about those two French agents — the troublemakers, as we've thought of them — who've been hanging around the neighborhood. I believe they go by the names of Gérard Le Blanc and Roland Durand." He glanced nervously around the group. First toward Sir John and then on to Nathan, who sat with his wife Graysie's hand in his lap. "From what Madeleine has told me, the situation is far more complicated than we realized. We're all likely to be affected — and Caleb too."

Madeleine moved uneasily in her

chair, shifting her weight from one buttock to the other. Graysie stretched out her legs and crossed one over the other. Everyone could hear the tension in Aristide's voice. He cleared his throat, as if reluctant to continue. "Madeleine has told me that the man Le Blanc — not his real name, I might add — is known to her. And he has intent to do harm to her and possibly others here."

Russell shot to his feet, his jaw rigid, his face clouded. "Harm?" he barked. "What kind of harm?"

Aristide held up his hand in a holding gesture. "He attacked her in the street yesterday. He's tried to coerce her to do errands for him under threats of awful consequences for the family if she doesn't agree. Right, Madeleine?" His voice was gentle and searching.

Madeleine nodded. Her mouth and

throat felt too dry to form words. She coughed uncomfortably. "That's right. It was vague. He particularly mentioned harm would come to Aristide and Mr. Stewart."

Aristide continued to hold his hand up in a gesture of containment. "Before we get into it, there's two things — well, three in fact — it's important that you know."

Madeleine fought a rising nausea. She was far too close to that fire. Beads of sweat trickled down her face.

Here it comes. My permanent disgrace.

"I mentioned that Madeleine knew Le Blanc. His real name is Philippe Coubert, and he comes from the same village as her. It was more than a passing acquaintance. She was married to him. Only for a matter of months, but married to him she was, and still is. They've never divorced. He deserted her in dire circumstances, and she thought for years that he was dead."

An abnormal silence fell at the word "married." So odd, Madeleine thought. She felt detached from the quiet that had fallen on the room like an invisible blanket.

Graysie was the first to speak. "Oh, Madeleine! How utterly ghastly for you!" She rose from her seat on the sofa next to Nathan and took two closing steps to Madeleine's chair, where she pressed her cheek consolingly against the side of Madeleine's damp face. "You've had a horrible shock, and I am so sorry." Her eyes were glittering with shared pain, and Madeleine's heart lightened.

"There's more," said Aristide, when Graysie resumed her seat. "Coubert originally deserted Madeleine because he was wanted for murder. He's a dangerous man, and he's already demonstrated that. He tried to get Madeleine to plant a gun in the Stewart stables."

There was a communal intake of breath. "He *what*?" said Sir John. "Tell us what happened, Mademoiselle, please."

Her cheeks burned as she scanned the circle of faces. She repeated what she'd told Aristide earlier. "I took the gun over there on the day of the round-up. I was so terrified of what he'd do if I didn't obey. But I couldn't go through with it. I threw it into the river when I went to town. That's why Le Blanc attacked me."

She coughed, and shook her head, clarifying. "He doesn't know about me throwing it in the river. He attacked me for not going along with him and planting it. To implicate Caleb. I think if he knew I've dumped it he really would have killed me. As it is, if someone hadn't interrupted him, I'm not sure that I'd still be here."

Graysie uttered a little cry, and Nathan drew his arm around her shoulder in a comforting gesture. "Oh, Madeleine! I had the feeling you hadn't just slipped on the street."

There was a heavy silence, and Sir John resumed his seat. "You realize this pretty well confirms what Caleb suspected, that Le Blanc was involved in those murders at his ranch. How could he have possession of incriminating evidence otherwise?" He looked to Madeleine. "And you realize you've destroyed that evidence? So it's impossible to take it to the sheriff's department?"

A cry of anguish rose in Madeleine's throat. "I know, but I didn't know what else to do! I was terrified he'd try and get it back. Kill me and then plant it at Caleb's anyway. Or plant it here and implicate Aristide and me. Arrange another raid with that sheriff he's got in the palm of his hand. Then everyone here would be under a cloud."

She looked around the circle, beseeching them to understand. "Don't you see? I've carried the label of 'the murderer's wife' ever since Philippe killed the first time — if that really was the first time. I had to face the wife of the man he killed every day at the market. Feel responsible for my husband's sins, over and over. So when Mother died last year I came to America for a fresh start. And now look what's happened." She felt the tears begin.

"I'm so sorry to have brought this evil on you all. I never thought I'd have to live with that awful label ever again. Or that he'd return to ruin my life."

No one stirred for a long time after she'd spoken. They sat or stood, gazing at the carpet, or into the fire, shocked into silence. Then Graysie wriggled on the sofa, her pretty flower-sprigged muslin skirts rustling around her. For a moment Madeleine thought she was going to get up and leave, but she edged herself to the front of the cushion, clasped her hands in front of her in a steeple pose, as if preparing to make a speech. When she opened her mouth her usually sweet singer's voice was cracked and rusty.

"Madeleine, you have absolutely no guilt to bear. You are not responsible for what your husband may or may not have done." Her lips pressed together in a slight grimace. "I'm sure I don't need to reiterate it to anyone here, but if you need to check it, I think the Good Book says that 'each will be put to death for his own sin.'"

She flashed Madeleine a quick smile. "It might be small comfort, Madeleine, but no one here will think any the worse of you because of this awful situation. Quite the opposite." She gestured to Aristide, who was still standing in a tense posture behind Madeleine's chair. "Sit down, Aristide. There's more. Another chapter." She gestured to her brother-in-law. "You too, John. I have a confession of my own. Nathan and I have not put you in the whole picture. It's time for us to correct that." She dropped her right hand to her thigh and Nathan reached across and covered it in his big square fingers and gently squeezed.

"You've been keeping secrets too, Graysie? Out with it then." Sir John's tone was mild but edged with impatience.

Graysie took a deep breath, and Madeleine sensed what she had to say next was not going to be easy. "That night the agents came here — New Year's Eve — rocked me. I was flummoxed. Not because of the men's sheer cheek, although there was that, but because I too have met Gérard Le Blanc before. But at that stage he still called himself Philippe Coubert." She swiveled on the spot, noting the sudden electric charge in the air. "And as you might imagine, the circumstances were only slightly less unpleasant than the ones Madeleine has described."

She pulled her hand free from

Nathan's grip and ran it through her hair in a distracted gesture. "There's no gentle way of saying this — so here goes. You see, this Philippe Coubert is Minette's father. He was my friend Francine's husband. And a no-good devil he turned out to be." She stared intensely at John, as if challenging him to interrupt her. He kept silent, but his face was thunderous. "I'm certain he has no idea we have his daughter here. If he did, I suspect he'd already have made trouble. I'm not even sure if he knows Francine is dead. He deserted her within weeks of Minette's birth. Rode out of town with another woman and Francine never heard from him again." She slumped against the sofa and her hand slipped back into Nathan's clasp. "And just like you, Madeleine, we thought — perhaps even hoped — that he had come to an end somewhere in the mountains, never to blight our lives again. As far as I'm concerned, it's a pity he's still breathing."

Madeleine's chest and throat had contracted into such a tight, hard wall as Graysie spoke that it was impossible to say a word. Instead, dry heaving sobs racked her, sending her ribcage into sharp convulsions as she fought for control of her breath, of her body.

She felt as if a dark veil had fallen over her, so that the full impact of what Graysie had just said could be only dimly grasped, like trying to make out a bulky figure across a meadow at dusk.

What is Graysie saying? Take it slowly.

Philippe had married again, here in California? And Minette was his daughter?

My sister was called Francine.

She didn't know if she'd spoken the words out loud, or just in her own mind. Her body shuddered with another wave of sobbing, but this time she wasn't sure if it was in grief or joy. *I'm going mad, I must be. He's finally turned me crazy.*

Was that just a coincidence, or had Philippe deliberately sought out her sister Francine, in some twisted way wreaking revenge on her? The one who'd been double-crossed, as he saw it, paying back the double-crosser?

Her hands felt so grimy that she scratched at them, expecting to scrape off a layer of dirt so deep you could see the line in her sweaty palm. "It can't be."

Madeleine couldn't sit still any longer. She rose from her chair, hands clasped in front of her, and paced in front of the fire. "It must be another Francine! It's not such an uncommon name."

Graysie's expression was kindly, sympathetic. "That's true," she said. "It is a common name. But how many Francines travelled with the Franconi family circus from Paris? Was your sister associated with that circus?" Franconi was an Italian who'd taken over a famous circus in Paris; one of his sons, Henri, had gone to America with a spin-off from the main show. And Francine had eloped with Henri's son.

Madeleine's cheeks were hot. She shook her head in disbelief. "I don't believe it. *C'est impossible*!" She dropped her hands to her sides and let them swing helplessly. "But yes. Francine eloped with Franconi's grandson, Jacques. The family originally settled in France because the old man got into trouble killing a man in a duel and had to leave Italy."

Graysie regarded her with steady, solemn eyes. "Then there's no doubt. Minette is your niece." She gave a wistful smile. "That must help to salve the hurt?"

"It's going to take a little time to get used to." Madeleine gave a half-laugh and collapsed back into her seat.

How could he?

When he got drunk, he would often goad her with how boring she was, always buried in books, the dusty schoolteacher.

Not like Francine, the darling of the village inn, pretty, pert, quick to dance and sing.

He'd only heard of Francine's reputation as a heartbreaker, he'd never met her, but still he'd baited her with it. And it was true. Madeleine had been the studious, sensible one.

Francine had broken a dozen hearts before she ran off to America with her love, never to return. She didn't know Madeleine had married a year after she left. She'd have had no idea Philippe was her brother-in-law.

A hundred cakes of soap won't wash away the shame.

And Philippe was a bigamist as well as a murderer and thief.

Aristide came around the side of her chair and crouched beside her, his arm around the back of her neck, a glass of water in the other hand. "Sip this. Breathe deep." He was consoling, coaching, encouraging her, while her sobs died away to be replaced by a dry rasping breathing.

"How could he?" Graysie tilted her

head on one side. "Madeleine, I am so sorry. You had no idea?"

Madeleine shook her head. "Just a few days ago — last weekend — when I was giving Minette her bath, she said something that made me think. She was talking about her maman. She had that circus toy there in the bath. You know the one?"

Graysie smiled. "I do. The painted wooden acrobat with moving joints. He's one of her treasures."

"She told me her mother had given him to her. And she said her father had been in a circus. She obviously got the stories a little muddled." She shook her head. "It did seem slightly odd. A strange coincidence. But there's been so much going on lately — I was too frightened to even try and talk to you about it. I was so terrified I'd brought something terrible on

238

the whole family because of Philippe. As if I was a curse on you all. 'The murderer's wife' — a bit like a witch in the Middle Ages. Only good for expulsion." She fiddled with the sleeve of her dress. Her cheeks were hot and tight.

"But that Philippe was Minette's father?"

She shook her head. "No, I never had a clue." She tapped her foot on the floor reflectively. "I'm pretty certain he doesn't know. If he did, I doubt he could resist gloating." When she raised her eyes to Graysie, her cheeks were wet. "Graysie, I'm sure you agree that's how it must stay."

Graysie jumped up and came across the room to hug her. "You're so right, Madeleine. The last thing in the world we want is for him to realize Minette is his daughter."

8

"I'm very disappointed at the news I'm hearing. The telegraph wires are positively humming."

Sheriff Wayne Arkwright socked back the last of his whiskey and stretched out his arm for more. Gérard sloshed a generous slug into the waiting glass and slammed the bottle down on the table with a loud crack.

"Careful with that," Arkwright hissed. "Or you'll be buying another bottle."

Gérard ignored the prickly irritation which was crawling up his neck and making him hot behind the ears. "What news?" he said, sharply. Too sharply.

Don't act interested. He's just baiting you.

"Apparently Sir John Russell has hired a fancy lawyer to bring proceedings against a certain French national who is unlawfully in California. Or so he believes. Seeking extradition, I understand, because of capital crimes."

Arkwright gave him a knowing stare, and Gérard's heart felt as if it did a full revolution in his chest. Was that even biologically possible?

Damn Madeleine's righteous soul.

"Really?" He picked up his whiskey and made a studied play of carefully sipping, savoring the burn as it slid down his throat. "You'll have to let me in on the secret of why I — why we — should care. At last count I believe there were — what, thirty thousand Frenchmen in California. Do we know exactly which one of the thirty thousand he's taking an interest in?"

Arkwright's mouth turned up in a genuine grin — the first Gérard had ever seen from him. "So glad you asked, Mr. Le Blanc. Although I have to say it's all being done with the *utmost discretion.*" He grinned again, but now Gérard could detect a malicious curl to his lips. Arkwright was enjoying this cat-and-mouse game, he could see that, as his mind went at a million miles an hour, trying to decide on his next strategy. Deny everything, admit everything, or find a cagey position somewhere in between?

He's always known it might be possible the California authorities would catch up with him, would realize they had a man wanted for murder in their midst. He'd been panicked into changing his name when that exact thing had happened a few years back. Someone had recognized him. Asked him if he was Philippe Coubert from Bordeaux. He'd denied everything, went back after dark and dealt with it. Shot the man. And then set about changing his identity.

But the chances of it happening a second time, especially now he'd changed his name and appearance, the idea of anyone being the least blt excited about it, he'd considered to be so infinitesimal as to not be worth worrying about. Sure, the US had signed an extradition agreement with France way back, twenty years ago, but no one had ever been deported, had they?

It would be just his luck for a big-wig like John Russell to get a bee in his bonnet. Because that was really the only way anything could ever come of it, if someone like him kept pushing. As his brain spun, Arkwright seemed happy to just sit and drink.

They were in Gérard's room at Ten Mile Station, having taken care to avoid being seen together in public. It was actually his and Roland's room, but he had Roland out on watch duty, keeping an eye on Madeleine, to make sure she wasn't tempted to make a run for it.

He'd badly miscalculated her. When he'd re-emerged in her life, he hadn't exactly expected an open-arms welcome. He'd expected she might run and hide — even go back to France to escape him. But he'd never have guessed she'd be willing to confide in someone like the mighty Sir John. Damn her soul in eternity.

"Well? Do you want to know who it is?" Arkwright was getting bored.

"I'm sure you're going to tell me, whether I want you to or not."

"Let's just say it's someone central to my inquiry into the death of Rory Mackinnon. Someone holding key evidence that would shuffle Mr. Caleb Stewart into jail and make the way clear for a syndicate very dear to my heart to acquire Rancho Del Oro. Or the parts of it that are in prime demand, like access to the American River. Such a sought-after commodity in these years of extreme drought, isn't it? Water, I mean."

Arkwright had begun speaking in a sing song voice, but as he continued it hardened into something else; a grating, insistent demand. He pointed his index finger angrily in Gérard's face. "You told me you had it all sewn up. That you had 'witnesses' who would put Caleb Stewart away for life, if not get him hanged. If you get caught up in this messy business with Russell, where does that leave me?"

Arkwright glared. "I don't know about you, but there's no way I'm going to be the fall guy for a failed takeover scheme for Buffer, Jones and Cottlesloe. Their patron saint, Senator Hector de Vile, would be most displeased. And if Senator de Vile is unhappy, so am I."

Gérard had risen from his chair and gone to stand by the window. Outside the usual frenetic activity with stagecoach and long-haul teams and their loads played out. Another electric California day, with the promise of riches and ease just within fingertip grasp. He turned back to Arkwright, his face set in a mask of serene confidence. "I understand your concern, Sheriff. I can assure you there is no reason to feel any concern. The witnesses are solid. Their stories will hold up in court. And Caleb

Stewart will go down."

The sheriff stood and took hold of his hat with one hand while he tossed back the remaining liquor with the other. He licked his lips in satisfaction. "That's what I wanted to hear. I told Stewart I'd be coming for him next week, and I don't want to disappoint him."

He picked up the gun that had been lying on the table as they drank and spun it on his finger, grinning into Gérard's face. "One good turn deserves another, right? I won't say anything about any murder charges in France, and you'll make sure Stewart is trussed up like a chicken by Monday. Don't let me down."

For a long time after Sheriff Arkwright left him, Gérard Le Blanc slouched in his chair, staring at his empty glass, not really seeing anything around him. He hadn't felt like this for a very long time — not since he was a twenty-year-old taking a close-to-knockout punch in the local tavern. His hands were clammy, his mind dazed and confused. Dammit, even his eyesight wasn't up to its normal clarity. He shook his head in disbelief.

He'd been so cocky, and he'd been bested by a woman. Not once, but four times. When would he ever learn? And by the same woman. His wife, the angelic creature who had promised on their wedding day to "have and to hold, for better, for worse." She had betrayed him again.

First she'd squealed on him to the gendarmes. Led them to where he'd hidden the bloody knife. Then she'd confirmed details of his embezzling activities — what she knew of them because he'd stupidly boasted they'd have plenty of money to leave with — and that had been more damaging even than murder. She'd refused to plant the gun to get Caleb Stewart. And now she had tittle-tattled to Sir John.

He'd been so wrong. He'd thought she'd be terrified of him. That she'd keep quiet out of shame; because if he went down, he was taking her down with him. She was an accessory to murder. Had she forgotten?

He recalled the sparkling aquamarine eyes, the delicately sculpted lips with their ready smile, and felt his body respond, despondent as he might be. She'd always had the ability to lift his spirits.

Then he thought of the way she'd looked at Caleb Steward on the night he'd been at the Russell house, as if seeking reassurance. The pleasure he'd felt rising within deflated quicker than a pricked balloon.

She has something going on with that pigeon boy, I'm sure of it.

Eight years in California and he was building himself a nice little castle of influence, only to have it collapsed by one elegant finger, like a cardboard house.

He wiped his hand around the back of his neck. He'd felt hot and sticky moments ago. Not any longer. His neck was like ice. That's what the mere mention of Caleb Stewart's name did to him.

And she's chosen that spoiled Californio ahead of me.

Yes. His first step in the new plan was to shut up his wife in a way that wouldn't see him swinging. Silently.

Surreptitiously. And then he would truss up that pathetic pretty boy she was chasing after and deliver him to Arkwright.

He slouched back in his chair, feeling suddenly relieved. The sense of being punch-drunk had gone, replaced by an almost euphoric light-headedness. Come to think of it, there was something else he needed to do as well. He'd go right over Arkwright's head to the big boys in San Francisco. He'd explain to Buffer, Jones and Cottlesloe why it was in their best interests to ensure that neither he nor his reputation suffered any harm. He knew they'd understand when he spelled it out because they had even more to lose than he did.

But first, he needed to teach his wife a lesson she wouldn't forget.

She is hot. So very hot. She tries to crawl away on her bare knees, over the green, green grass, the grass tickling her bare legs, over into the trees where he won't find her. But she can't lift her legs, and without even looking she knows she is held fast in honey. Or was it the blood? She looks down and her palms are red.

Her jaw drops wide open. And even as she stares, a bee flies into her open mouth. Flies right in, and before she can spit it out, it stings her tongue. She screams, then. She screams for a long, long time.

But she can't look away. From the topsy-turvy beehive. The scattered waxy honey frames. One of them is smashed by the shape of a man's boot. And everywhere, the clear honey oozing free … Running away . . . translucent gold and red, a brilliant red.

A black cloud forms, and it rises, buzzing, like a giant question mark. As it rises, her face swells. Further and further into the sky, the black question mark rises and her face with it. She's a pale pink balloon stretching on and on. Swelling and swelling until it reaches heaven.

And when it gets to heaven, she'll stop breathing. She knows this because your face can't stretch that far without something terrible happening.

She sits bolt upright, gasping for breath, arms and legs rigid, her heart racing like a train. She is staring into a darkness so dense she wonders if she will ever escape it. She shivers. She is cold. So cold.

She isn't in Pierre Bourreau's Bordeaux apiary, with his boxed beehives anymore. She's in her California bed, haunted by her dreams. She lies, eyes wide open, staring at the ceiling, terrified to go back to sleep and dream again.

What is that old proverb her mother always quoted? *Comme on fait son lit, on le treuve.* Yes, that was it. "As you make your bed, so you will lie in it."

"Josefa! Listen to me!" The exasperated tone in his voice would raise Josefa's hackles, so he fought down his rising irritation.

Why can't she see it?

Caleb softened his tone. "Sorry, I don't mean to sound impatient. But don't you see? Rory wasn't plotting against us. He was being used by others. He was expendable. Once they got him to sign the papers, they didn't need him anymore." He scratched the side of his face. "In fact he probably didn't sign them. That's why they dealt so badly with him. They probably forged his signature after they tortured and killed him."

The sun slanting through the window of the Chinese tea house was hot in the middle of the day even in winter, and his skin itched under its rays.

Josefa's eyes searched his. She massaged her left thumb in her right hand nervously, considering his words. She'd been reluctant to come out with him, to leave Bonaventura's. He'd skulked in the street until he saw Bonnie and Consuela go out, and she'd only acquiesced because they weren't expected back for a couple of hours. "I don't want them to know we're talking. I don't trust them," he'd explained. "Please. It's important."

Now Josefa gazed at him over her teacup. Her butterscotch complexion was dry and flat, the tiny fine lines around her mouth and eyes highlighted in the glare. "But those papers. It's his signature." Josefa peered around anxiously, as if fearful Consuela would appear out of nowhere.

Caleb reached across the table and covered her restless hand with his own much bigger one. "We weren't there, Josefa, and we'll never know. The people who were there won't tell us, even if we find out who they are. But if I was a betting man, I'd lay the farm against a milk churn that Rory was killed because he resisted doing what they wanted. They forced that signature out of him, or they forged it. But he didn't give it willingly, and he paid for that with his life."

Fat tears began to roll soundlessly down her cheeks. She pulled her hand away to dash away the deluge. "That sounds like Rory," she gasped. "He never wanted trouble. He always said the years his family was with Fergus and Valentina were the happiest years of his life. He never stopped missing us."

He considered how to phrase his next question. "Sheriff Arkwright seems to be so sure he has witnesses who will swear that I set up a meeting with Rory that night. Even that I was seen with him arranging such a meeting." He raised his eyes anxiously to hers. "You wouldn't be one of those people he was talking about, would you? He isn't planning to use you, is he?"

Her face darkened to light caramel, and she shifted her weight uneasily. "I don't know. Um, he might be."

His stomach lurched, and he had to fight to retain a neutral calm expression. "Tell me about it, Josefa. What exactly did he ask and what did you tell him? And don't be afraid. Truly. I have nothing to fear from the truth. I'm not planning on interfering with Arkwright's witnesses. I just want to get to the bottom of this. What does he think he knows? He seems to be pretty confident he has enough to arrest me — or will have by next week."

She made a choking noise and swallowed hard. "When the sheriff first came around, the day after you found Rory's body, he asked lots of questions, and I told him Rory had been invited to a meeting at the ranch. Because that's what Rory told me. He was excited about it. And I believed him. We both wanted to believe it. Wanted to think we could heal the scars and start again." She blinked rapidly. "You can understand that, can't you?"

"Sure I can. I very much regret it didn't happen."

"But really, everything I told him was hearsay. I was just repeating what Rory had told me. If he's saying anything more than that, he's lying."

Caleb shifted in his chair uneasily. "And what about Consuela? Have you any idea what she might have told him?"

She regarded him with serious dry eyes, as if trying to see into hidden mysteries. "Consuela hates our family, I have to admit. I've only realized since Rory died just how much she hates us. But she adored Rory." Her face flushed pink. "She was almost creepy about him, if I'm honest. I mean, she was his stepmother and ages older than him, but you'd almost think sometimes he was her beau."

She shook her head, and her fall of dark brown hair swung on her shoulders. She swiped it back with a distracted gesture. "I can't believe she knew about any conspiracy, if there was one. Not before he was killed, anyway. She'd never have wanted him put in danger, no matter how much she might want to get her hands on the ranch. But after his death? She was set on revenge. I don't know what she might have told them."

They'd barely made it back to Bonaventura's house when Caleb heard the warning whistle from the ranch hand he'd left on watch in the street outside. "That's Santiago." He grabbed Josefa's arm. "Is there another way out? Or somewhere I can hide? I don't want them to know I've been here. Arkwright might make a fuss."

Josefa shook her head vigorously. "Not another way out the front. Hide in my room. She'll probably go out again soon. Come on!" She shoved him down a dingy hall to the room next door to the family room. The walls were flimsy, and he could easily hear the sounds of visitors returning as he stood in the middle of the room, casting around for the best place to hide. Josefa pointed to a big oak wardrobe in one corner. "In there," she mouthed, pointing to the big doors hanging half-open. "Get in there."

He slid into the dark recess and was enveloped in slippery fabric and Josefa's sweet feminine fragrance.

She's so young, and so naive. She shouldn't have to be facing this.

The thought was interrupted by the

sound of Consuela and Le Blanc settling themselves down next door. Where Aunt Bonnie was, he had no idea. He peeked through the small remaining gap in the wardrobe doors and saw Josefa had assumed a pose of girlish innocence, seated in an armchair, standard lamp at her shoulder, knitting.

The boom of a familiar voice sounded through the wall, and her finely arched eyebrows contracted in alarm. "Doña Consuela, I'm relying on you."

Gérard Le Blanc's deep voice had taken on a sing-song French lilt that wasn't usually present when he spoke. Not exactly wheedling, but the tonal quality was close to it. "I've told the sheriff we will have him delivered like a trussed-up chicken ready for roasting by Monday. And you're the only one who can do it."

Josefa's eyes flickered toward the wardrobe in alarm.

"Of course, Monsieur Le Blanc," Consuela said. "I want to help in any way I can to catch my stepson's killer. What do you want me to do?"

"I understand you saw Mr. Mackinnon and Caleb Stewart together. You overheard Stewart making arrangements to meet on New Year's Eve?" Le Blanc's voice was briefly interrupted by coughing. "Think carefully, Doña Consuela. You have the power to put this meddlesome man behind bars, all at the power of your word."

"Yes, of course. Just let me think."

The silence was broken by the sound of liquor being poured into glasses. Sherry, or port, perhaps. He wasn't sure what Consuela drank. Then the sound of glasses clinking together.

"Here's to the destruction of the Stewarts." Consuela's voice rang out loud and clear. "I was with them in the Golden Eagle Hotel. Rory wanted to drop in there on our way home from viewing a house he was considering renting. He was so keen to set up house with Josefa as soon as possible. We called at the Golden Eagle for a quick bite on the way home. We were both famished. Rory was a real man, with big appetites . . . ."

Consuela's voice wavered, as if savoring her memories. There was a brief pause. Caleb guessed she was enjoying her port.

"Well, Caleb was there. In the dining room. Rory didn't seem surprised to see him. I got the impression it was pre-arranged. So, of course, he invited us to join him."

As Consuela wove her story, Caleb's

insides were turning to ice. He had been at the Golden Eagle dining room in the weeks leading up to Rory's death. He'd met Thomas Halliburton there to be briefed on the outcome of the last court case. But he had not seen Consuela or Rory. He wondered if someone had been watching him and had told Consuela he'd been there to add credibility to her account. His skin prickled with rising unease.

"Oh yes? And what did they discuss?" It sounded as if Le Blanc might be writing down Consuela's account as she gave it, like a policeman might a sworn statement. No matter that Le Blanc was no policeman, and this was no "sworn statement." Caleb guessed Arkwright wouldn't be bothered by such niceties.

"They chatted about what Rory had been doing — the winery, that kind of stuff. Rory expressed an interest in working with Caleb. Asked if they could let bygones be bygones. Reminded him how they'd always got on well together. All utter nonsense, of course," she snorted. "Fergus Stewart was a ruthless thief and his son isn't any better. They cheated the Mackinnons out of house and home. Rory knew that. But you know, he was trying to get back in there. For my sake. And for Josefa's. For the woman he loved. Who can blame him?"

Le Blanc gave a deep throated chortle of approval. "Nice touch, Doña Consuela. Very nice."

And then in a more formal tone: "And what did Mr. Stewart say in response?"

Caleb could almost see him picking up the pen to resume taking her statement.

"Oh, Caleb seemed friendly. He said he'd speak with his mother. He said why didn't Rory come to visit on New Year's Eve and they would work something out. One thing I thought was a bit odd, though."

Caleb imagined her taking another glug of port. He could hear the relish in her voice as her story grew. "He emphasized to Rory that he should keep the meeting private. Not tell anyone. And to come alone."

Le Blanc cleared his throat. "Really? Did he say why?"

"He said his mother would be upset if word got back to her before he had a chance to talk to her about it — I guess because of the court case. He said it was important it remained a secret until something was decided."

"I see. And that struck you as unusual?"

"Well, maybe not at the time,

although I thought it reasonable that Josefa and I could have been included. I mean it was going to affect us as well, wasn't it? And afterwards when Rory was so tragically killed — well, it seemed to me Caleb Stewart was setting up an ambush. Consuela's voice rose to a wail. "A cold-blooded, calculated ambush. And a perfectly wonderful young man was murdered."

Gérard Le Blanc's deep voice was a smooth as custard. "Caleb Stewart says he was at the Russell house that night and a number of witnesses can confirm it. What do you say to that?"

Consuela's voice was laden with contempt. "Oh, that man lies as fast as a dog can trot. He obviously got one of his lackeys to do it. That Santiago, perhaps. He's been there for years. It shouldn't be too hard to find out. He's got dozens of ruffians there who will do his bidding. But he's the one who set it up. And he should hang."

Josefa's hands had slowed around her knitting needles as Consuela's account dragged on. By its end her hands were completely still. At Consuela's final declaration she rose abruptly and bumped a tumbler of water from a side table to the floor. The glass smashed. Josefa squealed.

Consuela's voice barked out, "Josefa is that you?"

Caleb shrank back into the furthest recesses of the wardrobe, drawing the doors fully closed behind him. His last view was of Josefa standing frozen, watching the door, her knitting still in one hand, a little white garment like a baby's vest hanging off the needles. Then Le Blanc was there. "Ah, Josefa! It is you. We didn't know you were home."

Caleb could imagine him peering suspiciously around the room. "What are you doing here?"

"I was just resting. I fell asleep." She sounded breathy and defensive. "When I woke I thought I'd do a little knitting . . ." She affected a yawn. "What time is it? I've had such a restful morning." Her words became muffled, as if she was speaking against the back of her hand, stifling another yawn. "Quite lost a sense of the time."

"Really," said Le Blanc dryly. "And of course, you have no interest in anything we've been discussing?"

"Next door?" said Josefa vaguely. "Oh, you mean you and Consuela? I was quite wrapped up in what I'm doing here. Have you been here long?"

Caleb stuffed a fist in his mouth to

stop himself from laughing out loud. Josefa was making a valiant attempt to play the dumb brunette, but he doubted Le Blanc would fall for it.

"Only for the last half hour," he said sarcastically.

Consuela now chimed in. "Really, Josefa. This is too bad. Why didn't you tell me you were here?"

"I told you, I was asleep."

"Well, I'm pleased you find the room so comfortable, because you'll be spending a lot of time here over the next few weeks."

Caleb heard a heavy tread outside the room and then Le Blanc said, "Durand, tie her up and watch her closely. I don't want anyone getting the wrong idea, and I'm just not sure how reliable Miss Stewart is. Can't have her running home to mother now, can we?"

Josefa protested weakly but the sound quickly subsided.

"If you know what's good for you, you'll shut up. You've seen and heard nothing," said Le Blanc.

"But that's right," Josefa whimpered. "Exactly right. I've seen and heard nothing."

"Open it! Open it Tante Maddy!"

Minette jumped up and down excitedly, stretched on tiptoe to examine the rosette-topped floral-patterned gift box on the kitchen tabletop.

Tante Maddy.

It was fast becoming Minette's favorite name for her. She'd coined it after they'd explained she really was Minette's aunt, not just a pretend one. And it seemed to have stuck.

Minette fingered the red rosette which

topped the box, delivered by Wells Fargo Letter Express, but carrying official US Government stamps. A way to get around the US Post Office's mail monopoly. A local delivery then, from someone who knew how private express services worked in this part of the state.

Maybe it was from Aristide. Or Graysie.

Minette's chubby little fingers hovered. She itched to open it, Madeleine could see. "Is it your birthday?" she asked excitedly.

Madeleine shook her head, smiling.

"Do you think there'll be candy in it? Or toys?" she added hopefully. "Maybe it's cake." She gave Madeleine a buoyant smile. "Can we open it?"

"*Sûrement. Pourquoi pas?*"

Madeleine moved the box to a low stool and cut the ribbon that held the lid down. "There you are. Now we can look inside."

Eyes sparkling with delighted anticipation, Minette delicately edged the lid off the box and peered inside. The waxy perfume of honey arose from a smaller wooden box nestled inside on a storm of tissue. Minette's hand reached in. "Oh, there's a letter."

She handed Madeleine a sealed envelope and rooted around in the packaging. Madeleine tore it open and drew out a sheet of scallop-edged writing paper. Expensive. Perfumed. And carrying a hand-written message in a bold black hand.

Honeytrap! Snap!

Si je descends, tu descends aussi.

If I go down, you go down too.

Heart plummeting, she reached out. "No, Minette . . ."

The girl's hands were buried in the tissue, drawing something out. Simultaneously, a black cloud erupted from inside. Minette fell back, clawing at her exuberant curls, as the buzzing whine of dozens of angry bees boiled out of the box.

No! How could . . .?

Madeleine swept the flailing child up in her arms, scooping her skirt up around her stiff little body to protect her as best she could. Then she ran. Through a hail of stinging pricks, as the bees dive-bombed her head, pierced her neck, her arms. She ran.

"Aunt Bonnie! Aunt Bonnie!"

Caleb jerked awake, woken by the yapping of the two Pomeranians that accompanied his aunt everywhere. He could just make out Roland's protesting male voice through the barking.

"Aunt Bonnie! Aunt Bonnie!" Josefa called again.

Bonaventura must have pushed past Durand because he felt a gust of cold fresh air as the bedroom door slammed open against the wall. The laborious wheeze that was Bonnie's trademark was so loud he could hear it from the depths of the wardrobe. "Josefa! What on earth?" Bonnie's voice was sharp. "What's going on? Who tied you up like this, child? Has there been a robbery? For goodness sake." She turned to Durand, who was protesting. "Cut her free."

"Mr. Le Blanc, he'll be back soon. With the lady Consuela."

"Figs to the Frenchman. Free the girl. Now!"

A strong carnation scent, blended with

the musk of female body odor, wafted into the wardrobe. Bonnie was riled up, and that had to be a good thing.

The cramp in Caleb's thigh from being jammed first in the wardrobe and then crouched on Bonnie's roof was the only thing stopping him from dropping off to sleep.

Where is she? And how much longer will she be?

He was on the second story, back edge, of the multiple-roomed Victorian, waiting for Josefa to clamber out the water-closet window and join him.

Below was a shabby fire escape from the second to the first floor leading down a short ladder and then a long drop from the first floor to the ground. Not ideal for Josefa in her skirts, but if they were getting out of here without Le Blanc knowing, this was the only way.

They'd made the whispered arrangement when Josefa had made an excuse to come back into her room to collect a stole, and he wasn't leaving without her.

He rubbed his leg to ease his stiffened muscles and heard the low rumble of the window opening. Josefa thrust her head out, gave him a cheeky grin, and lifted a long skirt-draped leg over the threshold.

"About time," he breathed as he stepped forward to steady her. "I was starting to get worried."

"Bonnie was very informative. I'll tell you about that later. I made an excuse about having an early night, so they might not miss me till morning. But just in case, let's get out of here."

He grabbed the warm jacket and boots she'd given him earlier in preparation for her escape. "Quick, put on your jacket and boots." He handed them to her and pointed. "And then over the back. There's a fire escape."

He was halfway down the second-floor ladder when he heard the shout from above. So much for Josefa fooling them with an early night. He peered up at her. "You'll have to come now. I'll be at the bottom to catch you. *Que un coñazo.* What a pain."

He made a leap for the last few rungs, fearful the ladder might not hold both of them, and then flung himself over the edge down the next floor. The second ladder finished a good ten feet from the ground, but he didn't pause. As soon as he ran out of rungs he hung by his hands for the full length of his body and then let go.

The ground was boggy, the back lane

deserted. He landed evenly on both feet and braced himself to absorb the impact.

One down. One to go.

He was squinting up, trying to make out Josefa's progress in the twilight, when a figure loomed at his shoulder. He whirled, drawing his revolver as he turned.

"Woah, compadre! It's me, Santiago."

D'Oro's night manager held his hands up in mock-surrender, a grin on his face. Caleb let out a huge sigh. "Am I glad to see you!"

"Yeah, I saw they'd come home. Thought I might be more use around the back. And so it seems. But what's with the lady? We're taking your sister?" The disbelief in his voice rang clear.

"Yes, we are. We can't leave her there. She's joined our team." Up on the roof, Josefa had begun to make her way down the first-floor ladder and was nearing the point where the rungs ran out and she would have to jump. Her skirts were tucked up in her underwear, like a circus performer.

"Be careful!" he shouted up to her.

"Give me back-up," he grunted to Santiago, and turned to ready himself to catch her. "As soon as you hit the end, just drop. I'll catch you." Fleetingly he remembered the games they'd played in the hay loft when they were kids, jumping from height into soft mounds. Josefa had been fearless.

Oof! As she landed with some grace, her front facing the house wall and back to him, he latched on under her armpits and they fell backwards together. His back was wet with mud, but they were both safe and whole.

Nero's shiny black haunch loomed out

of the dark. Good old Santiago. The man for the job! The vaquero handed Caleb the reins. "Quickly," he hissed. "We've got no time."

Caleb hesitated for an instant and then mounted.

Santiago whirled to stand in front of Josefa, who was righting herself, smoothing her hair and skirts. "Miss Stewart. Excuse me." He grasped her about the waist with two strong hands and lifted her like a doll up to Caleb. Caleb in turn grabbed her around her hips and set her firmly on the saddle in front of him.

"Hold on, sis," he muttered in her ear. "This is going to be a bumpy ride."

They slid quietly out of the alleyway into the main thoroughfare of L Street. He planned to move at a leisurely pace so as not to frighten pedestrians or attract attention. But they hadn't gone more than a couple of streets before Caleb heard the steady drum of hooves coming up from behind. Fast.

"It's the Frenchman!" Santiago yelled. "He's got a gun. And he's got the other one with him!"

9

They hadn't fired yet, probably wouldn't want to risk attracting attention in the city center, but the sound of their hooves drew nearer. Caleb held Josefa close and leaned his body over hers, sheltering her from the line of fire, but his heart was exploding. They couldn't outrun bullets, and there was no time or space to wheel around and confront their pursuers without risking getting shot in the process. They were catching up too fast.

They left behind the busy sections of L Street, where workers gossiped on street corners before hustling home to lodgings on the pulsing Front Street waterside. The Rose of Lima church on K and

Eleventh where Rory had been farewelled was blocks behind them, and they were approaching the crumbling adobe ruins of the deserted Sutter's Fort on the outskirts of town. The haunt of the footloose and feckless, and not a place to go to after dark. But it could be somewhere, Caleb thought, to take shelter. The decaying walls sat on a grassy rise on the opposite side of the street from a church which was also closed up and silent.

He whistled shrilly through his teeth to let Santiago know he was going to change direction and abruptly plunged from L Street's hard surface to the uneven grass surrounding the fort.

"When we stop, jump and run," he hissed into Josefa's ear. "Don't worry about us. Just get down behind the wall."

He reined in Nero but maintained a steady pace up the rise to the remnants of the fort's thick walls. When they were within easy sprinting distance, he wheeled around to face their attackers and halted. He half lifted, half dragged Josefa off the saddle so she could slide to the ground with one hand, while grasping for his revolver with the other.

Josefa landed lightly, ducked around Nero's head and melted into a shadowed gap in the wall.

Good girl. One thing less to worry about.

Santiago had taken his lead and had followed him into the rough park. He too halted and turned to face their pursuers.

"Whoa there, Le Blanc," Caleb roared into the dark. "Any closer and we'll shoot."

It was plain that the ranchers had the

advantage on horseback. They were safely backed up with the crumbling wall behind them, aiming down the slope before Le Blanc and Durand had managed to pull off L Street.

"Thank God we were born in the saddle," he muttered to Santiago, who sat shoulder to shoulder with him. "At least we have that advantage."

The uneasy standoff was interrupted by the rumble of carriage wheels. An open-topped runabout pulled by a single horse slowed to a halt and a woman in a silky red gown stepped down to the street. The man beside her driving stared straight ahead.

Consuela! She strutted to Le Blanc's horse like the Queen of Sheba inspecting her troops.

He wasn't close enough to hear what she said, but she was gesturing angrily toward them and remonstrating with the Frenchman, obviously unhappy with the way he was conducting things.

Then she put her hands on her hips and took several long strides towards him. "Caleb Martinez Stewart." Her voice rang out strongly, laced with contempt. "How brave you are! Look at you! Back to the wall, pointing your gun at a woman. Are you going to shoot me, Consuela Valaquez, a *royales* daughter of Governor Valaquez? Your own cousin? A woman of your own blood — not that you recognize your blood!" Gérard had fallen into step behind her, his gun still drawn.

"You're no more a Valaquez than I am, Consuela," Caleb retorted. "I know you like to hug that heritage to your bosom like some fancy fan, but wasn't your father Brigadier Pico Alvarado, a failed army man forced to liquidate his holdings to pay his debts? Didn't he spend his final years in poverty?"

Consuela scowled.

"As for the appeals to family, is this the same woman who only hours ago held her own cousin a prisoner?"

Consuela threw her head back and laughed, a full-throated roar that echoed in the space around them and bounced back from the fort walls. "A prisoner? Who would believe that? Would Sheriff Arkwright, I wonder? Would he believe that?" She levelled him a wolfish grin. "I think not. Not when he *so* wants to put you behind bars for Rory's murder. And Josefa? Would she be willing to back up your story?" She curled her blood-red lips. "Josefa? You're hiding away back there, I know it. Back there in the shadows. Would you speak up for your brother, tell the sheriff I held you against your will? Knowing what I know about you?"

She waited, but Josefa did not step out.

"If you want to play it that way, I can have a word with your mother, the sainted Doña Valentina. Come on girl, show yourself. Tell your brother how it is."

There was a rattle of rocks falling against one another and Josefa stepped out from the shelter of the fort wall. "Caleb, I'm sorry." Her hair had slipped from its usual sleek pinnings to fall in bedraggled locks across her face. Her eyes flittered to his briefly, her mouth twisted into an embarrassed apology. "I couldn't . . . I can't . . . ." She bit her lower lip and fell silent.

Caleb moved Nero closer to her, surprised at the change in her demeanor.

She'd been so bold and confident. Now she was cowering under Consuela's contempt.

"She's got her own secrets, Caleb. She's not in any position to stand up for you. She's got herself to look after." Consuela turned her gaze on Josefa again. "Haven't you, little chickie? So why don't we drop this nonsense and you come home with Consuela? Come here, baby."

She smooched her big lips as if she was fussing over a baby or a lap dog, and Caleb felt his temperature surge. "Stay where you are, Josefa," Caleb barked. "You too, Le Blanc."

As Consuela had been talking, Gérard Le Blanc had sidled around her and edged into closer range. Santiago pulled his rifle from his saddle and leveled it threateningly. "Get back," he ordered in a voice that could crush rocks.

"Josefa come here." Santiago's voice carried the same tone of authority he'd used on Le Blanc.

With the dazed movement of a sleepwalker, Josefa stepped toward him. He switched the rifle to his left arm, leaned down and swept her up on the saddle in front of him with his free right arm, completing the maneuver in one smooth movement. The rifle barrel barely shifted from its position trained on Le Blanc. "Out the back," he muttered to Caleb. "See you back at the ranch."

Caleb wheeled Nero around and in two big stallion strides they were through the ruins and moving towards the K Street side of the block.

What a Pyrrhic victory. Josefa was coming home, but the taste of defeat was bitter in Caleb's mouth. No one had died, but if anyone had won it was Wayne Arkwright. His freedom was still imperiled by Consuela's false testimony. He had no clue what Consuela held over Josefa, but from what he'd just seen tonight, he doubted she'd be strong enough to hold out against it. Not when Arkwright was so desperate to patch together any lie to fit.

A thumping sound on the heavy, leather-studded ranch doors penetrated Caleb's drowning sleep. He'd been past exhaustion when he finally collapsed into bed, having answered Doña Valentina's many questions as fully as she could. She and Josefa had circled each other, accepting an uneasy peace without words. They were both hurting, and overcoming the chasm between them would take time.

I don't know what's going on, so how could Mother? Josefa has so many secrets.

The thumping reverberated through the house. Who was this, knocking at this ungodly hour?

Caleb grabbed his pistol and stumbled into the hall. His mother was there in her nightdress, looking remarkably alert. "Who is this?" he mumbled irritably.

She gave him a fleeting smile. "And good morning to you, too."

"Let me get this, Mother. Just in case it's trouble."

She padded after him in bare feet. "You're not handling this alone. I'm right here."

He readied his pistol, pushed the heavy door open a few inches and peered out.

"Hugo! *Mi amigo*!" He let out a long,

relieved breath. His mother pushed the door fully open.

A stooped gnome of a man grinned through a mouth which contained only half the teeth it should and stepped forward. He clapped Caleb on the shoulder and then turned his full attention to Valentina, bowing before her, hands clasped in front of him, and then extending both arms in a capacious embrace. "Doña Valentina. It's wonderful to see you, but I'm so sorry to have to come."

Valentina clutched at her chest and gave an anguished cry. "It's Bonnie, isn't it?"

Hugo nodded gravely, his hands clasped in front in a way that reminded Caleb of a priest about to deliver a sermon. "Yes. Doña Bonaventura." He momentarily turned his attention to Caleb. "She had a terrible row with

Consuela last night. After Josefa left. During the commotion, she took a turn." He faced Doña Valentina. "She's with the medicine woman. She's asking for you. And she sent this."

Hugo reached into the double-breasted woolen coat that swamped his shrunken form and pulled out a small object wrapped in cream silk. As he thrust it forward the light from the lamps picked up the fabric's sheen, creating for a moment a sense of a holy object.

Doña Valentina stepped back, both hands raised in surrender. "No! Oh no, Hugo. I don't want it. No!"

Caleb's jaw sagged as his ever-enduring mother collapsed sobbing onto Hugo's shoulder.

Doña Valentina fingered the clay talisman she clutched in one hand and prayed to the God of St Peter and the Holy Mother Mary she would get there in time. The totem was small enough to fit in her palm. When she held it in her fist it was completely concealed. She'd clutched so tightly at the edges of the spirit-shaped figure that it had dug into her flesh, leaving a rigid indent on the mound of her thumb.

She steadied herself on the edge of her seat as the coach lurched on a pothole. Caleb, sitting up front acting as reins-man, was in a hurry. Josefa sat beside her, pale-faced and mute, as they went full tilt on their early-morning mercy mission.

Bonaventura, the cousin who was twenty years older than Valentina and more like a mother than cousin, was in trouble. After her mater died when Valentina was thirteen, Bonnie had stepped into the vacuum. And now Bonnie was dying.

If she didn't feel it in her bones like a subtle but inexorable drain, the mere fact that she could run her index finger down the extended arm of the Rainbow Man talisman Hugo had brought her was the proof. The old man was Bonaventura's most trusted house servant. And when he'd knocked at her front door clutching the emblem wrapped in a piece of cream silk, she'd known instantly what it meant.

Hugo had explained the dreadful scene, where Bonnie had demanded answers. Consuela had refused to give them, instead unleashing on her mother a hailstorm of accusations. That she'd never loved her, never supported her, had betrayed her for Valentina's family. In a spiteful rage she'd struck

Bonaventura and stormed out, leaving her mother crumpled and wasted.

Bonnie had been taken to the *curandero*, a traditional herbal healer, where she said she would feel safe. But before she'd left the house, she'd insisted Hugo retrieve the Indalo talisman from a locked wooden box in her wardrobe. She'd begged him to take it to Valentina as fast as he could.

When Valentina unwrapped the fabric to reveal the figurine, she was instantly back in the Los Angeles pueblo, the house of her childhood, with its fragrance of beeswax polish and lavender and the singsong music of children's voices. That was where Bonaventura had first shown her the glazed clay figure, a treasured gift passed down through the maternal line ever since their families left Spain, to be transferred only at the point of death.

A premonition of disaster shivered up her backbone, chilling her to her core. She was not Bonnie's daughter. She wasn't the proper recipient for this family treasure. Consuela was. Passing the Indalo to her was only going to make a bad situation even worse.

"Madeleine! Your face! What happened?" They were the first words Josefa had uttered since Caleb decided to accompany his mother to Bonnie's bedside and seek John Russell's protection for Josefa while he was away.

Caleb could see why she'd not been able to stifle her shock. The Frenchwoman's fine-boned face was swollen and inflamed. One eye was partially closed by a puffy redness.

Madeleine raised her hand to her face, a quick involuntary gesture of concealment. "It's a long story. You probably haven't got time to hear it now. You've got an emergency, haven't you?"

"We do," Caleb said. "But not so much so that we can't spare a few minutes to hear what's been going on."

Aristide bustled in behind them, bobbing his head when he saw the matriarch. "Doña Valentina, Sir John will be with us any minute."

Caleb clapped him on the shoulder. "Thanks so much. I don't want to leave Josefa at home alone with the twins just now. There's too much weird stuff going on." He glanced towards Madeleine. "And it seems weird things are happening here too."

Aristide nodded. "Sir John wants to have a quick word anyway. Can we give you a quick coffee before you push on?"

Caleb flashed a wry smile in

Madeleine's direction. "I guess we do have time to hear your story."

Madeleine sank into a chair at the dining table, a protective hand cupping her face. "Aristide knows. He can tell you all you need to know."

Aristide began, "I think Sir John will fill you in, but as far as Madeleine is concerned . . ."

He related the tale of the bee delivery, of Madeleine's quick thinking which had saved Minette from the worst of the attack.

Josefa squeaked. "Oh, that darling little girl! Is she all right?"

"She got a couple of stings in her scalp when the bees got tangled in her hair, but Madeleine's skirt kept most of them off. Maddy's arms and face took the worst punishment." He shot her a loving glance and laughed. "She put

Minette in the horse trough and jumped straight in after her. That pretty much froze the bees."

His mouth tightened, the humor gone. "You were right to bring Josefa here. When you hear what Sir John has to tell you, you'll appreciate that even more than you might now."

Every time Caleb glanced at Valentina's drawn anxious face he knew they had to hurry, and he was thankful John Russell seemed to understand. Over a rushed coffee the business magnate laid out the extraordinary events of past days — Le Blanc's true identity and his attempt to coerce Madeleine into planting a gun at the Stewart ranch.

"He what?" Caleb's gut twisted painfully. He stared at Madeleine in disbelief.

Sir John continued smoothly, "Thankfully for us all, she refused to do it." He stared hard at Caleb. "But that explains why that sheriff thought he was onto a good thing when he raided your place. He was confident he'd find something."

"How in hell's name did Le Blanc get his hands on that gun unless he'd used it himself? Unless it was his?" Caleb placed his hands flat down on the table edge and pushed himself upright, unable to sit for another second. He glared angrily around the circle of faces. The women, pale and silent; Aristide dark and somber. "Doesn't Arkwright realize he's being duped?"

"Precisely." Sir John's tone was clipped and forceful. "He is either colluding with a killer, or he's been conned. Either way, it won't continue

much longer. I've already talked to
Halliburton."

Married! Madeleine Laurent is married!

As he propelled the carriage towards
Sacramento, Caleb could focus on only
one thought: the Frenchwoman had
acted as though she was single.

And that's what upset him the most.
Not that she might have seriously
considered planting evidence that could
have seen him hung. It wasn't entirely
clear from what Sir John said how close
she'd got to doing it. Even to consider it
was unforgivable.

But the other part of it, *that* felt to
him almost worse. He was a total fool.
From the first time he'd met her, she'd
played him. He hadn't known her well
enough to ask the bald question: "Why
aren't you married?" It just wasn't done

to be so blatant. But surely he hadn't mistaken the subtle little signs of interest? Had he got so out of touch that he couldn't recognize trouble when it was staring him in the face?

He cursed that his body had betrayed him so badly. How had he not picked that she was, without question, a black widow?

You have had a lucky escape, Caleb Stewart. Very lucky.

But as the miles unfolded to Bonnie's bedside, no answering sense of relief came. His body was a cold, unresponsive lump, permeated by a gray sense of loss.

Sacré bleu! Could things get any worse?

He'd had Durand watching them, so he knew what was up with Caleb Stewart and his sister. She was as sleek as a panther, a black panther, that one, and just as cunning.

He kicked a stone with his boot as he strolled for his morning coffee. Durand had seen Madeleine. Reported that Caleb had driven Josefa to the Russell establishment and left her there.

Why, he had no idea. But it looked as if Sir John and his new business partner were sticking together, even if Stewart was on the verge of being arrested for murder. And that was bad news for Gérard Le Blanc.

If his San Francisco masters got wind of this, there'd be hell to pay. Divide and conquer had always been his game. Get the winery signed up to the cooperative, and then acquire control of the water feeding Rancho Del Oro's five thousand acres. That was likely to take a bit longer, unless he found a way to speed up the process. He needed to go see the boss men in San Francisco. Set up a rear-guard action protecting himself, after Arkwright's unsettling news.

He strode past the alleyway where he'd had his little tête-à-tête with Madeleine a couple of days ago, his fingers twitching at the memory. He wondered how she'd enjoyed receiving the honeytrap, being the target herself for a change. He'd give her a few more days for the truth to sink in — that she wasn't going to beat him — and then he'd return on the attack. Meantime, he needed to talk to the San Francisco nobs.

Maybe he should up his fee. Men like that always respected you more if you demanded big money. He'd tell them how it was. Those city slickers didn't appreciate how tricky these things could get in the field. So what if he hadn't delivered Stewart to Arkwright trussed up like a chicken just yet? All was not lost. He still had Consuela on his side. And Madeleine would see the error of her ways any day soon. He'd make sure of it.

Bonaventura lay back, bolstered by brightly colored pillows, the light from the single window magnifying the deep lines, the sweaty sheen on the beloved face, now puffy with retained fluid. Her breath came in quick gasps, but her dark eyes were bright and steady, gazing out with the wonder of a child.

Valentina let out a barely audible sigh of relief as her son stood aside to give her precedence at Bonnie's side. The grand old lady might be in danger of dying, but she still had full mental command.

The room was pleasantly warm, scented with eucalyptus and peppermint from the steaming bowl infused with the herbs that sat on a side table. Valentina saw from the weak smile on Bonaventura's face, and the relaxation of her shoulders under her shawl, that she too was relieved to be graced with what might be their last meeting.

Within seconds she was across the room and gently hugging her cousin's motherly form, her head nestled against the warm folds of her neck. "Oh, Bonnie! To see you like this! I never wanted to see this day." She dropped her hands and slipped onto a bedside chair.

The medicine woman sat against the wall on the other side of the bed; she nodded an acknowledgment as Valentina's eyes searched her out. "Welcome, Doña Valentina. My patient will be a lot more at peace with your coming, which can only be good, *no es cierto*? She has been waiting for you."

The old woman's tanned face was calm and somber beneath a hatchwork of deep wrinkles. "I will go and make a tisane to help ease her breathing while you talk. Now, don't upset her while I am away."

Bonnie reached out her hand towards Valentina's side of the bed, and Valentina shuffled her chair closer to take Bonnie's dry bony fingers between hers. When had this precious woman grown old? She felt a sudden lump of loss in her chest for the wasted years, the rift forced upon them by Consuela's behavior. Bonnie had to support her daughter, whether she wanted to or not, and the cousins had barely spoken for the last few years.

"Bonnie, I am so pleased to be here. You can't know how much . . ." Valentina drew out the silk-wrapped figurine and held it in her lap. "It was such a shock to have Hugo come with this. But I am honored."

She searched Bonaventura's face. Her raspy breathing seemed to have calmed, even in the few minutes Valentina had been here. She leaned over and placed the silk wrapping on the bed. "But shouldn't this go to Consuela? If you give it to me, she'll just be angrier."

Bonaventura squeezed her hand, her fingers firm and steady on her skin. "No, my dear Valentina. There's no mistake." Her voice was whisper-thin. "I can no longer indulge my daughter's actions. The time has come when I must do what is right."

They stared into each other's eyes for a long moment, resting on so many good memories that had preceded the pain of recent years.

"You are the rightful inheritor of the figure. You, and I hope your Josefa after you." Bonaventura's eyebrows contracted together, as if Josefa's name brought her pain.

"What is it?" said Valentina. "Tell me."

"You've been badly deceived, dear Valentina, and I am ashamed to say I remained silent while things were done in my own house that shouldn't have been done. But I can no longer stand by. Consuela has overstepped all reasonable bounds." She sighed and slipped deeper into her pillows. "Once it seemed a simple case of jealousy. Now she appears to be willing to do anything, sacrifice anyone, to get what she wants." Her eyes were bright with unshed tears as she gazed out from her pillows. "She's ready to betray anything, anyone. Including me."

Valentina reared back, as if she'd been slapped, and then collapsed forward, racked with a fit of dry coughing.

Caleb had remained quietly to one side, but now he stepped to his mother and covered one of her hands with his. She glanced up at him. "I'll be all right, son."

She gently pulled her hand free and drew out a handkerchief from the folds of her skirt to wipe her damp eyes before turning back to Bonnie. "What are you saying? I know she hates us, but not you too?"

Bonnie shook her head sadly. "She really showed her true colors last night. I tried to talk to her. She'd be willing to swear black is white if she thought it would get her what she wants. And I'm sorry she's selling Josefa down the river too."

She slumped, as if the talking had worn her out. Valentina picked up a glass of water on the bedside table and helped her take some sips. "Josefa?" Valentina asked.

"I wanted to warn you, my dear Ina. You might think you know how bad Consuela is, but I don't think you have any true idea. You're too decent yourself to imagine what others can fall to. She'd trade decent men like your Caleb here for blatant lies. She's already betrayed Josefa."

Valentina's breath caught in her throat. "Josefa?"

"She encouraged the whole idea of a love match between Josefa and Rory. Pushed them into the idea of being betrothed. Repeatedly cheered them on with the notion that Rory could get back on the farm if Josefa and he were married. As if that's natural justice." Her voice had strengthened, as if getting a second surge of wind. "I believe she set Josefa up to wangle her way in by the back door. Not that Rory's feelings for Josefa weren't genuine."

She reached out for the glass and took another sip. Then she looked beyond Valentina to Caleb. "Water. That's so good. You know water is behind all this, Caleb?"

"Water, Aunt Bonnie? How so?"

"It became clear last night when we had the big row. Consuela says those big city lawyers the Frenchman works for are more interested in the water than the land. He says the water in the river is more valuable than the land it runs past." She shook her head. "I tried to warn Rory, but I didn't realize how calculating Consuela could be. It

316

was only this afternoon when I found Josefa tied up in my own house that it hit home what she is capable of. And when I asked Consuela about it, she was so furious! I think she might be jealous of Josefa. It was frightening. I'm afraid my poor old heart couldn't take it."

Valentina gently caressed Bonnie's weary face. Fatigue had deepened the dark shadows around her eyes.

"There is something else, Ina. Something Josefa hasn't confided to you."

Valentina searched the older woman's tired face for a clue. "What is it, Bonnie? What is it that my daughter doesn't trust me to know?"

"The thing Consuela thought was her trump card, dear Ina. The thing she's holding over Josefa. I suspect Josefa is bearing Rory's child. She hasn't told me straight out, but the signs are all there. You're going to be a grandmother."

10

"And ladies and gentlemen, I give you our very own Senator Hector de Vile!" William Chapman Ralston, founder of the Bank of California and a millionaire several times over thanks to a furious escalation in his Comstock Lode's silver shares, beamed and gestured towards his old friend.

Hector de Vile — another Comstock Lode multi-millionaire and first-term Senator — rose and surveyed the glittering crowd in San Francisco's Occidental Hotel, one of the fanciest places to drink and dine in the city.

The "Quiet House of Peculiar Excellence," as it liked to advertise itself, boasted San Francisco's first true cocktail lounge, run by "Professor" Jerry Thomas, a diamond-ringed showman said to have brought civility as well as creativity to the bar scene.

The exclusive group gathered in the bar tonight — fifty of the state's richest men and a scattering of women — were here to listen to a pitch for an exciting new venture, the launch of the biggest wine corporation ever proposed in the state, if not in the whole of America: the Bella Vista Vinicultural Society.

De Vile felt a fluttery, empty feeling in his stomach, even though he'd just enjoyed an excellent steak in the restaurant next door. It was so familiar — the love-hate jitters he always got at the start of a new challenge. He'd been asked to cheerlead here tonight — and that was the easy part. But for him the stakes were so much higher than whether his buddy Billy Ralston got enough investors to float his Bella Vista Vinicultural Society. For him, this was really the first speech of his re-election campaign as a state Senator later in the year. And everyone in the room knew it.

He straightened his shoulders, skimmed his notes, lifted his head and scanned the audience. At the back, Jerry's usually flying sparkling hands rested silent on the bar as he leaned forward with concentrated intent. In the middle Sir John Russell sat with a couple of fellows de Vile didn't recognize — not the brothers who were so often with him. And right near the front, the hustling lawyers, Buffer, Cottlesloe, and Jones with the French agent they'd engaged to push their land sales business, along with Billy.

"Gentlemen . . . and ladies." He flashed one of the wry smiles he knew women loved to a table where a couple of the women sat. "I'm delighted to be able to speak on behalf of my very good friend and colleague Billy Ralston," he gestured to the front table, "about this visionary project which will put California wines on the map. Not just here in the New World, but back in the Old World too. Billy tells me he's already had serious interest from French investors wanting our champagne."

For the next ten minutes or so he talked up Bella Vista's prospects: the articles of incorporation for the six-thousand-acre vineyard already drawn up and signed, thanks to changes in state law that allowed incorporation of larger agricultural blocks; the prominent names who'd already agreed to be trustees; the modern presses and techniques that would be used in the winemaking; and the expertise of the vintners charged with growing, harvesting and producing the wine and brandy.

All incorporated with $600,000 in capital, divided into 6000 shares of $100. He watched the room closely as he spoke. Jerry Thomas nodded in rapt attention; he'd probably snared a few shares there. At other tables too, there were signs of strong interest. Eyes were bright and fixed on him. A few whispered asides to their companions, others scuffed their chairs closer to him.

Billy had put up most of the money — with some help from other quarters, de Vile suspected — and he was on a promise of a twenty per cent shareholding to act as a cheerleader with no further money required. It would be a nice bonus, but as a senator, he had to be seen to maintain independence. There would be a lot of independent winemakers who would see the corporation as a direct competitor, rather than an effort to float everyone's boat higher, and he didn't want to lose out on their votes.

John Russell's face in the middle of the room was unreadable as usual. Now and then he turned to one of his companions and made a brief comment with a grim twist to his lips. No John Russell in Bella Vista then. He was going to compete with his interests in Vino d'Oro.

"Sir John, nice to catch up with you again."

The dark, hawk-like eyes gave nothing

away. The color flushed to de Vile's cheeks as he recalled the compromising situation he'd been placed in the last time they'd met. He was still paying out for an educational trust to help young men in return for Russell's silence in an intimate family matter. He probably would do so for the rest of his life.

He shuffled his fingers along the brim of his hat. "Thought I'd have a word before I'm on to my next engagement. How are you? I gather congratulations are in order. You're about to be a father, any day now?"

"Good to see you too, Senator." John Russell turned to the man beside him. "Can I introduce Aristide Laurent, my vigneron and vintner at Vino d'Oro." He gave de Vile a fleeting smile. "You will have heard of my latest venture? Agriculture is very new to me, as you appreciate, so I rely on Mr. Laurent heavily for advice."

De Vile gave an understanding chuckle. "Don't I know it. Mining has been more to our taste in the past, hasn't it? But we can't ignore the way things are changing. First with beef, now wine."

"You're referring to Miller and Lux, and the way they've been eating up old land grant country for their beef operations? You see something similar happening in wine?" Russell's dark eyes sharpened.

"I think it will have to, old boy. No one grower can put together the distribution system that California wine needs if it's truly going to make its mark. Even getting it into New York is a challenge, let alone Paris or London."

Russell nodded. "No argument there,

it's a problem. But I'm not convinced a corporation like Bella Vista is the way to go. It will be interesting to see."

"You're not tempted then? To invest, I mean?"

"Not me, Hector, no. What about you?"

Hector paused. "I'm happy to act as a cheerleader for Billy. I might get a few bottles of free champagne as a consideration." He laughed. "I've got to keep my focus on Washington."

"Ah, yes." Russell's mouth twisted. "So you're not involved with Cottlesloe and Co? With their efforts to corner the market in prime land for 'San Francisco investors'? You're not one of their investors?"

Dr Vile felt a warning surge pulse through him.

How does Russell keep up with it all?

He must have spies everywhere.

"Cottlesloe? No. Why?"

"Oh, just that Elijah and his cronies seem mighty friendly with good old Billy Ralston. And Billy's a good friend of yours. You know the old saying — Benjamin Franklin, wasn't it? — if you lie down with dogs, you get up with fleas."

The warm warning pulse turned to ice. "I don't know what you're hinting at, Russell. They're all perfectly respectable professional men."

"They might be, but do you know that Frenchman they seem to be using as an agent? I'd watch how close you allow yourself to get to him. You can't be too careful in an election year, can you, Senator." Russell made a small bow and gave him a tight smile. "We won't keep you any longer. Good night, de Vile."

"Josefa! We need to talk!"

As he stood in the Russell parlor, Caleb felt himself sway on his feet. His lack of sleep over the last twenty-four hours was beginning to tell.

Josefa sat across the room from him, rested and comfortable on a couch with her feet up on an ottoman, with Madeleine alongside. Two pairs of eyes, one of them a piercing aquamarine, met his. Caleb drew in a quick breath. What was it about this woman?

Seemingly unaware of the effect she was having on him, Madeleine spoke quietly, her eyes gentle. "Do come in. Josefa was just wondering how your mother and Bonnie are doing."

"Sorry to be calling so late. I've left mother with Bonnie. I drove straight back. Bonnie's weak but in surprisingly good spirits. Hard to say, though, what the long-term prospects are. There wasn't much point in me staying any longer. She's very tired. Mother and the medicine woman can meet all her needs. There's a couch bed if Mother wants to take a quick nap while Bonnie's asleep, and Hugo can bring her back whenever she needs to come. She'll be there for as long as it takes . . . but I need to get back home."

Josefa studied him. "Do you want me to come with you? Now?" Her voice was flat.

"No, not if you don't want to. And if it's all right with our hosts for you to stay, of course."

"That will be fine." The swelling on Madeleine's jaw had gone down a lot, but her eye still showed red and puffy. "Josefa fits right in. We'd love to have her for as long as she wants."

"Well, the twins and I will be out on the farm tomorrow so until Mother returns she'd be alone. I don't think that's a good idea."

"Have you had anything to eat?" Madeleine rose. "No trouble to collect some coffee and a tray from the kitchen."

After a moment's hesitation, he capitulated. "Thank you, that would be appreciated. Very much so. All I seem to have done the last day is ride."

As Madeleine slipped from the room, Caleb went to Josefa's side. He gave her a brief summary of the scene at Bonnie's bedside, the loving reconciliation that had taken place between their mother and her cousin. Josefa reached for his hand.

"Everything's happening so fast, Caleb. It's hard to accept it all. I just feel numb."

"Josefa." His sister watched his face, her eyes narrowed. "Everything's fine, it's just . . . Bonnie's told mother your secret. The one Consuela was referring to." A whisper of skirts at the door told him Madeleine had returned, carrying a tray loaded with cups and beverage.

"About Rory and me? It's okay," Josefa said. "Madeleine already knows. What did Mother say?" She held herself tensely, waiting for his reply.

Madeleine put a tray with a pot of coffee, three cups and a plate of cookies down, and began pouring.

"I'm not sure. I think she feels disappointed in Bonnie and Consuela mostly. That they didn't protect you better." He cupped the hot coffee cup Madeleine passed in his hands, suddenly grateful for its comforting heat.

"How long have you known?"

"Not long. I'm sorry it's happened like this, but I'm not sorry about the baby."

He took a long sip of the dark black brew and enjoyed the bitter tang as it slid down his throat. "I think Mother will surprise you. She's not going to be thrilled, but she's never one to make a fuss when there's nothing that can be done. If the horse has already bolted . . . You know the rest. No point in carrying on about the stable door being open. That's how Mother works. And it's in our blood to adore our babies — you know how we are."

Josefa smiled. "Sure do."

Caleb took another sip of coffee. "Is that why Consuela frightened you last night? Was she threatening to shame you?"

Josefa nodded. "Something like that. It's a bit rich, isn't it, when she's the grandmother. Well, step-grandmother."

Madeleine had settled back next to Josefa on the sofa. She put her cup down and took Josefa's hand. "I have an idea."

Josefa's face registered warm anticipation. "Oh yes? What's on your mind?

"You say you and Rory were secretly betrothed. Wasn't that recognized as equal to marriage in some old Spanish circles? And given your situation, it's feasible you did it. Like Romeo and Juliet." She gave a lop-sided smile. "Even if you just dreamed of it, talked about it. Who's to know you didn't do it?" She raised an eyebrow to Caleb. "I see no reason why you couldn't put that story about. Only the most mean-spirited of folks would object. I think everyone else would agree. You've had enough to bear already."

Caleb's eyes went to his sister. She was squeezing Madeleine's hand tightly, smiling in frank admiration. "What a grand idea, Madeleine. One I'm quite certain Mother wouldn't object to."

She glanced teasingly to Caleb for confirmation.

He dipped his head in agreement. "She might even dig into her jewelry box for an old family heirloom to seal it."

Her face sobered. "I'll tell you one thing, Caleb. I'm through with being frightened of that *bruja*. Consuela's a witch. And I'm willing to tell that sheriff exactly what she's up to, just as soon as you want."

"He's wanted on murder charges?"

The Senator thrust his right hand to his forehead and pushed his fingers back through his flowing gray locks. He fixed

Elijah Cottlesloe with a fierce glare. "Why in hell didn't anybody tell me before this?"

"We didn't know, Senator. Not until a couple of days ago." Cottlesloe's face with bright red as he shuffled on his little feet, his rotund body swaying from side to side, as if in danger of toppling over. "I'm sorry. We're doing the best we can to put a good sheen on things. We're—"

"Don't you blockheads understand?" De Vile's voice was strident. "I am a Senator of the United States Congress. I do not consort with murderers. I can't believe you've been so stupid." He let out a loud sigh. "I don't care how you fix this, Cottlesloe. I don't even want to know. Just get it done. Just tell me when you've done it. If it's not sorted out by the end of the month, you'll be getting no more investments or support from me. Is that clear?"

"I'll see to it, Senator."

De Vile stood up to leave. His legs were heavy, and it took extra effort to start towards the door. Cottlesloe's shuffling and sniveling gave him scant satisfaction. As he lumbered out, he was unsure who he was most furious at — himself for getting mixed up with this jerk, or Russell for knowing about it before he did. Because he would bet that John Russell already knew as much, if not more, about the Frenchman as he did. And that was always a bad thing.

"I see, Mr. Le Blanc. You have a problem you want us to fix, so you can continue taking care of our interests unencumbered."

Elijah Cottlesloe's oily voice carried an unpleasant, sarcastic edge which made

Gérard jumpy. He jerked his head up. Cottlesloe gave the impression of being nearly as wide as he was tall. He was sneering. "Is that what I understand you to say?" He tapped his fingers on the edge of his oak-paneled desk impatiently. "Well?"

Le Blanc was positioned in the middle of a semi-circle of leather-studded tub chairs in front of Cottlesloe's desk, with Jed Buffer on his left and Noah Jones on his right.

"Might I observe, you also don't seem to have made much progress on the case." Cottlesloe picked up a cigar he'd lit and left burning on the tray in front of him. He tapped the ash from it and took a hefty pull before setting it down again.

Gérard puffed out his chest and steeled himself. He was not going to sound defensive. "I don't wish to contradict you, sir, but we are making excellent progress. Sheriff Arkwright is about to charge Stewart with Mackinnon's murder, and once he's out of the picture the rest of it will collapse like a pack of cards." He leaned back in his chair, put his arms behind his head and stared Cottesloe down. "He assures me, he'll be arresting him in the next few days, thanks to the witnesses we've been able to identify for him."

"Good. Good." Noah Jones broke in, nodding. He was a softly spoken beanpole of a man with a shock of white hair who gave the erroneous impression of being timid. In Le Blanc's experience, he was the coldest and most calculating of the three. Now he tilted his head to Cottlesloe. A facial tic had started winking on his face, jerking like a malicious flashing sign under his right eye. "I don't see the cops being in the least bit interested in resurrecting ancient history. Le Blanc's problem was a long time ago. They've got plenty else on their hands right now."

Cottlesloe grunted and Buffer nodded assent. Angry demonstrations against Chinese workers had increased as hard economic times struck, and the city police were stretched handling frequent riot callouts.

Jones sniffed. "However, I suggest we take out an insurance policy, just in case. Especially with the Senator getting his monkey up. There's too much at stake for you to disappear on us now." His hands were trembling, but his gimlet gray eyes were piercing.

"An insurance policy?" Le Blanc was at a loss. What was he suggesting?

"That's right. You say Thomas

Halliburton has taken on the case for Russell? That man goes about as if he's got a walking stick up his bum, but he's damn good at what he does." His calculating eyes swept the circle. "We've found to our cost that you can't buy him, so we'll have to shut him up."

Le Blanc's heart pounded in his ears. "You mean—?" Le Blanc returned the cold gaze. He broke eye contact with Jones and scanned the room to see how the others were reacting.

Cottlesloe was staring at his blotter, as if disassociating himself from the discussion would also absolve him from responsibility. Jed Buffer was nodding sagely, a distant expression on his face, as if he was thinking about what he would have for dinner.

Le Blanc shifted uneasily in his chair and met Jones' continuing stare. "On what basis? I thought there were plenty of biddable judges in San Francisco. Plenty. You just have to ensure the case goes before one of them."

The lawyers remained silent.

"I see. I may as well be hung for a sheep as for a lamb, is that it?" His voice had a bitter edge, and he didn't care if they noticed.

They think I'm already a murderer, so I've got nothing to lose. Well, maybe they're right.

"Oh, I wouldn't put it that way," said Noah Jones. "But it would tidy things up. No one else needs to be bothered then. Especially not the Senator. We particularly don't want him alarmed."

So now I know the true power behind the throne.

"And might I ask what timing you're expecting for this new commission?" He was proud of how assured he sounded. "When do you want it done?"

"As soon as possible," Cottlesloe said smoothly, as if he didn't want Jones getting all the credit. He took another long puff on his cigar, sending clouds of smoke into the space above him.

Damn their smug self-assured faces. I take all the risk, and for what?

"I'd expect my fee to be doubled in recognition of the increased danger to me."

Buffer gasped and muffled it with a cough. Cottlesloe narrowed his eyes and took another draw on the rapidly shortening cigar.

The tic in Noah Jones' cheek flashed erratically, but the rest of his demeanor remained ice-calm. "Contingent on you completing all the business satisfactorily — not just Halliburton, but the whole

343

thing — I see no problem. We'll have the money to share. But just so it's very clear, we share the money but *not* the responsibility for getting it done." He gave a slow, spiteful smile. "I'm sure you'll manage admirably. After all, you have the experience, don't you Mr. Le Blanc? We didn't know your true colors when we hired you, but I can't say I regret taking you on. In fact, I'd say it gives us a distinct advantage." He turned to Cottlesloe. "Got any whiskey in that decanter, Elijah? I think this little arrangement deserves a toast."

"Caleb." Madeleine's voice cut across the dark. She bustled across the courtyard to stand at the foot of the Stewart coach, gazing up at him. "I wanted to explain, to apologize. I haven't had a chance. Everything's been so crazy." The dim light from the house windows cast a draining wash across her, leaving her looking ragged and depleted.

A war raged inside him. In his head the crystal-clear thought reigned: she'd damned well come close to destroying him, may she rot in hell. He wanted nothing more to do with her. And yet somewhere in the middle of him a warm feeling boiled up from down deep.

Stay. Listen. That's only fair.

"Madeleine, it's late. I have had very little sleep. Can't this wait?" His voice sounded plaintive.

"No. No, I'm sorry, it can't, Caleb. I can't sleep for worrying. I'll keep it really short." She took a deep breath, as if preparing to launch into a rehearsed speech. "Yes, I did take that gun to your house the day of your party. I was terrified of what my ex-husband might do. To me. To Aristide. To Minette. But I couldn't do it. I *didn't* do it. I knew it was wrong, whatever the consequences. I brought it home and destroyed it."

She gazed up at him, her face somber. "And I destroyed legal evidence. Something that might have helped prove your innocence. But don't you see? I was so frightened he'd come after me, try and reclaim it, and then plant it himself. I had to make sure that didn't happen. I don't know if it was the right choice, but at the time it seemed like the only one. The best of a bad choice." Her words were rushed, breathy, as if she had to get them out on pain of death. "I bitterly regret bringing this cursed man into your lives."

He jumped down from the driver's seat. "Madeleine, that's not your fault. You had no control over that."

"I know, but it's all such a mess." Her eyes were brimming with tears and something else. Hope. "I thought he was dead. I hadn't heard from him for eight years." She increased the gap between them. "I really enjoyed meeting you, Caleb. I haven't met anyone else like you. And now I've destroyed everything."

He wanted to step forward, take her in his arms, tell her it was all going to be all right. But he knew it wasn't. She was still Mrs. Philippe Coubert, when all was said and done.

As if reading his mind, she twisted her hands together and whispered, "I'm sorry." Then she turned and fled.

How am I going to get Arkwright off my back?

As Caleb rode out to check on the

cattle the next morning that one thought ricocheted in his head.

Now that Josefa is ready to talk, would Arkwright be willing to listen?

The growling doubt in his stomach told him probably not. For reasons he did not understand, Arkwright seemed determined to convict him.

It was ridiculous. He was an innocent man, being railroaded to the gallows. He'd no more have planned to kill Rory and Miguel than he'd plan to run for Governor. But where to turn? Was Halliburton the man he needed, as Sir John suggested the other night? Could he make it go away? And if not Halliburton, who? Or what?

He barely saw the pasture around him as a succession of thoughts chased through his head, each quickly replaced by another, possibly even more outlandish, idea.

He might be able to find a sympathetic judge to over-ride Arkwright and bring him to heel. But was there such a man, and did the system work that way? Who was Arkwright really working for, anyway?

The more he went over it, the little he truly knew about the situation, the more frustrated and discouraged he became. Rory wasn't the only one who was an innocent when it came to graft and corruption. He didn't have a clue what he was dealing with or how to fight back.

He turned for home with a heavy heart, and as he drew close to the house was surprised to see horses he didn't recognize tethered in the yard. He slipped off Nero and after he set him to munching from a feed box made for the house.

Gérard Le Blanc and the other Frenchman — Durand, was it? — were lounging on a garden seat by the front door. Le Blanc fixed him with an insolent expression as he approached. "Good morning, Stewart. Thinking about that jail cell you'll be occupying in a couple of days, are you?"

Caleb nudged him aside as he made to stride past. "Get out, Le Blanc. You're trespassing."

Le Blanc dodged ahead of him and planted his hand firmly in the middle of his chest, stopping him in his tracks. He was several inches taller than him, Caleb realized with a shock, and at least half a stone heavier. "You need to learn some manners," Le Blanc snarled, "if you know what's good for you."

The front door swung open and Santiago stood in the entryway, his Colt revolver drawn. "Let him go, *el tipo ascqueroso*. You dirty dog. Now!"

Le Blanc dropped the hand he'd planted on Caleb's chest. "A very foolish move, Mr. Stewart. Very foolish. And you too." He glared at Santiago. "I came here to offer you a deal, but I see you're intent on occupying that cell. Be my guest." He plucked at the lavender that grew by the bench as he turned with an arrogant swagger to leave. "One way or another, you're history."

Santiago stood on guard, gun at the ready. Caleb shook his head. "I know it's tempting, Santiago, but don't shoot. It'll only make things a whole lot worse." He flashed a wry smile. "If they could get any worse, that is."

11

"Halliburton could well be your man. He's cautious in what he promises, but he's thorough."

John Russell paused in front of a row of barrels and stroked the curved oak as he talked. Along with Aristide they'd escaped the house to inspect the cellars and take a late afternoon apéritif before joining the rest of the household for a light supper.

"Aristide reports this batch is showing promise. He might make us an award-winner yet!" He tapped the barrel and his eyes brightened.

Aristide made a demurring sound of protest in the back of his throat, then nodded. "What is it you Anglais say? Don't count your chickens?" He laughed and he too ran his hand over the barrel, as if conferring blessing. "Last summer's harvest is one of the best I've seen in my time here, I'll grant you that." He grinned at Caleb. "I think we've got something good happening here."

Caleb grimaced. "Glad to hear it's happening somewhere."

They'd left the womenfolk in the old hacienda's big family room, gossiping over coffee, Graysie with sleeping baby George in her arms, Minette pestering Madeleine for a story. Apart from wanting to be reassured there weren't any more bees around, she seemed to have weathered the bee-bombing well. Madeleine's quick thinking had saved her from being badly stung, though she complained her scalp itched from the stings she'd got from the bees caught in her hair.

Hugo had returned Doña Valentina from Bonnie's earlier in the day, and she was now settled with Josefa on a corner sofa, making her peace, Caleb guessed, after the turbulence surrounding Rory's death and the possibility of a baby on the way.

Nathan was attending to business in Grass Valley, so it was just the three of them who'd escaped to the cellar. They settled themselves around Aristide's simple wooden desk, and he produced three glasses and poured a tasting measure into each. "Bon santé!"

"Good cherry flavors coming through." John ran his tongue along his top lip and gave Caleb a barely perceptible wink. "Wouldn't you agree?"

They shared a brief chuckle as Aristide

gave them a rude sign. "You can laugh, you two. Just wait till it makes best in show."

John laughed again. "Yes. Well, getting back to what I was saying about Halliburton. He's so circumspect as to sometimes make you want to shake him, but he knows what he's doing. And he's incorruptible." He took another sip. "These days that's unusual in itself. Especially in the legal fraternity."

Caleb nodded. "That's the thing. I'm all at sixes and sevens with Le Blanc. Who is he? A criminal, that we know thanks to Madeleine. And one who seems to have some powerful allies. How does that happen? And why aren't the authorities after him? Surely if we reported him—"

John and Aristide shared an understanding glance.

"What?" Caleb straightened in his chair. "Is there something you're not telling me?"

John gave a slightly embarrassed shrug. "I am doing something, but I don't want it advertised. It will mean less of a risk for Madeleine and Minette — for us all to be honest — if Le Blanc doesn't know."

"What is it?" Caleb fingered his glass. "This affects me too, you know."

John raised his hand in a conciliatory gesture. "I know, Caleb, of course. I only met with Halliburton last week, and I didn't want to mention it till I'd heard back from him. I've asked him to start proceedings to have Le Blanc deported. He lodged the papers yesterday. There was a bit of a delay while he checked a few things out, but he's advised he's going ahead.

"We've got the laws to do it, although I admit they're rarely used. I'm not certain what success Halliburton will have. We'll probably need Madeleine to swear he's not who he says he is. And God knows how long it will take."

Caleb nodded, understanding John's drift. "I hear what you're not saying. Not fast enough to be of much help to me. And it could be very dangerous for Madeleine if he gets wind of it. I get it." He thrust his glass towards the bottle.

"This is good stuff, Aristide. And I suddenly find I need another." He flashed them an ironic grin.

"I wonder where this leaves me with the Arkwright business. Say Le Blanc's being paid by those criminals at Buffer, Jones and Cottlesloe to suck up property on behalf of their rich clients wherever they can, using whatever means they can. It seems fairly obvious that's what's going on. How can I stand up to that? I've got to find another way to stop Arkwright."

John flicked his finger against the top of his glass, making it ring. "Scoundrels like him have always got their price. We've just got to find it."

"And who's paying him?" chimed in Aristide. "It would help to know that."

"That's right. Who's his boss?" asked John. "He'd have to be getting a lot of grease money for it to be worth risking his sheriff's badge."

Caleb's heart rose at the sense of camaraderie among them. John and Aristide; they were all in to help. "Would Halliburton know?"

"He might have an idea," John said. "But whether he'd have any direct influence? Hard to say. Arkwright's boss might be a friend of his. He might be able to drop some quiet hints. Or warnings. It's worth finding out."

When Russell's cook Mrs. Snively called them in for supper, they walked in on a cozy domestic scene. Minette was bathed and in her nightgown, ready for bed, snuggling into Madeleine's side on the sofa, a Hans Christian Andersen story book open on Madeleine's knee.

"Shall we read your favorite or try a new one?" Madeleine teased, fluffing up the child's damp curls.

"The Emperor's New Clothes. And then a new one," Minette giggled.

Graysie's lips curved in a fond smile. "Oh, you're a cheeky poppet. You're lucky Tante Madeleine is reading you *one* story!" She gave Madeleine a warm grin. "Thanks for keeping her entertained."

"My pleasure." Madeleine smiled up from the book and caught Caleb's eye as he paused in the doorway. She hesitated, her hand hovering on the story.

He dipped his head slightly in her direction. "Mademoiselle. I see Minette is keeping you busy."

"Indeed she is." She paused awkwardly.

He filled the gap. "How is the face?"

"Improving by the day. It'll be back to normal soon."

"Just give us a few minutes, can you Mrs. Snively? We've got a few matters to finish up." John gestured for Caleb to follow him to the corner sofa where Josefa and Valentina had last been seen.

"To resume where we left off, Caleb," said John. "Aristide mentioned that Le Blanc came to your house. When was that?"

Caleb felt his skin prickle under John's hawk-like gaze. He had a predatory edge, no doubt about it. Just as well he was on his side. "Earlier today. He wanted to make me an offer."

"And what did you say?"

"Santiago ordered him off at the point of a gun and I cheered."

The cast-iron justification he felt lasted as long as it took for Russell's dark brows to close in a frown. "Why would you do that?"

"I'm not doing business with that slime. Not under any circumstances."

Russell's hawkish eyes glittered. "No one said you had to do business with him. But wouldn't it be an advantage to know what he's offering? You can't win a game of chess unless you can anticipate your opponent's next move. And here he was coming and offering to tell you. Even if it was lies, you'd be in a better situation to fathom what he really wants."

Why didn't I think of that?

Come to think of it, he was always a bit inclined to see things in black and white, his mind already made up on the rights and wrongs. His thoughts flicked to Rory, the one-time heart-brother he'd never given a second chance because of the way his parents had behaved. A few days ago he would have been ready to condemn Josefa too. Now, when he was more aware of how she'd been drawn into Consuela's web, he wasn't nearly as confident he had all the answers.

His eye wandered to Madeleine, still engaged with the story-telling. Her too. He'd been too quick to judge her, to make assumptions about her as well.

"You know, John, you're right. And

I'm embarrassed to admit I haven't appreciated it until now. I have to start handling things differently if I'm going to beat this thing." He examined the backs of his hands. "You too, Aristide. I'm all ears to hear your advice. What I've done up to now clearly hasn't worked. I've been thrashing around with a club when I need to be using a foil."

By the time Mrs. Snively hurried them along ten minutes later, they'd agreed on what he should do next: see Halliburton by all means, but also make discreet inquiries with anyone who might know about the Midtown Sheriff's office and who ran things there. Even more tricky, John urged him to find a way to tickle details out of Le Blanc of the proposed "offer."

"And while you're at it, use any trick in the book — flattery, guile, evasion, deceit — to uncover his motives. What does he want out of it? What are his 'not negotiables'?' The things he'll never put on the table?" John grinned. "I hope I don't need to remind you, all's fair in love and war."

Caleb gave an ironic wince. "I hate to admit it, but I do need reminding."

Especially when seated next to the enchanting Madeleine Laurent, he thought a few minutes later, as Mrs. Snively bustled in with a supper of meatball soup. *Sopa de albóndigas*. He raised his glass in a toast. "To the cook. This smells delicious!" Even Mrs. Snively, it seemed, was showing them she cared.

As he savored the tiny meat balls in the deep rich vegetable broth, he mused over the way he'd treated Madeleine on the night of Le Blanc's "invasion" and after. As an object of suspicion, he admitted. His cheeks tingled. She had perfectly good personal reasons for being circumspect. Naturally the poor woman would be frightened. Terrified.

He inclined his head. "Enjoy your story?"

Her lips bent in a winsome curve. "I love reading to Minette. She's such a bright little button. She doesn't miss a thing. I find it interesting that she likes that story the best. It's quite a subtle morality tale for a small child to grasp, but you'd be silly to underestimate how much she understands."

"Yes. I guess we're all prone to personal blindness at times. I know I am." He set his spoon down with a satisfied sigh. His plate was empty. That soup had been good. "Which brings me to something. I feel as if I may not have treated you very fairly. Obviously I don't know the full circumstances—"

She raised her hand, palm outwards. "No. No, Mr. Stewart—"

"Caleb."

"Caleb, then. You were fully within your rights."

"Technically, maybe. But I didn't need to blunder in the way I did. I'm afraid subtlety doesn't come naturally to me. A bit of a blunt Scotsman, I'm afraid."

She twisted her elegant neck, checking the company, but no one was taking any notice of them, all engaged in other chatter. "A very likeable Scotsman," she said in almost a whisper. "So I wouldn't worry about it. I don't." Her face brightened to a soft pink. "And thank you."

He took a sip of the coffee that had been served as they spoke. "I noticed Minette was calling you Tante today.

You're obviously getting along well together."

Her aquamarine eyes flashed with uncertainty. "Graysie's suggestion. She wasn't happy with us carrying on with using Mademoiselle, and Madeleine didn't seem appropriate either."

"I think that's lovely. You make a sweet pair even if you aren't blood relations."

Her eyes fell to her plate, and he had the uncomfortable feeling he'd put his foot in it again. *Really, I am hopeless at talking to women. No wonder I'm still unmarried at thirty. I'll be in the same state at forty if I don't buck up my ideas.*

"Aristide and Sir John have been coaching me on how to deal with the situation I'm in, with Le Blanc seemingly trying to push Arkwright to arrest me for Rory's unfortunate demise."

A little voice piped up at Madeleine's side. "Tante Madeleine, what's 'unfortunate demise'?"

Madeleine's face lit up in one of her inexpressibly beautiful smiles. "The little dove asks the darndest questions." She turned to Minette and gave her shoulder an affectionate squeeze. "As your Uncle Nathan says, there's no flies on you."

Minette giggled. Her pearly-white baby teeth bit her lower lip. She lifted her sparkling eyes to Madeleine. "What does 'no flies on you' mean?" She dissolved into more giggles.

Madeleine smiled across the table at Caleb. "I think it's time I got this little one to bed before she wears that fertile brain out asking questions." She rose, hoisted the six-year-old onto her hip, and gestured down the table towards Graysie, who responded immediately, sensing her move. "I'll get her settled," she mouthed, and Graysie smiled and nodded.

She dropped a light kiss on Minette's curly head. "My goodness you're getting to be a big girl. I won't be able to carry you for too much longer." Her eyes vaulted over Minette's head and met his in a wordless message. He was locked into something he didn't want to end, and then Madeleine took a deep breath and smiled. "Say good night to Mr. Stewart, *ma chérie*." She paused awkwardly, as if reluctant to leave. "Good night, Caleb. And thank you for our talk."

Caleb relaxed back into the warmth Madeleine and Minette had left behind, basking in the afterglow, reluctant to let go of the unfamiliar sense of mutual sweet adoration. Made up of equal parts mischief and innocence, he mused, and so rarely seen. He had glimpsed true love in those few minutes.

A yearning he'd never acknowledged before gripped him. He wanted that warmth in his life. The soft joy of mother and child, of nurture and fun. He'd been wrong about Madeleine Laurent, and she'd been gracious in return. Maybe Aristide and John were right. He needed to stop being such a stickler, think a bit more creatively.

If he did that, maybe he and Madeleine Laurent could see more of one another, and he could decide if that sense of promise that hovered around them was fake or real.

Madeleine barely registered Minette's gay chatter as she settled her down to sleep. She was fizzing with a joy she had never felt before, and she knew why. It was due to Caleb Stewart's presence at the supper table. The man affected her like no one else. She knew her cheeks were flushed pink with excitement; she savored the bubble of anticipation rising from deep within. She barely knew him and yet she was falling under his spell.

A little voice within protested. She hadn't exactly flirted with the man. They'd only shared a few well-meaning exchanges. So why did she feel this way? As if they could have some sort of future?

The ridiculousness of it gave her goosebumps. She was eight years into enforced spinsterhood, married to a man who had the worst of intentions toward Caleb's life. And she'd promised Sir John she would not reveal anything more about Le Blanc to anyone, particularly his paternity, to preserve Minette's safety as much as possible.

If he ever realized, if word somehow leaked back to him . . . They couldn't risk it. Keeping the information within the tight family circle was the only option.

So she couldn't even squelch whatever it was that was willfully rising, refusing to be suppressed, by telling Caleb the whole story. Her whole story. She could never tell him that. If he ever found out . . . Her husband was correct. She could be accused of collusion. She choked back the thought.

She couldn't have a trusting relationship and not tell him. He'd guess something was wrong, just as he had earlier. She'd have to tell him. And then he'd do what any decent man would do. He'd walk away.

He was the most eligible bachelor in the Valley, a man who'd put family honor and the security of his loved ones ahead of his own desires and wants. She shivered to think of his reaction when he discovered how much she'd kept secret. He thought he knew her darkest secrets, but he hardly knew anything about her.

Minette was snuggled down under her covers, cuddling her favorite, soft, blue bunny rabbit, her eyelids hovering on the edge of sleep, when she rolled towards Madeleine and fixed her with those big luminous eyes. "Tante Em, why did everyone pretend the Emperor was wearing clothes when he wasn't? Isn't that telling lies?"

Madeleine drank in her wide, open face, her lightly flushed translucent skin that was as transparent as her soul. "Yes, *ma chérie*, I guess it is."

"So why did they do that? Isn't that wrong?"

"It is, my sweetheart. You're quite right. I suppose they were scared the Emperor would be angry if they told him the truth. He would feel very foolish, and Emperors don't like feeling foolish."

The child gave a little sigh. "Oh, I see. But he's silly, then, isn't he?" She stuck her thumb in her mouth, rolled over and instantly fell asleep.

Madeleine sat in the dim light cast by the low-burning night light on the bedside table and let the peace of the room engulf her. It took long minutes for the tumult inside to subside.

Emperors, or men. Or women, come to think of it. No one much enjoys appearing foolish.

There was really only one thing for it. She was going to have to exercise rigid control around Caleb Stewart from now on. She'd be cool and distant and give him no reason to think she had any feelings for him. Because she didn't. She couldn't. Not unless she was ready to expose all her dirty linen. She could see it now. The thought of them together was patently ridiculous. She just had to somehow convince her unruly heart.

12

The lure of the elephant had been their undoing. That, and Graysie's celebrity, which meant she was recognized wherever she went.

Madeleine stared into the ringmaster's face and repeated her question for a second, maybe even a third, panicked time. She'd completely lost track of how long they'd been standing there.

"What do you mean, you can't find her?"

The Franconi Family Circus's top man stammered his apologies. The child who'd accompanied them backstage after the performance couldn't be found — but Mae, the elephant trainer's daughter, was also missing. It was likely they had just run off to get an ice cream. There really was no cause for alarm.

Madeleine stared into Graysie's chalky blank face, and then scanned the backstage area, seeking any glimpse of a little girl in royal-blue velvet edged with broderie anglaise.

"Minette!" Her yell was propelled by a fierce, not-to-be-denied fervor. "Minette! My little darling, *mon ange*. Where are you?" She buried her head in her hands in despair and prayed she was just a mischievous kid who'd run off with her new friend.

The circus folk had done their best, instigating a full search of animal enclosures, private caravans, even up the aerialist ladders in the Big Top — but they had failed to find the two girls.

They'd now been missing for nearly an hour, far longer than it look to play hooky and buy an ice cream.

"I can't believe this is happening," wailed Graysie. "If only we hadn't accepted that invitation to go backstage."

They'd both been so excited to arrange this treat — a surprise visit to the Franconi Circus, the show Francine had accompanied to America as the wife of Jacques Franconi, one of the founder's grandsons.

When the ringmaster had recognized Graysie Castellanos, the famous stage and singing star, and then discovered the link that Minette's mother had with the show, he'd been ecstatic about hosting them backstage. Minette could feed the elephant and marvel at the aerialists practicing their routines, he'd said.

Minette had been dancing on tip toes with excitement.

And then, the fatal interruption. A bumptious clown had thrust himself upon them, insisting he'd known Francine, seeking Graysie's autograph — and that was all it took. Minette had been ten feet away, fascinated by a pair of small monkeys being trained to ride bareback.

A moment's inattention. One minute she was there, the next she was gone.

"We can't go home without her." Graysie's distraught eyes were red-rimmed. "But she's been gone for nearly an hour now. Maybe one of us should go to the police and report her missing, while the other stays here just in case she comes back."

Madeleine nodded. "We've done everything else. It's our last resort. I agree, we can't leave here without her.

I'd hate her to think we'd deserted her."

They were turning to tell the ringmaster of their plan when a freckled urchin tugged at Graysie's skirt and held up an envelope. "S'cuse me, miss. The man said to deliver this to the ladies out back."

Graysie glanced down at the paper and frowned. "Madeleine, this is for you. It looks very odd. Here."

She thrust her the message and Madeleine glanced down. Written in the same cursive black ink handwriting as that on the gift box delivery of some days ago was a name: "Mrs. Philippe Coubert: Urgent."

She gasped. "Oh, Graysie. No! It can't be."

She ripped it open. Inside was a slip of white paper, the same expensive notepaper as in the bee delivery. On it in the fine script was a hand-written message:

If I go down, you go down. Understand?

Beside it was a black drawing of a bee swarm flying skywards, like a big black comma. Or a question mark.

She grabbed at Graysie's shoulder as her knees buckled. "Oh Graysie," she wailed. "This is all my fault!"

"There are a thousand places the child could have been taken, Mademoiselle. We don't have the manpower to search even a dozen of them."

Sheriff Roscoe Honeyman seemed a decent chap, but Madeleine wanted him to say something else. That he would immediately put all the members of Sacramento's sixty Benevolent Societies on high alert. Or call up Sacramento's military men — the light infantry, the territorials, even the Hussars — for an all-out search.

Instead, he'd asked her where Gérard Le Blanc was staying and offered to send an officer to his address, but of course she had no idea where he lived, or even if he was in Sacramento.

She sat for the second hour of Minette's vanishing in tortured indecision, not wanting to leave in case Minette was brought in but feeling useless for not doing something practical herself.

She had just decided she would visit the nearest newspaper offices and place a notice of reward for information when a street urchin presented himself at the sheriff's desk. He looked remarkably like the boy who delivered her the first note — freckled, dressed in ragged clothes and a cheeky demeanor — but it was a different boy, taller and older, old enough to display a mouthful of strong white second teeth.

"Sheriff," she whispered urgently. "Look!"

Honeyman's head jerked up as the boy slipped the note across the desk, then twirled to dash for the door. Madeleine was upon him, swooping and grabbing him fast by one ear. "No, you don't!" Some good had come of her years as a school mistress, after all, she thought grimly.

Roscoe Honeyman was not pleased. He handed her the unopened envelope and gestured to the boy. "Let him go. There's no law against being paid for delivering a message." He turned to the boy. "Sit down son. You're not in trouble. I've got some cookies here. Help yourself — and while you're eating tell me where you got that letter."

Madeleine glanced at the clock on the office wall: 3:15 p.m. The last note had come at 2.15 p.m. Minette had gone missing at 1.15 p.m.

She broke in. "You see what he's doing, don't you?" She gestured to the clock. "Crowing triumph. On the hour." She ripped open the envelope. The same message, with an addition in the same confident script:

Careful, or that sheriff will start asking questions. Then where will you be?

She guessed she looked guilty as she glanced up. She couldn't help it.

Honeyman was a serious-faced man with dark brown eyes and a steady presence. He had a reputation as a man of integrity. "Well?" he demanded. "What's he got to say this time?"

She passed the paper across without comment and he read, his eyebrows lifting as he reached the last line. "Do you know what he's referring to?"

She nodded. "I think so." She looked pointedly at the lad, who'd been chewing his way through a canister of cookies.

Roscoe nodded towards the boy. "What's your name, son?"

The boy scowled. "Frog. 'Cos I can jump high."

"Well, Frog, tell us about the man who gave you this message. Where did you meet him, and what did he look like?"

The man he described matched Roland Durand more closely than it did Gérard Le Blanc. Apart from that, he had nothing new to add. He'd been in a crowd. The man had given him his instructions and some gold coins and disappeared before Frog could say a word.

Honeyman let the boy go, saying, "If you see that man again, or anything else unusual, come back and tell me instantly. I'll make it worth your while."

Madeleine headed for the door. "I'm going to as many newspapers as I can to place missing-person ads. I'll be back before four-fifteen."

"I'll send someone to Mrs. Russell with an update," said Honeyman. "Then I think you need to get back here and tell me everything. A rather odd type of demand, I must say. It's not clear yet what he's asking you to do, or whether he's even seeking a ransom."

It took her nearly the full hour to do the rounds of the papers, but she'd been gratified to discover two of them promised to treat her plea as a news break and give it prominence in their late editions. When she returned Honeyman was waiting impatiently. "So tell me, what's he getting at? 'If I go down, you go down'?" His eyes narrowed. "What's that all about?"

Madeleine felt sick to the stomach, though she'd been expecting the question. "I told you before, Gerald Le Blanc is wanted for murder and embezzlement in France. I'm sure these notes are from him. It's just the sort of low blow he'd find amusing." She steeled herself. "I should know, because I was his wife. Only for six months, but it was six months too many. He's trying to make me guilty by association. I don't know what he wants me to do, but there will be something, and it will be horrible. You can bet on it."

She reached over and picked up the note, examined it again. "I had nothing to do with his crimes. In fact, I gave the police evidence against him. He's bluffing, to intimidate me." She met Honeyman's eyes without flinching. "But I'm so frightened for Minette. She's only six years old! I don't know how far he's prepared to go to get what he wants."

She stared at the sheriff, wanting him to make it right, but all he could do was shake his head. "I know, Mademoiselle. It's a bad situation."

Madeleine choked up. "She shouldn't have to handle this! She's been through enough already."

All the way in on the train Doña Valentina had reassured Josefa she had nothing to fear in simply telling the sheriff what she knew. The truth. Caleb had done nothing wrong, and all they had to do was tell the truth and stand firm. It was the job of the law to ascertain the facts, and she was confident the sheriff would do that.

Caleb pushed aside the memory of searching Rory's room — that was a technicality, surely — and wished he could share his mother's optimism. However, he doubted that their wardrobe — Valentina had insisted on them wearing their Sunday best, saying it suggested respect for the position Sheriff Arkwright occupied — or his flat denial of any wrongdoing would have the desired effect. Despite his overriding worry about the coming interview, a quick image of Madeleine's smile, with its quicksilver charm, flashed before him. He gritted his teeth.

The train was drawing to a standstill, the Front Street station just a short walk from City Hall and the Water Works masonry fortress on the riverside where the police department and Arkwright could be found.

Caleb stood aside at the entrance, giving Doña Valentina the chance to sweep on ahead. Clad in imperial purple, tall and straight-backed, her hair drawn into a chignon, she looked every bit a ruler's consort.

Past the Mayor's office, the city councilors' rooms, the offices of the city waterworks, they swept. The edifice had been built a decade ago as a municipal catch-all, with the police department on the west corner above a dank, six-cell, station-house-cum-jail in the basement.

They halted at the heavily reinforced police department doors, and one thing became immediately obvious. Being situated one floor above street level did not protect them from the noxious marsh dubbed China Slough, so-called because of the close proximity of Chinatown. The west side of the building backed straight onto the swampy water, and the smell let them know it. Doña Valentina sniffed, paused, and drew an impeccable white linen handkerchief from the soft bag that hung from her wrist and dabbed it under her nose. The citrus fragrance of Eau de Cologne briefly overwhelmed the muggy scent. But only briefly.

A controversy had raged in the newspapers about the stink of the Slough, which one *Sacramento Daily Union* correspondent described as a cross between "a buzzard's breath and a glue factory." A smell, he warned, warming to his task, that was "able-bodied, vigorous and aggressive. It didn't creep along the slough on its belly, weak and apologetic. It got up on its hind legs and howled."

It was howling today. Catching the

revolted expression on his mother's face, Caleb couldn't suppress a smile. He turned to his sister, who followed in his mother's wake, seemingly oblivious to the odor. She too was stunning in a cherry-colored gown with a matching hat. Her jet eyes shone with a quiet defiance, and Caleb felt a jolt of pride. A finer mother and daughter pair you'd never find.

He braced his shoulders, the slight tightness of the jacket around them unfamiliar to him. He rarely wore fancy city clothes, as he called them, and he hoped that just this once it might be worth the trouble. He pulled open the heavy door and brought up short, a surge of alarm pulsing through him. "Madeleine?"

Beside him his sister froze, and his mother exhaled a surprised breath.

"What are you doing here? Is everything all right?"

"When will those afternoon newspapers be going out, the ones with your ad in them?"

Caleb's tone was matter of fact, business-like, and for that she was grateful. He seemed to sense that if they started lamenting, or even sympathizing, she'd fall apart. She had to stay strong for Minette and Graysie.

"Any time now, I think. It's a very long shot, I know, but wouldn't it be wonderful if someone sees them? And thinks to report it?" Madeleine produced her best counterfeit smile.

When they'd been told of the emergency Madeleine and Graysie faced, the Stewart trio had dropped any thoughts of seeing Sheriff Arkwright and moved straight into being of service in any way they could. Madeleine's spirits had lifted being surrounded by friends willing to share the load.

They'd gone up to see Graysie, who was still waiting at the circus, and had filled her in on what was going on at police headquarters. They'd satisfied themselves that she had sent a messenger to the vineyard so that Aristide and the Russell men would be advised of the drama.

And as the clock hand crawled towards 4.15 p.m. they returned to give Madeleine moral support as she awaited the next message. They sat in a tense semi-circle facing the door, attempting to make light chit-chat when they had only one thing on their minds.

The tap of wood on wood jolted them to attention. Five pairs of eyes stared in sick anticipation as a wizened old chap in rags hobbled in, leaning heavily over a walking stick nearly as gnarled as the hand that clutched it. His eyes widened at the reception committee. Sheriff Honeyman stepped forward and said reassuringly, "Please come in. We've been expecting you."

The old chap glanced around, as if momentarily entertaining the idea of bolting then thinking better of it. He thrust his hand out to the sheriff, who took the envelope. Honeyman gave Madeleine a hard look, one eyebrow raised, and she nodded assent.

Yes, you open it. I don't know how much more of this I can stand.

In reply to Honeyman's questions, the hobo wheezed that he had been accosted by a man in a bar and had good money thrust in his face to deliver this note to the police station. So here he was. He remembered nothing about his benefactor, he said. "My eyes aren't so good, gov'nor. 'Cept he had a pretty big conk."

That could describe half the men in Sacramento.

Honeyman ripped open the envelope. He took a long minute to read its contents before raising his eyes to catch Madeleine's. The dark pools were shining with tenderness, and her breath caught in her throat. "What? Is she all right?"

"He's finally made a demand. He wants to do a trade. The child for you."

He passed the paper to her and she stared down at the words written on it.

"Till death us do part, for richer for poorer." Now is the time to fulfill your vows. I claim you as my wife and will redeem the child in your place.

She passed it to Caleb. Her throat had closed over, and she could barely speak. "I can't . . . I can't . . ." The words were a raspy whisper. "You read it." She looked abruptly away, then glanced back in time to see the stark shock on Caleb's face as the impact of the message registered. He *did* care. And that made everything so much worse.

The shocked silence in Honeyman's office was shattered by Wayne Arkwright's jeering figure in the entryway. "Well, well, who do we have here? Is the president visiting?"

Honeyman straightened. "Not now, Sheriff. We're dealing with a serious situation here."

Arkwright's brow furrowed in an aggrieved scowl. He remained planted in the doorway, his stance challenging. "So a kid's gone missing. Happens every day of the week. She'll turn up."

"Sheriff Arkwright, now is not the time—"

Arkwright puffed out his chest and glared at Caleb. "It so happens I've been wanting to interview this fellow, and here he is, in at the station. Seems to me that's too good an opportunity to miss."

Caleb mirrored the implied threat and stood. At full height he stood shoulder to shoulder with the burly sheriff. "We have a situation here, Sheriff. I'm happy to come in another day."

Arkwright's voice was chilled. "I don't think so." He turned to Honeyman. "I'll use the interview room next door. Get Lumpy to bring in some chairs, will you?" Then he stepped closer to Caleb, chest to chest, like a dog summing up a rival. His eyes were narrow and hard. "I'll see you next door in five minutes — with or without the harem."

In the deathly silence that followed Arkwright's exit, the old tramp who'd delivered the note crept out without a backward glance, glad to have escaped without being locked up. And then, as if a shot had gone off for the start of a race, they all started talking at once.

Caleb: "Madeleine, Le Blanc's a thug! It's a ridiculous idea. You mustn't. We'll think of something."

Doña Valentina: "We're coming with you, son. You're not seeing that man on your own."

Josefa: "Oh, Madeleine, I'm so sorry."

Madeleine: "Minette. She's the one that counts."

The roar of voices meant they each heard only snatches of what the other was saying.

Sheriff Honeyman stepped in and held

up the hand of authority. "Woah. Stop right there, everyone." He gave a dry coughing laugh. "We're not going to get anywhere, all talking at once. Now Caleb, much as I hate to admit it, you need to follow Arkwright's direction and get in there." He tipped his head to indicate the room next door. Then he glanced between Caleb and Madeleine. "Say whatever it is you want to say, and then get on with it."

He turned to Josefa and Valentina. "I presume that means you'll be going with him. Rest assured we do have the men to handle this. You've raised Madeleine's morale, no doubt about it, but you can't be of much practical help at this point. This is police work."

"Isn't there another option?" Caleb's voice was strained. "The man's a predator. It's just not reasonable to expect—"

Madeleine stepped to his side and touched him on the arm. "It's all right, Caleb. We'll work something out. I married the man. I brought this on myself. Minette has done nothing to deserve it." She went to hug Josefa and Valentina. "You've both been a great comfort. Thank you. From now on the only thing you can really do is pray. Pray for us as hard as you can."

When the Stewarts had gone, Roscoe Honeyman sighed. "Right. Let's get down to some strategy here. I guess we'll be getting the instructions for the trade in the next missive, at 5.15 p.m. We want to be as well prepared as we can when it comes. First, are you carrying?"

Madeleine was perplexed. "I don't understand."

"A gun. Have you got a gun concealed on your person?"

Her cheeks flushed. "How did you know?" She opened her capacious carryall and drew out the Remington.

Roscoe shook his head sadly. "Because when a woman has to deal with a man like Le Blanc, it's natural they resort to carrying a firearm. And one of our first rules for this trade is, there's going to be no guns."

"Oh." Madeleine felt a dark hole open in the pit of her stomach.

I've comforted myself with the thought I could shoot him if the worst came to the worst. And now you're taking that away from me?

"We're going to free both of you and no one's going to die doing it."

Despite the tingling fear that ran through her, Madeleine felt a strength flow into her from his calm sureness. "Well, that's good news," she said with a wry smile. "I just want you to know, the most important thing is to rescue Minette. Everything else comes a faint second. So how are we going to do that?"

Roscoe answered with a broad grin. "I understand. And that's what we're going to sit down right now and work out."

"As an officer of the court, I'm sure you'll want to administer the highest truth, and we're here to help you find it."

Doña Valentina allowed her gaze to sweep the interview room. Not that there was much to see. Three of the four walls were windowless; the fourth had small barred windows high up. Caleb wondered how the smell still permeated everywhere when no air circulated. The space already felt crowded and fetid. There was one bucket chair and a small rectangular table alongside it backed against the wall. A butt-filled ashtray sat on the table. Valentina's eyebrow arched. "I presume you've got chairs, Sheriff."

As if on cue, a pimply youth appeared in the doorway carrying two chairs which he awkwardly deposited beside the two women. Caleb leaned against the wall and folded his arms. "I'm happy standing."

Arkwright turned an oily eye on Josefa. "Miss Stewart, good of you to come in. I was intending to call on you." He slumped back in the bucket chair, and as if to assert his authority pulled the table away from the wall with a dragging screech and put his feet up on it. He pulled a cigar out of his shirt pocket and began methodically to peel and light it. When he'd exhaled a mouthful of tar-tainted smoke he fixed his eye on Caleb. "So, Stewart, I wanted to see you, but why did you come to see me? I'd like to know. Hiding behind your mother's skirts, aren't you?"

"Hardly hiding, Arkwright. It so happens my mother and sister have information they think relevant to your inquiry. They're happy to swear to it."

"Sworn testimony, eh? And why should I be interested in what a couple of woman have to say?"

The rancor and malevolence Arkwright had displayed in Rory's room was back. Caleb sensed he grew in confidence with each puff of his cigar.

Valentina broke in. "As I am one of the 'couple of women' you are referring to, perhaps you would do me the courtesy of allowing me to answer?"

Arkwright regarded her in silence and

then exhaled another cloud of blue smoke. "Very well, then. Go ahead."

"I've only recently become aware that a very old friend of mine has inside knowledge of the events surrounding Rory Mackinnon's death. I feel sure you'd be interested." Valentina faltered. "She's not in good health, so it would be best to take a sworn statement from her as soon as possible."

Arkwright tapped ash into a wastepaper basket beside him. "Oh? And who is this person?"

"Bonaventura Alvarado."

"And how is she in a position to know anything of interest?" Arkwright's voice was reluctant, skeptical.

"The dead man was her grandson who lived in her house, and she was closely involved in his life."

Arkwright's eyes flicked uneasily to

Josefa. "And you? Why are you here?"

Josefa's shoulders stiffened, but she replied calmly, "I too wish to make a statement about events before and after Rory's death."

Arkwright's words were mocking. "And I suppose this 'evidence' has nothing to do with the fact that your brother is one of the main suspects?" He sneered. "Dragged you in to vouch for him, has he? Really, Miss Stewart, I thought you'd stay faithful to your . . ." He paused suggestively. "Your *paramour* for a bit longer than that. Quickly forgotten, eh? He's been dead for what? Less than twenty days."

Josefa took a sharp breath. Her hand flew to her mouth, as if to hide her shock. "I know more than anyone else in this room about Rory's wishes. And I know what Rory would want me to do.

He was an honorable man."

"Such fine sentiments. What a pity his 'honor' didn't protect him."

"Isn't it?" Josefa bit back. "But that has nothing to do with any of us here."

"Really, Miss Stewart? And what would you say if I told you I have witnesses who saw Rory Mackinnon and your brother together a couple of nights before his death?"

"I'd say they were lying. I believe I know who they are and why they're not telling the truth."

"And why should I believe you, a person with a conflict of interest? How can you be objective? Naturally you want to save your brother's skin."

Josefa's voice took on a stressed, shrill edge. "You should believe me because I know what's been going on. I know the truth."

"Ah, the truth." Arkwright took a final deep pull and stubbed the cigar out on the heel of his boot. "Forgive me if I remain a little skeptical. You had nothing to say in the days after your beloved's death, and now suddenly you've got a whole tale to tell? Isn't it simply a matter of realizing your lover won't be coming back to take care of you, so you need to go home to Mummy?" Arkwright's lips curved nastily.

Valentina rose angrily. "Those personal comments are quite unnecessary, Sheriff. Your job is to discover facts, not fit them to your own fiction."

Arkwright pulled his feet off the table and leaned forward with an intense concentration. But before he could speak Lumpy limped back in ahead of a dark-haired woman in full sail.

"Sheriff, Sheriff . . ." Lumpy's weak

voice trailed off helplessly as Consuela stopped short and stared. "What are *they* doing here, Wayne?"

She glared from Caleb to Valentina, who had swung around to meet her face to face.

"Just trying to sell me bull dust, Doña Consuela. Don't worry your pretty head about it."

Pretty head? Consuela must be coming up for fifty, Caleb thought. *Long past being a 'pretty head,' if she ever was one.*

His mother drew herself to her full authority. "Bull dust? If you're not interested then I'll find someone else in the department who is. Your superior perhaps? Or Sheriff Honeyman. Josefa and Bonaventura are more than prepared to tell what they know."

Consuela's lips simpered in a show of

false sympathy. "Bonaventura?" Her hard, black eyes bored into Valentina's. "Oh, I don't think so. I'm terribly sorry, Doña Valentina. Haven't you heard?"

Valentina's eyes sharpened to an eagle brightness. She clutched at the side pocket of her skirt, where Caleb knew she'd deposited Bonnie's figurine, and her fingers worked silently under the fabric. "Heard what?"

"I'm afraid my sainted mother died a few hours ago. She had another one of those bad turns, but this time she didn't come back."

Valentina pulled her hand free from her pocket and clutched at the edge of Arkwright's table with both hands, her haughty reserve draining away. Her mouth drew back in a stricken gasp, exposing her eye teeth. For a flash she reminded Caleb of a wolf caught in a trap. And then she was his aging mother again, sinking into deep grief.

Consuela stood like an ice statue. "So sorry, Valentina. We won't be able to hear from her, though what she could have had to say that I haven't already told the Sheriff, I can't imagine."

"Good point," said Arkwright. He pointed a finger at Josefa. "What do *you* have to say that's any different from what Consuela's already told me?"

Josefa's face was pale. She stood beside her mother, stroking Valentina's shoulder and upper arm, consoling her. "I don't know what Consuela has told you. I know Rory told me he was meeting my brother. But I believe he'd been misled by someone. Caleb never met up with him before that night. Of that I'm certain. He would have mentioned it."

"Why? Were you with him every waking minute?" Arkwright sounded triumphant.

"Well, no, I wasn't, but—"

"Then how could you know? Really, Miss Stewart, all you have is hearsay and supposition."

Doña Valentina placed her hand on top of Josefa's. "We're wasting our time here, Josefa. We can come back to this. Right now I want to pay my last respects to Bonnie and talk to the *curanderos*."

Josefa's eyes sparkled with unshed tears. Her jaw clenched as she fought to maintain her composure. "Of course, mother." She threaded her arm through her mother's. "Sorry, Caleb. We will get back to this. But Aunt Bonnie was so good to me. I can't bear to think she's gone."

Caleb stood to leave with them.

"Not so fast, Stewart," snapped Arkwright. "You have unfinished business here. I'm arresting you for the murders of Rory Mackinnon and Miguel Chico. The usual warnings apply."

Caleb's insides turned to ice. "You can't be serious!"

"On the contrary, Mr. Stewart. I am deadly serious. And we've a lot to see played out here yet, I assure you."

13

"I'm not happy about this, Madeleine. Not at all happy." Graysie punched her fist into her hand in futile protest. "I'm not allowing you to give yourself up to that man." She turned to Roscoe, eyes wide with appeal. "Tell her, Sheriff. There must be another way. Isn't that what you're here for?"

Roscoe leaned back in his chair, hands clasped behind his head. Only the nervous flicking of his index fingers betrayed his inner tension. "I agree, Mrs. Russell. The ideal outcome is for us to free Minette without having to surrender Mademoiselle Laurent." He rocked forward and put both elbows on his desk, the clasped fingers still twitching. "It's a matter of working out how to achieve that happy outcome."

The 5.15 message had been delivered by a young woman who looked vaguely familiar to Madeleine, a café worker who — like the others — said she'd been paid to deliver a message.

The instructions she carried were terse and specific:

Come to the Embarcardero, corner of J and Front streets, at 6 p.m. BRING NO ONE WITH YOU. You will receive further instructions when you arrive.

Roscoe had sent someone to bring Graysie back to join Madeleine at police headquarters because — as he'd explained to them both — she'd need to be present for Minette's return. "Assuming a trade is to be made, Minette has to be handed over to someone she knows." His eyes were dark with doubt. "I don't want this, Madeleine, but we have to be prepared."

Now they were sitting in Roscoe's office discussing how to proceed. Graysie was adamant. "We're not just going to allow you to go there alone and be carried off to who knows where. We lose all our bargaining power if we allow that." She turned to Roscoe. "Don't you agree, Sheriff?"

"Quite right, but I'm not sure how to communicate that without possibly endangering Minette. It's a very delicate situation and he holds all the cards."

Madeleine took Graysie's hand, as if comforting her. "I agree we can't trust him. And once he's got me, if he hasn't released Minette already, he's quite likely to double-cross us. So yes, we have to be devious." She smiled. "But

Graysie, more than anything, I want that little girl returned to you! More than anything."

"Our biggest problem," said Roscoe, "is we still have no idea where he might be holding Minette. If we knew that, we'd have some leverage."

A timid tap on the door had them all looking up in surprise. The café worker who'd delivered the note a few minutes before was standing there, nervously wringing her hands. "I've got something to say." Her eyes flitted around the room, as if fearful to come to rest. "I saw your notice. In the paper. The missing person notice." She licked her lips, arms tense at her sides. "I didn't realize … I thought . . . ." She fell into silence, her eyes wide and anxious.

And then in a rush she took two quick steps further into the room. "I know where she is." She stared around her, took another step toward them. "I know where the child is."

If silence had a sound, it would be like the long, hollow thrum of a kettle drum, rolling, rolling on, thought Madeleine. The hush grew in palpable intensity as the three of them sat transfixed, staring at the white-faced, wide-eyed woman before them.

She spoke again, hurried, garbled. "Until I saw the newspaper, I didn't know. Truly."

The gas lights strung like pearls along the Embarcadero waterfront threw puddles of light onto the oily waters of the Sacramento River, little bursts of brightness in a black and cold city. It was an icy January night, and dusk had already fallen. No one was out and about on the boardwalk in winter.

Madeleine shivered and pulled her coat collar more tightly around her. It was 5.55 p.m., and she was here for her rendezvous with her murderous husband, the bait to keep Philippe occupied while Graysie and Roscoe raced with Elspeth the café worker to the National Theater ice cream shop. Or more precisely, the boarding house next door to the ice cream parlor, where Elspeth insisted Minette would be found. They were gambling on being able to rescue the child and get her back home before Le Blanc got his hands on her.

Never had she felt more alone. She prayed for the ordeal to be over soon. She was so frightened she couldn't blink, though her eyes stung from the chill wind and tears rolled down her cheeks. Funny, she thought, how the tears started out hot, and by the time they reached her jawline and dripped onto her coat they were like ice.

She thrust her hands deeper into her pockets. She knew she had to spin this encounter out as long as she could to give Roscoe time to find Minette and get back here, but part of her just wanted it over. Philippe was such a blight on them all, and the prospect of being forced to live with him again so alien to every fiber of her being, she died a little inside every time she thought of it.

There was a faint change in the background noise of water slapping against the wharf pillars and creaking ropes from moored vessels. She went in to high alert. Yes. Footsteps, coming from below. She inched closer to the wharf edge and glanced down. Planked steps led to a smart schooner bobbing on the current, its deck neatly level with the wharf's lower platform. And coming up those steps, a man, moving with stealth. She darted back into the protection of the shadows and watched. Philippe's dark head appeared, then his muscular form. He paused with the intense focus of a cat on the hunt; his eyes searched the darkness.

"I know you're there, Madeleine. I can smell you."

She shuddered and wished she hadn't worn her favorite perfume.

"Show yourself."

She stepped into the gaslight and stood stock still. "Where's Minette? It's not a trade without her."

"All in good time." He gave a smile of eerie satisfaction. "So how's the cowboy?"

"Who?"

"Don't play dumb with me. The Californio rancher. Starting to feel as if his tail's on fire, I hope. His woman gone. His arrest completed."

"You're talking rubbish, Philippe. I saw him this afternoon, and he was in fine fettle."

"Not for much longer, he won't be."

"Where's Minette? I'm not going anywhere without you producing the child."

"Is that so?"

With a sixth sense for danger, she heard a soft padding noise behind her. She thrust her hand into her bag, pulled out the Remington, and whirled to face the sound. Roland Durand loomed up out of the murky night.

The deadness she'd felt just minutes ago had gone, replaced by a burning will to live. She was so glad she'd blatantly ignored Sheriff Honeyman's orders not to bring the gun. Philippe didn't have Minette here. He'd never intended to do anything other than lure Madeleine to this rendezvous. As she clutched the cold metal, she prayed that Minette was already safe in Graysie's arms.

She ignored the awareness that she would probably die on these cold bare boards by the river. She just knew, with a warmth radiating from deep within, that she was not going to be Philippe's woman, ever again. She stood her ground, gun raised, finger determined on the trigger, and fired. There was the dull thud of a bullet hitting wood, an empty echo. She whirled to where Philippe had stood seconds before. The wharf was deserted. Her quarry had already fled.

Then Roscoe Honeyman's quiet bass reached her through the blackness. "It's over Madeleine. Now for goodness sake put that gun away. You're making me nervous."

"I've got to give it to you Le Blanc. You know how to get what you want."

Noah Jones relaxed in his capacious armchair and picked up the whiskey glass that sat at his elbow. He raised it to Gérard in a toast. "Here's to your continuing success."

The two men were sitting in the Sacramento branch of Buffer, Jones and Cottlesloe, on the first floor of a commercial block on Third Street in the heart of the city. The best hotels — the Orleans, the Western — were within easy walking distance, and Buffer and Co.'s offices had the aura of a posh hotel. The sort of atmosphere created by leather-covered chairs, oak panels, silver trays holding crystal decanters. The thick carpets absorbed sound, creating a sense of a haven. The faintest cooing of the pigeons on the sills above them was the only outside noise that penetrated.

The affluence made Le Blanc twitch. He pushed up from his chair and went and stood by the window. He was only a couple of blocks from last night's debacle on the waterfront.

Hot anger flamed within as he recalled the scene. Honeyman arriving with his men. He'd barely escaped onto the salmon boat he had waiting. And then to discover that Roland's tart had turned the kid in. He wasn't sure if it was for the money or because she felt sorry for her, but she'd live to regret it.

Still, there was one thing he could savor. The rancher was behind bars. That victory was sweet. The rest of it was mere entertainment. He turned back to Jones. "Get someone to arrange his payment, will you? Arkwright's, I mean. I don't want him pestering me."

In truth, Arkwright's weak-willed malice had affected him like the measles. He wanted to scratch himself whenever he was near the fellow. He acted as though he was the man running this project. And no one bounced Gérard Le Blanc from his rightful place. No one was as good as him at what he did.

He held the glass Noah Jones had poured when he arrived and brought it to his lips. The smooth rim was cold and strangely comforting. He took a sip of whiskey and enjoyed the warmth as it slid down. "He was slow to play ball, but he's come through in the end."

Jones answered the conversation with a matching sip. "What were his objections?"

"Oh, I think he was concerned that if it came to trial, the witness statements wouldn't hold up," Le Blanc said. "He doesn't realize we've no intention of letting it go to trial. We just want to frighten the living daylights out of the sod so he's ready to make a deal." He allowed himself a contemptuous grin. "He was so hoity-toity the first time I tried to get him to see sense. It will be different next time round." He tapped his glass with his finger, and the wedding ring he'd slipped on the day he married Madeleine chimed against the glass. The only time he'd taken it off was when he was romancing her flighty sister. "Nothing like the carrot and stick to get a result with a donkey."

Jones laughed, a low gurgling sound, like a drain losing water. "And the deal? What do you have in mind?"

Le Blanc swung away from the window and, nursing the glass to his chest, resumed his seat. "From what I understand, you and your colleagues want to acquire the western half of the boundary line with access to the American River. Is that correct — your clients are interested in the water? It's good wine country so your city farmers can play at being vignerons as well?"

He couldn't hide his snide mocking tone, but Jones didn't appear to notice. Instead, he nodded his approval, licking his lips as he did. The lank lock of hair that always hung over his right eye moved back and forth as he nodded, and he swiped it aside irritably. "That's right. The consortium we are part of will be delighted to hear things are so close to resolution."

Jones leaned forward and pulled open

a drawer at the right-hand side of his desk. From the drawer he drew a metal canister. He unlocked the lid with a small key he carried on a chain around his neck and drew out a fistful of the large denomination $10 notes issued by the US Treasury in recent months — the so-called Rainbow Notes — printed with blue borders and a green and red overlay. Very pretty. Le Blanc's palms felt sweaty.

Jones stacked them in a pile in front of him. "I must say your work has been most pleasing, Mr. Le Blanc. I'll be delighted to report back to the others on your progress. You've shown enormous foresight, you didn't panic when things didn't go your way, and you've completed the dirty work without a hint of remorse. Most commendable." He closed the lid, locked the box and put the key back around his neck. It disappeared beneath the collar of his shirt, hidden from view.

Wouldn't someone love to know about that key, Le Blanc mused.

Jones pushed the pile of notes across the desk towards him. Le Blanc acted surprised, though his heart was fluttering frantically. "What's this? I wasn't expecting to be paid today."

"I wouldn't complain, if I were you, Le Blanc. Cottlesloe's a tightwad. Be grateful I've managed to extract it from him when I did. The next lot may be a long time coming."

Le Blanc reached across to retrieve the notes and brushed fingers with Jones' bony icy hand. A shiver ran down his spine. The man was a walking ghoul. Did red blood actually flow in his veins?

"I think you deserve an advance, and

I told Elijah so. What you've achieved for us in a short time is quite remarkable." He nodded to the money, which Le Blanc was tucking into the inside pocket of his bearskin jacket. "There'll be plenty more where that came from when you complete the job."

"That's when Caleb Stewart turns over half his ranch for a nominal sum in return for being busted from jail?"

"We're only interested in the ranch. He can be busted from jail or not, I don't care. We just want to get our hands on the real estate." Jones drew the round tortoiseshell tray carrying a half-full decanter toward him and poured himself another glass of the golden liquor. "Another glass?"

"Sure. Comes a distant second to French brandy, I have to say, but needs must when the devil drives." He thrust his glass forward with a grin.

"Very funny. Speaking of the devil, does killing people bother you?"

"Not unless they're young and female." He laughed as if to indicate he was joking, but Noah Jones's tic was flashing his discomfort.

Interesting. The man was feeling under pressure.

"Well, that's very good, because you won't get your final payment until Halliburton is dealt with." His eyes searched Le Blanc's face, as if trying to read its hidden depths.

Le Blanc maintained the cold, bland expression that was his trademark. Shut down and repelling any further inquiry. "Halliburton?" He said the name lazily, distantly, as if it was a faint memory, of the least concern to him.

"That's right," said Jones. "We're very

happy with your work, Mr. Le Blanc." He grinned. "Very happy. But we can't possibly allow news of your past misadventures to reach Capitol Hill. Senator de Vile. Elections are in November and he can't afford any scandal. Not this year, not next. If we want to continue to use your services — which I hasten to add we do — we need to be protected. Reputation counts, you know, in the law as much as in politics. We can't be seen to be associating with a known felon. I'm sure you understand."

Le Blanc nodded. His hands, which minutes before had been sweating, had turned to ice, and underneath his granite wall of indifference he sensed a rising sense of dread. He must be getting soft in his old age, but he felt a sense of doom bearing down on him. For a few moments he wished he could shove the cash back across the desk and get up and walk out.

This is what comes from wanting power. You have to step up. Do whatever is needed. And never look back.

The sense of Madeleine's seductive curves flooded him, so real he imagined her standing next to him. He could even smell her, the fresh green fragrance he'd smelled again last night, that was always there when she was around.

Never look back. God knew he'd tried to live by that. So why in the hell couldn't he leave her behind? Even bedding her pretty sister hadn't done the trick. His thoughts always returned to the woman who wouldn't heed and obey. Who'd turned away from him and chosen someone — and something — else.

"Where were you, Tante? They said you were coming to get me."

The plaintive appeal in Minette's distress rang in Madeleine's ears as she gazed around the peaceful Vino d'Oro bedroom that had been her haven for the last few months.

She had never wanted Minette to feel abandoned. The bewildered light in the child's hurt eyes last night? She never wanted to see that again, either.

Elspeth had led Roscoe and his men to the rooming house where Minette had been held. She was locked in with no captors in evidence when Roscoe and his men broke down the door. An empty nausea washed over her as she recalled their reunion. By the time she'd joined them, Graysie and Minette were installed in a comfortable family room in St. George's Hotel on K Street, close to the theater where the saga had begun and favored by families visiting Sacramento.

The child had suffered no physical harm. As had been suggested, she'd been taken for ice cream with her newfound friend Mae, the elephant keeper's daughter. She told Graysie, "The nice lady said we could play." She'd spent a couple of hours playing in the family's rooms before she tired of the games and asked to be returned to "Sissy." She'd become increasingly upset as her pleas were fobbed off and she began to worry that neither Graysie nor Madeleine were coming to get her.

"Why didn't you come? I was scared."

"It was a terrible mix up, *ma chérie*. A big misunderstanding. And we did have enormous fun at the circus, didn't we?"

Graysie shot her a grateful look. No one was admitting to anything. Minette had seen no one except the circus mother and daughter, and they weren't talking. But the incident had left its mark. Minette was fractious and upset, frightened to sleep without a nightlight, anxious for Graysie to stay with her. It would be some time before she regained her breezy confidence, Madeleine could see that.

She picked up her leather carry-all and turned at the doorway, willing herself to remember every detail of the room. The slotted shade that spilled bands of light across the rug from the window shutters. The light fragrance of the purple lavender on the bedside table, collected on one of their little garden expeditions. The glow of the red velvet eiderdown, reflecting on the butter-yellow adobe walls. She wanted to remember this room forever because she never expected to be as happy as she'd been here, ever again.

She glanced to the crisp white linen pillow, where she'd left a note for Aristide. By the time he came looking for her, and found her letter, she'd hopefully be far gone. She'd brought nothing but danger and misfortune to the people she loved. She was a liability to the house, to her brother, and particularly to Minette.

The greatest gift she could give them was to leave, go far away, where Philippe couldn't find her, and she wasn't a lightning rod for his venom.

One night in the Sacramento County jail was one too many. If Caleb hadn't guessed that before he'd spent fifteen hours in the frigid, mouldy-smelling basement, he sure knew it now. He rubbed his upper arms to stimulate some warmth. Scratched his itching right hip. It was breaking out in a rash that looked suspiciously as though it had been caused by bed bugs, although how the little critters survived the near freezing overnight temperatures, he had no idea. The thin blanket Arkwright had provided gave no comfort at all, and if he was going to have to stay here another night, he prayed Josefa would bring some relief in the form of a mercy parcel.

The thought of Josefa had hardly entered his mind when Lumpy's bulky, doughboy form loomed from the other side of the bars. The boy's erupting adolescent complexion was pinker than yesterday, and he glanced nervously behind him as he planted himself at the cell door. "Your sister's here. Sheriff says she can't come in and you can't come out, so you'll just have to talk through the bars."

He retreated awkwardly, glancing

sideways at Josefa with a moony expression. He hovered, reluctant to leave. Just a dumb kid with no idea of what's going on here, Caleb thought.

Josefa looked at him kindly. "Thank you, Ned. I'll come and get you when I'm ready to leave."

He backed away blushing.

"Ned? Is that his name? How did you find that out?" Caleb gave her a weak grin.

Josefa reached through the bars to grasp his hand and he pulled away. "I think I've got bed bugs. Best not come too close."

"Ned Honeyman." Josefa said. "Roscoe's his father — you didn't know that?"

Caleb shrugged. "I had no idea. How do you know all this?"

She gave a slow, questioning smile.

"What? You don't know everything, you know. Ned's got an older sister, Teresa, who was at the convent school at the same time I was. I know the family."

"Not well enough to get Wayne Arkwright's foot off my neck, I suppose?"

She shook her head and her expression sobered.

"But before we get to that, how are Minette and co doing? Roscoe was good enough to drop by last night and let me know they'd successfully rescued her. Is everything all right?"

Josefa shrugged. "We haven't seen them, Caleb. What with mother wanting to see Bonnie and everything. They stayed in town last night, I hear, and went home this morning. No one was seriously hurt, and I suppose that's the main thing to be grateful for. Though it was terrifying for them all, I'm sure."

Caleb kicked the toe of his boot on the stone floor. "The sooner we get that Frenchman out of our lives, the better. He's a total menace."

"Speaking of which." Josefa perched on a chair Ned had deposited by her while they were talking. "I did try for Roscoe's help. He says he can't interfere with Arkwright's cases, even though he suspects he's a measly baggage — he called him a right boodler who'd sell his own grandmother if he could see a profit in it. But Roscoe's not had any involvement with Rory and Miguel's case. He can't just step in and take over." She looked at him soulfully. "I'm sorry, Caleb. I did try. The only thing he did hint at was if we managed to stir up a public stink about it — you know, if you got a newspaperman to write something

443

about corrupt cops and innocent ranchers — that might make the higher-ups sit up and take notice. It's been known to work in the past — they hate that kind of controversy. It can stir up all sorts of problems for them."

Caleb shuddered. "Arrrgh. At present, what have I got? It's just my word against his — and Consuela's. I don't have much of a case to talk about. 'I didn't do it, your honor.' I mean, doesn't every jailbird claim he is innocent?" He slumped back down on the hard frame that served as a bed, his elbows on his knees. "It's hard to believe this is really happening. But I'm grateful for everything you're doing. Really I am."

Josefa shrugged. "I've got some stuff for you out there. Ned wouldn't let me bring it in until he's searched it. A thick blanket, some of Mother's chili con carne and piglet molasses cookies. I know it's not much. I wish I could bring better news."

"How's Mother shaping up? And what's happening with Bonnie's funeral?"

"She's taken a knock, no doubt about it. Bonnie's funeral is later today. Santiago is bringing Mother into town — they'll swing by here, I'm sure, to see you."

"Yeah, seems like I'll still be here. I'm glad Bonnie isn't here to see this. She'd be going loco."

The outer door of the holding area screeched on its iron hinges and Ned reappeared holding a burlap bag, followed by the erect, unhurried form of Thomas Halliburton. His well-tailored, gray suit seemed strangely out of place seen through the dim bars, but Caleb's heart leapt into his throat at the sight of him.

Halliburton's lips were pressed together in a thin tight line. The spike of hope died.

Josefa stood and embraced the solicitor. "Mr Halliburton. Good to see you."

"You too, my dear, though I'm afraid I don't have anything to make you smile." He turned to Caleb and doffed his hat. "Caleb. It's deeply regrettable you are being put through this, it really is. But at present there's nothing I can do to interrupt the law's due process." He dragged a wooden chair across to the bars and squatted to meet Caleb at eye level. "I did my best. I called on Judge Seb Wade. He's one of the county judges who presides over the court — he might even be the one to hear your case if it gets that far — but he is adamant justice has to be seen to be done. He's not going to interfere in the sheriff's case. He says it gives the impression the legal process can be swayed. *Fiat justitia rual coelum* and all that."

Caleb stared back at him, barely concealing his disappointment. "Which to ordinary plugs like me means?"

Halliburton's vaguely benign expression sharpened. "My apologies. I'm talking like a lawyer. 'Let justice be done though the heavens fall.' That's how the ancients saw it. We're more inclined to say 'justice at any cost.' Or even 'justice is blind.' They can't be seen to be partial to influence."

Josefa protested, "But they've been partial already. This isn't justice, what Caleb's experiencing."

"Yes, and we can only trust that when the evidence is all aired in court, it will be shown for the flimsy nonsense it is."

Caleb hugged the bars. "And meantime I have to stay and get eaten alive by bed bugs. Forgive me if I'm not impressed."

Halliburton gazed at him, his eyes warm and concerned. He was no longer the vague professor but a kindly father. "I can understand your frustration, Caleb."

"The thing is, the longer I'm in here, the less chance there is we'll catch who really was responsible for killing Rory and Miguel. Arkwright is certainly not investigating any further, trying to find anyone else. They're not getting justice either!"

Halliburton nodded. "There *is* one other option. You've discounted it in the past, but maybe now you're ready to rethink it."

Caleb frowned. "What?"

"Consider doing a deal. With Arkwright. With Gérard Le Blanc. With whoever is pulling the strings here. It's not entirely clear who the puppet master is."

"Well, it certainly isn't Arkwright. He hasn't got the brains. And Le Blanc? He's the middleman. How much freedom has he got to negotiate? Who knows? But he did try and get me to parlay a few days ago." He scratched behind his ear. "What do you reckon, Josie? John Russell's already suggested the same thing, I must admit. Seems I have to get a bit cunning. Being the up-front country boy isn't working."

Josefa grimaced. "For you or for Rory. Two country boys devoured by city wolves. I'd say go for it, Caleb. What have you got to lose?"

Halliburton rose and put his hat back

on with a flourish. "I'll go and tell Arkwright you're ready to talk turkey."

The burlap bag lay on the floor, overflowing with the blankets and food sent by Valentina. Ned was skulking near the door. Halliburton gestured to the bag. "He won't be needing these, son. Tell the sheriff I want to see him immediately. Mr. Stewart is willing to talk."

The youth's face was lively and intelligent, "Lumpy" no more. "Certainly, Mr. Halliburton. Right away."

Halliburton bowed to Josefa and raised a hand in salute to Caleb. "With any luck we'll have you out of here by bedtime. Perhaps not quite in time for you to go to your aunt's funeral, I'm afraid, but you can escape another night with the bedbugs. Just don't sign anything until I've had a chance to approve it. Make that a not negotiable condition."

"You won't be needing that ticket."

Madeleine's hand was stretched across the ticket booth of California Steam Navigation Company, her two-dollar fare in her fingers, when a male arm reached over her shoulder and stilled her hand.

"Oh!" Her heart jumped to her mouth. Last night, a stroll away from here on the Embarcadero, Philippe had been close to abducting her in a salmon boat. She struggled to remain calm, reminding herself as she whirled to face the intruder that she knew his voice well. "Aristide! What are you doing here?"

"I could be asking you the same thing, *ma soeur*. Now put that money back in your purse and come home."

She hesitated and then palmed the fare and stepped out of the way of the next customer. She glared up at him, doing her best to look annoyed when inside, every nerve ending felt alive, enraptured. "What are you doing?" she protested. "I have to get on that boat!"

Her brother's handsome face gazed back, a reassuring curve to his lips. He took her hand and squeezed it, shaking his head. "Graysie won't hear of it. Minette would be distraught if she knew what you're planning. We've told her you're visiting a friend and will be back soon. And your brother? He is the most adamant of all. I've only just found you again. I'm not ready to let you go." He turned and linked his arm through hers, keeping hold of her hand.

She pulled back, stopped him in his

tracks. "How did you know? How did you find me?"

He grinned. "I put myself in your shoes. I figured you wanted to get as far away from Philippe as possible. So that almost certainly meant going back to France. The one place on earth you can be sure he won't return to. And the quickest way to do that is to get a steamer to San Francisco then a train to New York and sail from there. I've been waiting here for you pretty well ever since we discovered you had gone."

He gave a guiding tug on her arm. "Now stop this nonsense about bringing shame and misfortune on our heads. We are all in this together, and we need you to help us get out of it."

14

"What does he want?" Sir John tapped his cigar ash into an ashtray. "Any idea?"

"He's bringing maps from his San Francisco masters showing what a reduced Rancho Del Oro will look like. At least I suspect that's the idea."

Caleb cracked his knuckles in disgust. "After that rubbish yesterday, I'm surprised he can show his face in the state of California. Thank God they rescued Minette. But why in glory's name hasn't he been arrested?"

John gave a frustrated sigh. "Not enough hard evidence, believe it or not. He never signed any of those notes. No one saw him anywhere near the child. The only connection was him standing on that wharf near where Madeleine happened to be. The cops have concluded it was a 'marital dispute and a misunderstanding about who was looking after the child.' Minette was with the elephant-keeper's wife the whole time, playing with the daughter. And the police don't like getting in the way of a husband claiming his rights. It can get very messy."

"What about the fact he's wanted in France?" Caleb tipped his head back and briefly closed his eyes. "Or doesn't that count?"

John's jaw tightened. "This is Gérard Le Blanc we're talking about. Not Philippe Coubert. It's all just a bit too complicated for the sheriff's daily run. Plus Le Blanc's got friends in high places. He's the devil's own gutter-blood, that one."

A gust of icy air blew into the study, and Caleb shivered. He was at a low ebb, feeling the cold and light-headed from his sleepless night in jail. He'd made this quick call on the Russell household to check up on how they were coping after yesterday's drama. That, and to get Sir John's advice about how to handle his dreaded meeting with Le Blanc tomorrow. But he was finding it hard to focus. He was dead on his feet, barely coherent. "I'm whacked. I should be going." He picked up his hat and stood to leave.

John tipped his head to one side and gestured for him to hold on. "Just a minute longer. I think that's Aristide back." The magnate ducked his head out of the study and called down the hallway. "Aristide, is that you? Come on in and say hello to Caleb."

Aristide's feet dragged on the hall floor. His breath sent a faint cloud of warm mist as he paused in the entry. His sister stood alongside him, her shoulders slumped forward, damp in a heavy winter coat.

John's eyes glittered with a delight Caleb couldn't fathom. "I'm so glad he found you." He stretched forward and gave Madeleine's shoulders a light squeeze. "Graysie and Minette were beside themselves. You've no idea."

Caleb's ears tingled.

What is he talking about?

John caught Caleb's dull confusion. "Oh, Caleb, sorry. Explanation needed. We haven't been talking about it, but Madeleine took herself off to France this morning."

Caleb's heart bolted like a shying horse. "She what?"

"She decided she was a liability to us all if she stayed. The police weren't willing to act, and she thought we'd be safer if she wasn't around." He gave her a quick smile. "She just didn't check with any of us before she left."

Madeleine's cheeks flushed. "I thought it would be best." Her voice was soft, low and hesitant.

Caleb's light-headedness was now a wave of dizziness. His head was too fuzzy for him to speak.

There was a long silence, and then Madeleine spoke again in the same uncertain, tentative voice. "I thought maybe Philippe would leave you alone if I wasn't here."

Caleb's mind was suddenly crystal-clear. "Oh, Madeleine! That's crazy." He gave a quick breathless laugh and drew his fingers through his hair. "Sorry, I'm not making any sense. It's just, well, Del Oro wouldn't be the same without you."

There was another long silence. Caleb sensed a rising embarrassment, his neck flushing red, his discomfort visible to all.

Then Sir John covered for him. "And so say all of us, Caleb. That's just what we said."

Caleb was turning to go when Madeleine spoke again, her voice powered with new determination. "He thinks he's got you beat, Caleb. He got away with yesterday's horrible game, and now he's pushed you into parlaying. He thinks he's winning." Her face was pale and drawn but lit by an inner glow that made her translucent. Her eyes were gleaming. "Go on the offensive, Caleb. Don't let him set the agenda." Her voice cracked, but she pushed on strongly, her eyes suspiciously bright.

"Surprise him. There's nothing he hates more. It's your only chance. Make the first move and you've doubled your chances of beating him."

She was as beautiful as the day he'd married her. Maybe even more so. Then she'd been innocent, certain of everything, what was right and what was wrong. Was it fair to call her *too* principled and predictable? To his soured soul, yes. She'd been a typical schoolteacher, twenty-one years old and sure that if she was a good girl, life would be kind to her.

Now she'd matured into a creature far more complex and beguiling. He'd noticed it in her voice, which had dropped in register and now whispered an allure that the young Madeleine couldn't have dreamed of. Her facial expressions, too, had deepened into a rich gravity, far more cautious and complicated than the earnest young woman she'd once been.

He credited himself for the changes. Nothing like the cut of despair to mellow easy optimism into something more profound and enduring.

He'd stepped off the late-morning stagecoach in Goldtown, the village closest to the Vino d'Oro cellars, still with plenty of time before he had to meet Caleb Stewart, and there she was, in a general store-cum-ice-cream-parlor and coffee shop, with the child.

He ground his teeth as the events of last night flooded back. He should have guessed that Durand's infatuation for his circus tart would turn his brains to cheese. He shook the thought away. Reminded himself they couldn't pin anything on him. At least it might have given Caleb Stewart the reminder he needed about what he was up against.

He was on his way to their rendezvous, but he could afford to take a leisurely coffee in the watery morning sun. To play tourist, if watching Madeleine was part of the show. He bought a coffee from a canteen near the one Madeleine was frequenting and sidled closer. He spotted immediately that they'd stepped up their security. Two muscle-men, both wearing irons, stood at a discreet distance, not obvious unless you were looking for them but with clear purpose. He pulled his hat down low over his face and turned to stare into the general store window, his back to the woman and child, apparently enthralled with the display. The best he could do was eavesdrop. No one would

be getting near his quarry today. Or
tomorrow.

Minette. That's what they'd called the
child yesterday. He'd only become aware
of her value when he'd been looking for
ways to pressure Madeleine and, through
her, Stewart. As he studied them now,
he kicked himself for the missed
opportunity.

From the way the child and Madeleine
interacted it was obvious they were
close. Madeleine had one hand draped
over the child's shoulder, the other
pointing at a counter where ice creams
were being served. She bent over, intent
on explaining the choices. As he
watched, she stood upright again in
response to a tap on her shoulder from
behind.

Another woman, roughly Madeleine's
height and age, greeted her with kisses

on both cheeks in the French way, before presenting another little girl who'd held back shyly.

"You must be Lisette!" Madeleine's voice was barely audible above the morning traffic. "And this will be Séraphine. Minette, you remember Seraphine?"

A side-long glance had shown Minette gazing into the glass-fronted cabinet where the store staff were assembling ice creams, but at the mention of Séraphine's name she turned with a beaming smile.

"Séraphine! I am so excited to see you!" She clapped her hands in delight. "It seems like ages since we played!" The girls grasped hands and danced around in a circle, ignoring Madeleine's half-hearted attempts to shush them. The two women sank into chairs at a round corner table and he heard snatches of his native language as he leaned forward, too far away to hear the full conversation.

It occurred to him that the children, too, were speaking his mother tongue. There was a momentary lull in the street traffic and the bright little voices drifted across. Just hearing them carried him back to an earlier, simpler life. The muscles in his shoulders, his thighs, relaxed and a weight of longing rolled over him like a goose-feather eiderdown, wrapping him in memories. For a split second he asked himself how he had got so far away from those unencumbered times. He smelled the fragrance of hot-from-the-oven baguette and roast duck breast, felt the creamy meltingness of newly cured goat's-milk cheese, the rich warmth of a good red wine. His mouth flooded in anticipation.

Then a child's tinkling, silver voice cut through his reverie. "This is my Mummy's magic man. His name is Pierrot."

He wasn't back in France. He was in the canvas lean-to he shared with Francine, the "consolation prize" he'd claimed for being betrayed and rejected by his wife. The familiar heat of rage roiled in his gut. All these years later, the memory of Madeleine's disloyalty, leading the gendarmes to where he'd hidden the knife, telling them all about it. When he got home, she smelt of vomit and the police were waiting for him.

His eyes flew open, his reverie broken by the crack of a teamster's whip. He was more on edge than he had realized.

The little girls had moved closer,

edging out of the ice-cream shop onto the sidewalk. Minette was holding up a brightly painted wooden toy, the sort with moving parts held together by twine or elastic which allowed them to be manipulated to do somersaults with ease. She was wiggling the toy's legs, showing her friend what Pierrot could do.

And it came to him in a rush. The last time he had seen that worn plaything it was hanging on a cord from Francine's mirror. It was the one thing she had retained from her ill-fated marriage to the grandson of the circus owner after he died of yellow fever or smallpox or some other pox within months of their arrival in America.

He had hated the thing. It had jeered at him, a reminder of the men preferred ahead of him. Francine's Jacques. Pierre Bourreau. And now Caleb Stewart —

they'd all taken precedence ahead of him.

He edged out of the coffee shop and ducked into the general store with its smells of oats and turpentine, feigning interest in the merchandise stacked to the roof, while he studied the child. And it came to him in a rush, as if scales had fallen from his eyes. His heart was bouncing in his chest; he could feel the rush of blood to his temples.

She is mine. I am standing here on a rough California street, feet away from my daughter.

He'd never bothered to give her anything more than fleeting notice, like a nuisance dog. Now he studied her with an intensity which gripped his entrails with such force he had to resist the urge to bend double from the cramping. He could see Francine's sparkling dancing eyes, her charming irrepressible brown curls, in the replica locks that feathered the child's face. He searched her countenance for something of himself, but there was nothing recognizable. Perhaps he was to be seen in her sturdy frame, her strong stance, her air — even at this young age, even after last night — of being willing to take on the world.

His fleeting sense of wonder was quickly swamped by rage. White-hot rage, that Madeleine was somehow able to enjoy his child, when he'd not even been aware of her existence. He'd always taken comfort in the knowledge that while she might have rejected him, she would never be free of him, never free to marry again, or to have the children he knew she desired. Not unless she was willing to do it outside the blessing of Church and the law, which he could never see the old Madeleine being willing to do.

And now he'd discovered her secret. She had her sister's child! How had she accomplished that? And did she know he was the girl's father?

He clenched his fists at his sides. He was overlooked again. Marginalized again. Thrown on the rubbish heap. Again. Through a red haze he saw the burly store manager edging between the narrow shelves towards him. "Can I help you with something, sir?" He had a ruddy, broad featured face, his mouth filled with crooked and missing teeth.

"Just looking thanks." He ground out the response and turned sharply away. The women, the girls, had finished their ice cream and coffee. They were leaving with their guards.

He turned back to the store man. "On second thoughts, do you stock ammunition for a Smith & Wesson Army Model 2?"

The store man shuffled back a step or two, as if caught by surprise. "No, sir, we don't. You'll need to go to the gunsmiths across the road for that."

He nodded. "I see. *Merci beaucoup*."

He loitered, hands hanging uselessly at his sides, flexing his itching fingers, willing his rage to subside. He told himself it was all of no consequence. He had much more important business to attend to. He was close to achieving his mission to make himself rich and powerful.

I don't care about the child. Really, I don't.

His infatuation with Francine was long over by the time she told him she was expecting a baby. She'd been an easy conquest. He'd only wanted her to assuage his rage over Madeleine anyway, to take out his revenge on her sister, and he'd done that. It wasn't hard to leave town with a whore. He'd heard vague rumors that Francine had died in a gambling hall fire, but he'd never bothered to check on them, or to ask himself about the child. He realized now that he'd conveniently assumed they were both dead.

L'enfant n'a pas d'importance.

But he knew in a rush there was one thing he would see fulfilled. Something that was nearly as important to him as power. One thing he'd ensure over his dead body. Caleb Stewart and *his wife* Madeleine were not going to be getting together, living in sin or any other way, and raising his daughter.

Over my dead body.

But preferably, over Stewart's.

Spot on at noon, as arranged, Gérard Le Blanc announced his arrival at Rancho Del Oro with the click of his leather boots on the tiled entryway.

Caleb had been up since dawn, checking on the new bulls and giving the deerhounds a run. He watched his visitor swagger out of a hired hack from his vantage point in the stables. He'd had little sleep overnight as he'd wracked his brains for a smart way to win and had failed to come up with one. But he knew Madeleine was right. No matter how much her earnest appeal had disturbed him because of what she wasn't saying, she knew what she was talking about. He wasn't going to pretend to be something he wasn't in a city suit. And he'd do everything he could to rob Le Blanc of the initiative.

One thing had chimed with him repeatedly in the post-midnight hours: ever since Miguel and Rory's deaths he'd been reactive, waiting for someone else — Arkwright, Halliburton, even Le Blanc — to make a move and then responding to it. That was finished. From now on he was going to meet Le Blanc head to head, just as he was, a robust native son of the valley, capable of being as wily as any of the coyotes out there on his domain. This was his land. His roots were planted here, and it was where he and his children were meant to live and die. No foreign agent of big-city money was going to take that away.

He crossed the yard with the dogs bounding at his heels and closed in on the Frenchman from behind. "Good morning, Le Blanc."

Le Blanc whirled at his voice and his eyes went straight to the dogs. His jaw tightened and his fists clenched.

Interesting.

As if responding to the tension, Jupiter narrowed his eyes and went half-down on his haunches, as if about to spring, emitting a low growl as he took up his position. Venus pressed up against Caleb's other side. He stroked her neck fondly. "The dogs are okay. They're bred to bring down a deer by the throat in one bound, but they're fine with people. As long as they behave."

He grinned, playing the fresh-faced country boy who only knows dogs and beef, and studied Le Blanc as the fear — because it was fear — in his eyes faded.

Very interesting. Almost as if he's seen the dogs before. As if he's scared they might remember him.

"You can open the door. It's not locked. We don't generally expect trouble around here. That's one reason we've found the double homicide so shocking." He stared into Le Blanc's face, deliberately giving the impression of trying to read his mind, and he saw once again a fleeting shadow of uncertainty flick across it.

He is definitely ill at ease. Strike one to me.

Le Blanc turned abruptly to the door and wrenched the handle with more force than needed. It turned easily and he hesitated, as if gathering himself, before stepping cautiously over the threshold. The dogs followed Caleb in, and he allowed them to flop on the Mexican rug in front of the warm fire. If Le Blanc didn't like having them around, they were definitely staying. He raised his voice and called, "Are you there, Santiago?"

Santiago poked his head around the door jamb from the study, as they'd pre-arranged. "Here, boss. Just working on the accounts."

"Bring them through here. I'm sure Monsieur Le Blanc won't mInd." He gestured to the room next door casually. "We're still ill at ease about using the office. Doña Valentina's woman hasn't managed to get all of Miguel's blood out of the carpet yet." He levelled Le Blanc with his stare. "That's where he was killed." He tipped his head toward the office. "In that room next door. Of course, you wouldn't know that, because you haven't been inside before, have you?"

Le Blanc gave him a frigid glare and

jerked his hand into the leather duffle bag he'd set down. He drew out some rolled-up maps. "That's right. I haven't been here before. Oh, except for when you threw me out — last week was it? I'm so glad you're starting to see reason." His voice was oily. He gave a fake smile. "I know you needed an incentive. So let's get down to business, shall we?"

Santiago settled himself on the sofa next to the dogs, the ledger propped up in front of him, and went about his work.

For the next thirty minutes Caleb and Le Blanc hung over the maps, which showed professionally prepared views of the southern side of the American River system, the lakes it fed into, and the boundaries of the Stewart property and the neighbors on Caleb's borders. The names of the property owners were marked, as well as some of the historic boundary lines for the old Mexican land grants. A lot of the first settlers and grant owners — Leidesdorff, the first African American millionaire; the sea-captain owner of Rancho Del Paso, Eliab Grimes; and Folsom, who dunned Leidesdorff's heirs out of a fortune — several of the old names were there. But there was a new one too, one he'd never seen in this context before: Mackinnon.

His index finger went to the spot. "What's this? Are we rewriting history? Dougal Mackinnon never had a grant. The land was always my father's. He just farmed it."

Le Blanc gave a nasty smile. "Of course, you would say that. You might be surprised to find we've found a full record of Dougal Mackinnon's papers — even the *diseños* maps — and Spanish witnesses to swear half the grant was always Mackinnon's. The half that runs all the way along the river, as it happens."

So this is why they forced Rory to sign those papers — and then killed him.

Caleb shook his head. "You'll have to do better than that, Le Blanc. It will never stand up in court. And it will take years. I'm sure your city-slicker sharks don't have that kind of patience."

Le Blanc's black eyes shone with amused contempt. "I concede, you're correct about that. But the Spanish land claim is only the first part of the strategy. Why not let me continue?"

They were standing shoulder to shoulder at the table, and as he spoke, Le Blanc leaned over Caleb, his bulky shoulders intimidating in their closeness. Caleb straightened, occupying the space between them, bumping into Le Blanc's lowered shoulder as he stood. The two men locked eyes and after two or three seconds Le Blanc moved away, giving Caleb breathing space. Caleb allowed the silence to hang for another ten, fifteen seconds, before indicating to the table. "Continue, please. This is better than a bedtime story."

"Yes, the Spanish claim is a long-haul gambit," said Le Blanc. "But so inconvenient, so time-consuming, so expensive to defend. All those hearings to attend. Lawyers to brief and pay. And judges can be so unreliable these days, don't you think? Why, I heard just the other day about the Santa Rita settlement. Virtually no evidence to support that claim but the judge approved it. And I gather he had a hefty debt against him 'forgiven' at the same time.

Such a coincidence, don't you think?"

Caleb had heard of the Santa Rita claim. It was notorious as an example of likely, but unproven, judicial corruption.

"And then, what about Buri Buri?" Another old Spanish claim where new owners successfully redrew boundaries, depriving an original Californio rancher next door of important water sources, which meant he had no watering holes for his cattle. "Poor old Francisco Sanchez at Rancho Pedro. His complaints fell on deaf ears. No water, no ranch."

"So what are you suggesting here?"

"I'm suggesting, Mr. Stewart, that my clients have already bought up access to the water sources for Rancho Del Oro." Le Blanc made a wide sweeping gesture along the map's river margins. "And we can already legitimately deprive you of water. We will be doing so this coming summer. I think we both know where that will leave you and your animals." His face was triumphant. "You're beaten, Stewart. Face it. You can't win against these men. They have the money, and they have the power."

Caleb fingered the edges of the map. "Oh, I don't doubt they've got money and power, but I'm not convinced they understand the land. And I'm very surprised you expect me to come to an agreement just standing around a map. I'm going to need time to ride out there and take a look."

Something in his voice — perhaps it had lifted in pitch, become more insistent in tone — excited Jupiter. The hound's ears pricked up and he suddenly stood, erect and twitching in anticipation.

Animals are amazing, the way they can read their owners.

Le Blanc's eyes flicked to the dogs, momentarily fearful. "On the ground? Now?"

"Why not? You weren't expecting me to surrender thousands of acres without careful consideration?"

"Well, no . . . I'm not exactly dressed for riding." Le Blanc gestured to his striped trousers and loose-fitting cutaway coat.

"Oh you'll be fine. You're not scared, are you, Mr. Le Blanc? Of being out on the range with two ole cowboys?"

"Two?" Le Blanc's powerful body swung toward Santiago, who lifted his deep brown eyes from his books with a studied vague expression.

"What? Oh, are you ready to go now? Good. The dogs could do with another run." Santiago slammed the ledger shut. "Come on Jupiter, Venus. Time for bunny rabbits."

15

Gérard Le Blanc did not have to go riding in his striped trousers after all. It could hardly have surprised him when Roland Durand turned up driving a fine new hack with padded, black-velvet seats and a jingling, silver-trimmed harness. But what did appear to have caught him off-guard was that the cold-eyed limp-wristed fellow who sat in the back.

The hack bore the signage of a local livery stable operating from the stage stop from Sacramento. Le Blanc grudgingly introduced the passenger to Caleb as a lawyer named Noah Jones. And it was plain that while the transport might have been comfortable, the countryside was not to his liking. He regarded the raw vine plantings from the hack window with a curled upper lip. "I wanted to make sure you understood the utmost urgency with which we regard this matter, Mr. Stewart. Not that I doubt Monsieur Le Blanc's abilities to get the job done. He's been very effective in pressing our case, I know." He hooked an expensive gold watch on a chain from inside his jacket pocket and clucked with impatience. "If you're insisting on some wild goose chase to see the land under discussion, then let's get moving. I'm due back in town soon." His disdain for anything rural was amplified by the wintery sniff that concluded the sentence. "If this is some prevaricating tactic on your part, then I warn you. We want those papers that Le Blanc's given you signed and delivered by Monday.

You've got two days." He rapped on the outside of the hack door with his hand. "Get a move on, Durand. I can't waste any more time out here."

Caleb sent another silent thank you heavenwards that he'd followed Madeleine's advice and chosen not to go it alone. Amazing, he thought, that he could have been naive enough to imagine this was a business negotiation, when it was actually a planned annihilation. But Noah Jones was probably as much a liability as an asset in a fight. The attorney's chilly autocratic manner didn't bother him.

Caleb patted the holster on his hip, a routine check he usually made when leaving the house, and saw Le Blanc's eyes flicker in awareness that both Caleb and Santiago were armed.

Le Blanc was by far the most

dangerous of the three men accompanying them, of that Caleb was sure. But between him, Santiago and the dogs, he was confident they could handle any situation. He communicated the thought to Santiago with one raised eyebrow and saw by the barely visible answering nod that Santiago understood.

It was great to be out with the wind in his face and the broad rippling expanse of the American River's South Fork glittering through the trees. He could almost forget the bizarre purpose of the trip: to see for himself just which part of his birthright Le Blanc thought he was going to give up.

With Le Blanc giving directions, Durand eventually drew the hack up on a grassy knoll overlooking the river. Caleb rode over to the hack while Santiago remained mounted on the crest of the hill, watching the dogs chase for gophers and rabbits, his eyes on a distant horizon.

Le Blanc and Jones had their nether regions firmly anchored in the hack's plush, padded seats, with Durand perched up front running the pair of horses. They had no intention of stepping into the dirt, or of soiling their shoes. To them, Del Oro was nothing more than real estate sprouting greenbacks.

Caleb leaned through the window as Jones unrolled a map across his knees. "Tell me, what are you proposing, Mr. Jones? It's always good to hear it from the horse's mouth."

Jones flushed, and a tic started up on his cheek.

Another good sign. He's

uncomfortable, maybe even a little riled up.

"Not that it's any of your business," Jones snapped, "but we're planning to control both sides of South Fork for a considerable stretch of river before it discharges into the lake. That way our clients will have access to water for agriculture, ranching and any other purpose they may propose — mining, industrial, dams. You've seen this already with the diversion from the North Fork a year or two back." He stabbed at the map with his index finger. "We can't let some ancient Spanish grant stand in the way of progress — and that's what you're effectively doing here, Stewart. Standing in the way of progress. It's not the California way."

Caleb knew that Natoma Mining and Water already had ambitious plans under way for a dam on the American River using convict labor provided by the State of California. Amazing what political patronage could achieve. He plucked a grass stalk and chewed on its end as he took his time in answering. "There is also such a thing as private rights and due process, Mr. Jones. As a lawyer I'd have thought you might've taken some notice of those concepts."

"Of course, of course. Unless there's a higher public good." Jones tipped his head toward Le Blanc. "And I think Mr. Le Blanc has already explained how we believe there is a higher public good involved here."

Caleb turned to face the river, his eyes distant. "And just where do you propose to build the dam — or divert water? How many other ranchers are going to be affected, apart from Del Oro?"

Inside the shadowed compartment, Le Blanc's eyes jittered towards Jones, as if unsure which of them should respond. When Jones stayed silent, he spoke. "I don't think there's any need to discuss our clients' plans any further. For a distance of five miles upstream from here — and from where we're standing to the lake entrance, of course — our purchasers already have control of the water rights. There's nothing you can do about it, Stewart, except retire gracefully and save your family more heartache. We'd hate to see any repeat of the violence that occurred at your home so recently."

A thinly veiled threat. The audacity of the man.

Caleb took a deep breath. "According to you and Sheriff Arkwright, I'm responsible for that bloodshed, Mr. Le

Blanc, so any repeat would be well out of your hands, would it not?"

An amused smirk played across Le Blanc's face. "Have your little game, Scotsman. You're not left with much else, are you?"

Caleb turned away again to the broad view. Santiago had been positioned with his back to them, but now he turned towards the hack and made the lariat signal — a man circling an overhead rope to bring down a bull — they used as shorthand for "something's up."

"Excuse me a moment, will you?" Caleb said. "Santiago's seen something."

He spurred Nero over to Santiago, who gave a suspicious tilt of his head back to the hack and gestured to the river below. "There's a surveyor working down there. Close to the bank. So it occurs to me, why is he still here? He's

493

got all his gear set up. He's working on something." He grinned. "Thing is, don't they want you to believe they already own the riverbank?"

"That's right." Caleb's eyes brightened. "Doesn't add up, does it?"

"Certainly doesn't. If they've already got ownership, then why is that fellow hard at work on his devil's-chain down there?"

"Good question," said Caleb. "And one we'll be asking him very soon."

Caleb and Santiago rode back to the hack together. "Nothing to worry you, gentlemen. A bull down there that seems to have damaged a leg. We'll take care of it later."

"Is there anything else you want to ask before you sign?" Le Blanc's voice carried a high note of anticipation. Noah Jones' cold eyes gleamed. Caleb wondered if they had cold drinks stored somewhere and were impatient to crack them open.

"Not so fast. I made it clear any paperwork has to be delivered to my solicitor, Thomas Halliburton, for his perusal. I'm not signing anything without his say-so. Isn't that normal, for a man to check with his lawyer?"

A black scowl darkened Le Blanc's handsome, square-jawed face. "Halliburton?"

The two men in the cab shared a silent exchange that said, louder than words could, "Him again."

Noah Jones flicked open his right hand and examined one of his nails. "Mr. Halliburton has been very successful in defending land claim cases." He fixed Caleb with a gimlet eye.

"But I hope you are not setting any

unrealistic hopes on his undoubted brilliance and cunning, Mr. Stewart. He won't be getting you off the hook this time, of that I am quite certain."

He straightened himself in his seat, sitting a couple of inches taller. "I'll make sure the papers are with Halliburton by five this afternoon. You have two days to get them signed. After that? Well, I can't be responsible for the consequences." He turned to Le Blanc.

"We're finished here." He reached out and flicked a small blind across the window on Caleb's side of the carriage, shutting him out of sight.

One way to conclude a negotiation, thought Caleb, as the vehicle gathered speed, leaving a small plume of dust in its wake. But not when you're anticipating a successful outcome. Noah Jones needed to learn better manners, and Caleb Stewart might just be the one to teach him.

As soon as the hack disappeared from sight, Caleb and Santiago rode on down to the riverbank. It was a glorious January afternoon, the best time of year because the air had a clarity, the temperature a moderation not found at other times. The air was clear, the sun pleasantly warm, bald eagles circling overhead and then dive bombing for salmon in the sleepy current. The unsuspecting fish, betrayed by the silver flash off their backs spotted from on high, were scooped up by the birds' talons in a swift braking movement that barely skimmed the surface.

Caleb had often been out here with his father. They'd shared memorable expeditions in this country, exploring the higher reaches where the river exploded through rocky canyons into white-water rapids that surged between banks which in springtime were a yellow-and-gold carpet of Californian poppies. Even after all these years his heart pinged with the loss. It was so much more than the land. To sign all that away, the memories of his father, his irreplaceable heritage, to these highway robbers, without a thought? These men had no idea what they were destroying.

The surveyor heard them approach and Caleb saw him stiffen. They quickly hauled in and dismounted. Santiago called in the dogs and they introduced themselves. "This is Del Oro land — our ranch goes right down to the river — so I'm interested to find you here," Caleb said. "It always pays to know what the neighbors are planning." He smiled to try to set the man at ease.

The surveyor uncoiled to his full height, stepped around the tripod he had been sighting through and extended his hand. He was tall and thin and had the self-contained air of a man who preferred his own company. He wore an old Union peaked cap. His hair was a lank, grizzled gray, his face lined by hardship, but Caleb guessed he was probably only ten years older than himself. Kind eyes gazed out of a weary face. Life had left heavy marks on him.

Another one who's still living with his ghosts.

"Elias Hardacre. Pleased to meet you." He shook hands and gestured to his equipment. "I'm just the patsy called in to perform a service. I haven't been brought into any confidences about what they might use the information for. The guy who commissioned me held his cards very close to his chest. A Frenchman, I guessed, though he didn't say. Just wanted the job done. Not someone I'd want to meet alone on a dark night, if you get my meaning. I'd trust him as far as I could throw a bull by its tail."

Caleb laughed. "If it's who I think it is, you've got that right." He sobered up. "They've told me they've already bought up the riverbank, effectively locking me in without access to water. That's nonsense as far as I know. Unless there's been some jiggery-pokery, I hold title. So I wonder what their game is. They can't sign up the neighbors without the survey, can they? Or if they do, its dependent on the survey being completed before they can register them with the General Land Office. Would I be right about that?"

Elias nodded and narrowed his eyes shrewdly. "They only called me in a week ago and they want both sides of the river surveyed for several miles on either side. It's going to take me a month at least to get it all done." He winked. "I'm happy to make sure it takes me at least that long. That guy put me in mind of something slippery."

"A truer word never spoken, my man." Caleb gazed out over the river, breathing in the serenity of the afternoon. How he wished he didn't have to spend his time on this strife. "Elias, I might need to ask your help with something."

The veteran's soft gray eyes were inquiring.

"Something that's potentially dangerous."

Elias shrugged and tipped his cap.

"I've seen my share of danger. Seems to me life's dangerous. You can't avoid it if you've got a pulse."

"We'll do our best to protect you, but they've already killed at least twice, and I don't really know how far they're prepared to go to get what they want."

Elias took his cap off and ran his hand through his woolly locks. "What do you want me to do? Shoot."

"I want to call a meeting of all the landowners in the area and tell them what these guys are up to. Warn them of what's coming. Some may already have been approached. They've probably all been made to feel they are the only one affected and are powerless to do anything. I want to get it all out in the open, let everyone know what's what, and try and get some sort of resistance going. Stir up public opinion, do whatever we need to do to put them out of business."

Elias gave a short, sharp laugh. "One thing you can count on is public officials don't like it when someone creates a stink. They like their lives to be quiet and uncomplicated."

Caleb grimaced. "Well, I'm about to try and ensure their lives are pure hell."

He and Santiago laughed, and Elias joined them, a deep rumbling sound like the rolling boom of a deep South Fork canyon. "Happy to do anything I can, if it's likely to help. I hate to see ordinary folks cheated. It's not what we fought for, a country where the rich have everything, including the justice. And I've lived long enough to discover that avoiding risk can be just as deadly as meeting it head-on. So, you tell me where and when, and I'll be there."

SCANDALOUS NEW LAND GRAB —
Exclusive Report

Local Ranchers Under Threat

Thousands of acres of productive north Sacramento ranch land may be flooded under a secret plan to force local farmers off to make way for big-city interests. Outraged ranchers will meet tonight to discuss the plan, which threatens the future of beef and wheat farmers along the American River and its tributaries.

Doña Valentina tapped the latest edition of the *Sacramento Daily Bee* and frowned. "Well, son, you've certainly met fire with fire. I hope you know what you're doing."

"I'm doing the only thing I know how, Mother. And that's taking the fight to them. According to them it's a done deal, and there's nothing I can do about it. Well, we'll see."

As soon as he and Santiago had finished chatting to Elias Hardacre, he'd gone straight to the newspaper office to place an ad calling a public meeting.

He knew from what he'd been told by Le Blanc and Elias that most of the properties in the area would be affected by their plans, and a quick check with a couple of nearby neighbors showed none of them had been approached by the Le Blanc parties. It seemed as if they'd targeted him as one of the biggest landowners in the area, perhaps assuming that once they had his land the other farmers would be forced to capitulate.

He patted his mother's hand. Her fingers were thin, the blue of her veins showing clearly through her icy skin. "I'm not at all certain of how it will turn out, but I'm not going down without a fight." He banged his coffee cup down. "There is something we have to discuss, though. While Santiago and I are at that public meeting tonight, I want you and Josefa to stay over with the Russells. John's coming to the meeting, but he's agreed that Nathan and Aristide will stay back to protect home and family. It makes sense for you to join Lady Pania and Graysie and the children. I'll have men on standby here to ensure the house isn't burnt down, but I'd have more peace of mind if you were at the vineyard. Is that all right with you?"

His mother nodded, her eyes narrowed and watchful. "You're right. After all that's happened, we have to be cautious. I understand."

He stroked Valentina's silver-streaked hair. "You're both too precious to put at risk," he said. "You know that. I'll leave the dogs inside as well, with instructions this time to guard the place." He grinned. "I don't know why they didn't last time."

His mother stood and began to clear the breakfast dishes. "You've well and truly set the cat among the pigeons with that story. The bureaucrats and their friends won't be pleased. Be very careful. Promise me?"

"I will, I will. Tom Halliburton is coming, and he's convinced the sheriff's department to send extra men, so hopefully it will go off without incident."

Doña Valentina crossed herself, unusual for her. He couldn't remember the last time he'd seen her do it. "Amen to that. Josefa is with child, so the next generation is on the way. We need to stick together more than ever before." Her lips were dry and warm on his forehead. "Now we've both got work to do." She picked up the tray of dishes and walked briskly to the kitchen.

16

Gérard Le Blanc had never cared about having children or being a father, and he still didn't. But he hated being bettered by a woman. Or women. And since he'd discovered his daughter was being cared for by his wife — okay, his ex-wife — he'd been in volcanic turmoil, and he couldn't figure out why. He'd known Francine had a baby. He'd vaguely heard she'd died. And he'd never done anything about it. He'd been indifferent to the whole episode.

But now he couldn't bear the thought that other people knew his daughter better than he did. Knew her and knew *about* her. And him? He didn't know a damn thing.

So what if that wasn't logical. He had a thunderstorm banging around in his head and it was all Madeleine's fault. If she'd come with him to California all those years ago, he'd never have needed to exact revenge on her little sister. He'd never have got her pregnant, though God knows he still couldn't work out how the child had ended up in the same house as Madeleine, even if she wasn't officially raising her.

And now he'd had his face rubbed in the pig trough again. He stared at the headlines in the Sacramento rag left behind by some other customer in the Goldtown coffee shop and brought his fist down on the solid wooden table with such force it rattled teaspoons on tables all around him.

The burly house manager scowled from behind the counter. "Are you all right there?"

"Yes, yes. Sorry. Just this stupid newspaper."

The headline screamed "Scandalous New Land Grab." He'd bet that within a couple of hours he'd have a messenger from Noah Jones standing over him demanding what he was going to do about it. This was a nightmare for men like Jones and his cronies, doing their smelly deals in dark corners but never wanting to stand up in the light. They always had someone else to do their dirty work.

And Caleb Stewart was giving them their worst public nightmare. He could already see how it would play out. The corrupt judge they had got buttoned down would take fright. The General Land Office commissioner would examine any papers they filed far more closely than before. Farmers for miles around would be suspicious when a Frenchman came calling offering them a "great deal." And with the public interest stirred up, it would be that much harder to get to Caleb Stewart and shut him up.

He cursed under his breath. He was beginning to regret he hadn't got rid of Stewart when he could. Weeks ago, when no one would have cared. Now the Scot was assuming the mantle of public crusader. He'd seized the initiative so completely Le Blanc was at a loss as to how to grab it back again. Where were Caleb Stewart's weak spots?

He slumped back in his chair and signaled for the manager to refill his cup. The grand prize he'd been slowly working his way towards ever since he'd arrived here was just within his grasp, and now it was in danger of being ripped away. He'd set his sights on getting enough funds to make himself a player and the contacts to give him the playground. He was this close, and he could see it all vanishing away like melting snow.

No money. No power. And no daughter. As if he had never existed. The wind blows over the field and you're gone. His daughter would never know who he was. He thought back to the ice-cream shop. What was it she'd said? "My daddy worked in the circus." Did she think Francine's fancy circus boy Jacques was her father? Had he been written out of the story completely? No, that wasn't quite it. "This is my Mummy's magic man." That was it. "This is my Mummy's magic man." He didn't even feature.

A hack drew up outside and the driver, dressed in a smart black suit and matching hat, bounded into the shop clutching a letter. "Are you Monsieur Le Blanc?"

For a fraction of a second he considered denying it, getting up and walking out. And then the rage surged back in. He'd see this through to the bitter end.

"Letter for you, sir."

It was the fancy hack company Noah Jones used, and Jones knew Le Blanc frequented this shop, so he knew before he even opened it who it was from. He withdrew the one page of thick scallop-edged paper from the envelope and read Jones' looping fancy calligraphy.

What in Jove's name are you playing at? I thought you had this under control. I've been summoned to the General Land Office on Monday. The Commissioner is furious. You'd better do something. And fast.

He ripped the envelope into tiny pieces, then spread the letter out before him. His rage had been replaced by an icy calculation. What was Caleb Stewart's weakest point? His mother? His sister? Sure, possibly. But even better, what about Madeleine?

Yes. Madeleine. He could still have the satisfaction of knowing she'd never see his daughter live to adulthood. She'd never get to play happy families with someone else. She might even regret she'd betrayed him. And if he played it right, he might just catch Caleb Stewart in the same trap.

Jones' fancy hack man was loitering outside, talking to someone on the street. He jumped up and hailed him as he turned to leave. "Just a minute driver. I have a reply message for Mr. Jones."

He turned the expensive notepaper

over, took a pen from his jacket and he wrote in his distinctive French script: "Everything under control. Expect good news shortly." And handed it to the driver. His headache had vanished. Suddenly the day felt a whole lot better.

"You think I ever cared for you, you silly bitch?"

His arm was hard across her windpipe. She couldn't breathe. Black spots danced before her eyes. She was slipping, sliding away.

He must have sensed her body collapsing from under him because he suddenly released his hold on her throat, moving one hand in a flash to her breast. He gripped the soft flesh so hard she cried out, but the sound was barely audible, muffled in a stream of saliva. Le Blanc's big hand covered her mouth, jamming her jaw closed.

She'd simply stepped out of the house and crossed the courtyard to call Aristide for morning tea. A mere few feet from the front door. So close, she hadn't thought to call for an escort. She hadn't really thought he'd be this reckless. And then Le Blanc had appeared out of nowhere and grabbed her. "You think you'll escape me? Never! You never will."

He hoiked from the back of his throat and spittle splashed down her skirt onto her shoes.

"That's what I think of you. I never loved you. You know that, don't you?" Pinch. "You always were just for show." Another pinch.

He whirled her around to face him and held her at arm's length, his hands encircling her throat. "Make one sound

and I'll finish you right here. So fast
you'll be dead, and I'll be away before
anyone hears."

He leered at her. "Clever, beautiful
Madeleine. Every man wanted her, but
she pined after Bertrand LeBeau, her
married school principal." His voice was
sneering. "Everyone knew the pathetic
story of beautiful lovelorn Madeleine and
the anemic Bertrand. You couldn't even
choose a red-blooded male."

He turned her violently towards him,
jamming her backbone hard up against
his body, his hot breath in her ear. "And
then you betrayed me in front of the
whole village. I didn't care about the
murder charges. Bourreau had it coming.
But I did care about my wife turning me
in. Refusing to come with me. What kind
of outrage is that? A wife goes where her
husband goes."

Madeleine convulsed forward and retched, unable to stand his closeness. "Philippe! Let me go! I'm going to faint . . ." The words came out in snatches between long painful gasps.

He leaned into her ear again. "You're the reason I went after Francine, you know. I had to get my revenge, so your little sister had to pay."

He let her go, and she pitched forward onto her knees. She tried to scuttle out of his reach, struggled to rise. He reached down and yanked her back to him. "Oh no. Not so fast. You're not escaping just yet." He ran his finger down the side of her face in a horrible caricature of a caress. "You thought I was so stupid that I wouldn't realize that child you have in there." He pointed in disgust across the yard to the house. "That I wouldn't realize that child is my daughter?" His voice was broken and rasping. "How stupid do you think I am?"

She gave a low keening cry, and the tears began to fall. "No, Philippe. Not Minette. You've destroyed Francine and me. Let that be your satisfaction. But not Minette!"

"You had my daughter and you didn't tell me? I suppose you thought that was funny. Poor dumb Philippe. Doesn't even know I've got his daughter. Well, don't go to sleep. That's all I can say. Because I'm coming after her. I didn't pull it off last time, but I didn't know she was my daughter then. Next time I won't fail."

Beneath his hands Madeleine was trembling. "Oh yes, Madeleine, you're getting a taste of what I've been living with for the last eight years. Always watching my back. Never able to sleep. And you won't be sleeping either. Because

I'm coming for Minette. And soon."

She heard the creak of the cellar door hinges as someone emerged into the yard. With an almighty burst she pulled free of Le Blanc's hold and screamed.

It seemed like mere seconds before Aristide was with her, his arms around her, comforting her. But of Le Blanc there was not a sign.

"Oh Aristide, how could I?" Madeleine huddled on a chair in front of a hot coffee in the Russell dining room and wept. "I bring bad luck on everyone near to me. Truly. I'm cursed." She put both hands in front of her face and sobbed into them. Her neck was hot and stinging from her husband's rough handling, and she guessed that within a few hours her throat and breast would be mottled black and blue.

"I should go away. I should just go away. If I'm not here, perhaps it will be safer for everyone." Her voice was rising to a keening pitch, and she realized she was close to becoming hysterical. The last few minutes with Le Blanc had been among the worst of her life.

"It was so frightening, Aristide. He was venomous. Poor Francine. To think she had to put up with him! And now he knows about Minette. I don't know how he guessed he's her father, but he has. What are we going to do?" All the grief she'd been holding in, banking up, was flowing now, and she could do nothing to stop it.

Her brother sat opposite her, a kindly, patient expression on his face, and let her cry herself out. He got her a glass of water and took her feverish face in his cooling hands. "If he knows about

Minette, I think we can assume you being here or not is no longer going to make any difference. The way he sees it, she's his daughter and no one else should have her."

She gulped down the water and set down the glass. "I suppose. If you look at it that way." She stood abruptly. "We have to warn Graysie and the rest as soon as we can. Sounds like we might be needing the extra security for longer than we thought."

Much later, after she'd warned Graysie and had a chance to lie down and cry some more, she was back with Aristide in the drawing room. "I've decided. I'm going to see Thomas Halliburton. I'm going to see if I can get Phillipe Coubert declared officially dead. I mean, he claims he's Gérard Le Blanc. And it's coming up seven years since anyone heard from Philippe Coubert. So isn't it reasonable to assume he's dead? And then Gérard Le Blanc can have no claim on Minette."

There was a sparkle in Aristide's eye. "Good luck with that one. If Coubert was furious before, I can imagine he'll be apoplectic if he hears you're trying to get him declared dead. Though it's perfectly logical. I'll be interested to see what Halliburton says."

Madeleine smiled, suddenly exhausted by her day. "I do hope everything goes well at that meeting tonight, but I'm far too tired to wait up to hear about it. I'm done." She stood to gather herself and leave. "I know I told Caleb he had to go on the offensive. I maybe wish he hadn't taken me quite so literally. I do hope they'll be all right." She kissed Aristide on the top of his head. "I'm going to rest now, *mon frère*. Thank you for rescuing me today. If you hadn't appeared when you did, I hate to think what would have happened."

17

The American Fork House was buzzing with angry, expectant energy. For the first time since he'd conceived of this idea of calling a public meeting to lay it all out in the open, Caleb was pierced by an arrow of doubt.

A couple of hundred farmers, miners, teamsters and nosy observers seeking scandal were crowded into the spacious bar room. A speaker's platform had been set up along one wall so Caleb and the others could be seen and heard above the masses, but the bar was doing a roaring trade. Surely they'd stop serving beer as soon as the meeting got going? He'd imagined something sober and sedate, not this excited, half-drunk crowd already spoiling for a fight.

He surveyed the room and the tingle in his fingers was calmed at the sight of a good number of local sheriffs dotted around the room. It seemed Halliburton's cautions had been taken seriously.

The attorney sat beside Caleb, a professorial figure puffing on his pipe, looking as if he'd given many a lecture to a crowd as unruly as this one. Halliburton narrowed his eyes and gave him a quick smile. "Ready for this, junior? You've got a croc by the tail, this time, that's for sure."

Caleb warmed inside at the approval in the older man's gravelly voice. This was madness, but it was also right. He saw Elias Hardacre slip into place, unobtrusive in the crowd, and a warm gloating sang in his veins. His ace, but he didn't want him revealed just yet.

He picked up the gavel Halliburton had supplied and brought it down on the table. "Let's get started, shall we?"

Halliburton was probably the only man to hear him above the roar of voices. He thumped louder to get attention, and the chatter subsided. Within minutes Halliburton had the mob eating out of his hand, speaking with the unquestioned authority of a principal conducting an assembly. For the next ten minutes he outlined the situation and the concerns. Ranches, orchards and vineyards in the rapidly growing agricultural area being deprived of water. Smaller mining operations hobbled by possible diversions. The devaluation of property that would occur as land deprived of water supply dropped steeply in value, probably ultimately becoming worthless.

The room settled into attentive silence as Halliburton outlined the likely outcome if another corporation was allowed access to the South Fork's waters. When he'd completed his spiel, he introduced Caleb, whose part was to explain what he knew of Buffer, Jones and Cottlesloe, and the shadowy men they represented.

His throat closed over as he saw Le Blanc and Noah Jones standing right in front of him, surrounded by a gang of toughs, grim faces indicating trouble was on the way. He cleared his throat and began talking. He told of the approaches he'd had from agents of a San Francisco law firm which advertised widely in the local press offering to buy out struggling farmers. How the "offer" had been accompanied by two unexplained deaths, attacks on his stock and a threat to resurrect a false land claim to muddy the waters and send him bankrupt with legal fees and court costs.

"Were the deaths of Rory and Miguel anything to do with what we're discussing tonight? We can't know until we find out who was responsible. But as you know, Rancho Del Oro is one of the oldest land-claim ranches left, dating back to the Mexican era. Many of the others around here — you know them, Rancho del Paso, Rio de los Americanos, San Juan — have already disappeared."

"So what?" yelled one of the men lurking near Le Blanc. "When they're broken up it means more land for everyone. That's how many of us came to be here."

Caleb raised his voice. "I'm not saying it's wrong, if it's done legally. But this attack on Rancho Del Oro is an attack on all of us. They're going after the biggest landowner first so they can pick off the smaller properties afterward. If they succeed in stealing my place, you guys will be easy prey."

The atmosphere in the bar escalated from solemn and attentive when Halliburton had been speaking to explosive. Caleb could feel it, the sense of that moment when the fuse is lit, the spark is traveling down the string, but it hasn't yet touched the payload.

Le Blanc raised his fist and yelled, "Mr. Chairman! I demand the right to speak. I represent the buyers. They're honest men, offering good deals. They deserve to be heard!"

The men around him began chanting "A fair deal! A fair deal!"

Halliburton rose. "Very well. Say your piece."

Le Blanc nudged Caleb aside and

planted his tree-trunk thighs astride the platform, commanding the space with the confidence of a born rabble-rouser. "This Californio!" He gestured dramatically toward Caleb and sneered. "What does he know? He's from the old times. He wants to preserve the old ways. You know how they are. The old privileged ranchos. Always spending, always in debt, always visiting with the family. Fiesta and siesta. Living like there's no tomorrow."

A few men cheered. Others got restless. Men shuffled their feet and muttered. Le Blanc was hitting the spot of their tenderest prejudices. Where they told themselves, "That won't happen to me."

"The Californio days are over. Listen to him and you'll do yourselves out of good profits! When this deal goes through, you'll still be able to farm. In fact, it will be better than before because the new owners will introduce irrigation schemes none of you could afford individually. You'll have *more* water, not less."

The crowd rippled and swayed. Then one of the hustlers in front interrupted. "Yeah and what about the 'unexplained deaths' he's referring to? This guy is a murderer! They had him in jail until a couple of days ago, until that fancy lawyer sitting beside him pulled strings to get him out. It's always the same, one rule for the rich, another for the poor. I see no reason to feel sorry for him!"

The crowd erupted.

Halliburton jumped to his feet and thumped the table with his gavel. "Silence! Order in the house!" He waited expectantly, his eagle eye surveying the room beneath heavy brows. Again, the headmaster magic worked. He signaled to Le Blanc. "You've another minute to finish off your case, sir. Starting now."

Le Blanc took a deep breath. "None of you have anything to fear from the activities of Buffer, Jones and Cottlesloe. Quite the opposite. They represent capital investment, which the region needs. They've got the contacts with the power players in San Francisco where the decisions are made. If you want to join the winning team, they're the ones to go with." He looked around the room, the picture of confidence. He'd dressed to impress in a soft leather jacket and moleskin trousers, looking like he was just one of the boys. "My name is Gérard Le Blanc, and I am the agent for Mr Noah Jones — who is here tonight — and the other investors. If you're interested in talking to us, join us at the bar afterward. Drinks are on us and you've got nothing to lose."

Men cheered and clapped and there was an awkward silence as Le Blanc stepped down. Caleb rose. "I just want to put it on the record, here tonight. I have not killed anyone. Miguel Chico and Rory Mackinnon were murdered in my home when I was nowhere near. The sheriffs know that. The killers have not been apprehended, but I had *nothing* to do with it."

The men in front of him shifted and rustled, whispered comments to one another. Doubt hung like a cloud in the room. He glanced across to Halliburton, who frowned, as if querying the wisdom of Caleb's denials. Too bad. He wasn't going to be labeled a killer if he could help it.

"We have one more speaker before

we close here tonight. I want you to hear what Mr. Elias Hardacre, the surveyor working for Buffer, Jones and Cottlesloe, has to say. Then I propose that those who oppose this purchase remain behind to discuss the benefits in starting a farmer's coalition against it, while the rest of you disperse."

"You're throwing us out?" yelled one of the rabble-rousers with Le Blanc.

"Not at all," replied Halliburton. "Wait till you hear from Mr. Hardacre, then decide."

As Elias made his way to the front, Caleb glanced out. Le Blanc's face was thunderous. Elias swayed on his heels as he took center stage, his long legs clad in the same hardy, dust-stained pants, one knee poking through, that he wore for his work. His pale face twitched under his kepi.

"I'm just a surveyor," he began. "Not one much for public speaking. But I met Mr. Stewart here on his property down by the banks of the South Fork yesterday, and I agreed to speak tonight to tell you what I've been doing. Been paid to do." His voice was like his body, thin and reedy, but it was compelling, nevertheless.

It's his authenticity. You can't miss the ring of truth in every word he speaks.

Elias reached into his scuffed duffle bag and pulled out a large roll of paper, which he unfurled with the ease of a man used to handling maps. "This shows you the picture better than words can, and you're welcome to come and take a closer look if you want to later." He proceeded to show the boundaries of the areas he was being asked to survey, how far in from the riverbanks the claims extended, the proposed areas likely to be favorable in terms of geology and gradient for damming or diversion. Men crowded forward to peer at the drawn lines, and Le Blanc and his crowd got pushed further back.

"What I'd ask," declared Elias, "is why they've gone to all the expense of preparing a survey like this — I've been working for weeks to get it all done, and they've got another guy working on Middle Fork — unless they were damn certain they already had a highway right through to approval.

"You know how the world works these days. The ordinary man doesn't stand a chance against big business." He doffed his navy-blue kepi. "I was with the Union at Gettysburg. Fought for the rights of the least of us. And I don't like what I see happening around us today. It's not what I fought for." He glanced at Caleb. "That's why I agreed to come and say my piece here tonight. They don't even need to come and talk to most of you about buying your land. If they drive off Caleb Stewart here, they've got it won. They've already got the water rights sewn up. They don't have to talk to you or tell you what they plan. They don't even have to buy your land. They just have to sit back and wait for you to go broke and walk off it."

The crowd fell into a shocked hush as he looked around the room. "I'm a simple man, and I ask myself. Why would you let varmints like that into your vineyard?"

The place erupted into cheers, whistles and laughter.

Elias rolled up his map, placed it back

in his duffle and walked off. He positioned himself in the corner and lit a pipe.

The night was winding up. Farmers had surged forward to shake Elias's hand, and talk some more. Someone asked him to unroll the map and show them the details again. He'd been the hit of the night, the plain-spoken man whose words struck straight to the heart.

Halliburton stood to one side, ready to answer questions as men filed up to register their names and signatures on a Farmer's Petition they'd already prepared, objecting to the proposed development on South Fork River.

A newspaperman pressed in alongside Caleb. "Mr. Stewart, are you hinting that someone's trying to frame you for the murders at your farm?"

"Oh, no. Nothing so dramatic. I suppose I'm disappointed the sheriffs don't seem to have made much progress in finding out who did it."

He outlined his version of what had happened, occasionally glancing at Halliburton for guidance. He was satisfied that without making any outrageous claims, he'd given the man a good story.

Finally Elias said his goodnights and Caleb turned to shake Halliburton's hand. "You were essential here tonight, Mr. Halliburton. I wouldn't have made it through without you. Let me walk you across to your hotel." Halliburton had taken a room at a smaller, quieter hostelry across the street, rather than return to Sacramento late.

They stepped out of the bar onto the Fork House veranda. A crowd had gathered in the road outside, circling a man in the dust. "What's going on?" Caleb asked a bystander, a grim-faced man in a miner's red shirt, a striped neckerchief at his throat.

"Guy got mugged. Someone looking for a quick buck, no doubt." He shook his head. "The old dog who just spoke inside there. The war vet. Bleeding shame."

Caleb gasped for breath, then stumbled on numb legs down the hotel steps into the street. Elias Hardacre lay sprawled on his back, mouth open, eyes staring, his denim check shirt ripped, bloody grazes showing on his ribs through the gaps in the fabric. "No!" He fell to his knees at Elias's side.

A restraining hand on his shoulder pulled him back. Roscoe Honeyman. The sheriff who'd dealt with Minette's disappearance the other night. "Afraid there's nothing more you can do for him, Mr. Stewart. His earthly toils are over."

Caleb rocked back on his heels, regarding the man who'd just demonstrated such quiet courage.

"What happened? Someone said . . ." A rocky lump was forming in his stomach. He couldn't swallow.

The lawman regarded him with solemn dark eyes. "A lot more to it than a random mugging for a few dollars, I'm afraid. If the knife wound in his side is anything to go by, someone wanted him dead." Roscoe turned to one of the other officers who'd appeared in the crowd. "Take him back to town and put him in the morgue. We'll see if we can get an autopsy done tomorrow."

He turned back to Caleb. He shifted his feet in the dust. "I was in there just now, heard what he said. You'd think someone didn't appreciate it, wouldn't you?"

"Exactly." Caleb spat into the dust. "I'd bet on it."

18

It was Sunday, the day of rest. But didn't they say there was no rest for the wicked? There was certainly going to be none for Caleb. He waited as long as he deemed decent before pushing Nero at full gallop along the backwoods track that would take him to the Russell's place, Sabbath or no.

Sir John had been at the meeting last night, had seen what had happened, but they'd had no chance to discuss the implications. Caleb was hoping in the clear light of day he'd see what he needed to do next with more clarity. And for that he valued Sir John's advice above anyone's.

There'd been a light frost overnight, and Nero felt just as ready for a good run as he was. The brown plains' grasses sparkled as tiny ice crystals melted into diamond droplets and slid down dry stalks. Mist rose from the damp ground, carrying with it the bracing tang of coyote mint.

By the time he pulled up in the Russell's yard the stuffy nose and foggy mind he'd awoken with were gone. As his feet hit Vino d'Oro's paving stones he realized with a jolt that he wasn't just here to see John. Seeing his magnate mentor would be great. But he was here for more than that. He couldn't let another day go by without talking to Madeleine. *Really* talking to her.

"Madeleine, there is no easy way to say this." Caleb was standing at her side, arm resting on the top board of a paling fence, gazing out over the bare brown ground that would soon be planted in more vines.

It reminded her of the day of the round-up. They'd stood shoulder to shoulder by another fence, and he'd protectively held Minette against him on the top bar as he apologized for unfairly accusing her, Madeleine, of not being honest. And all the while she had the gun Philippe had given her concealed in her bag. She shuddered at the thought.

We've always been out of step.

"Are you warm enough?" Caleb's eyes were narrowed in concern. "Do you need my jacket?"

"No, no, I'm fine. It's nothing. Just goosebumps." She glanced up and got caught in his penetrating gaze. The moment hung, like the air around them, motionless.

"Caleb, I shouldn't be here with you. For pity's sake, I'm a married woman. Married to a man who kills without conscience."

Caleb sighed. "You're a woman who has suffered because of things beyond her control. From what I've seen, you've only cared about those you love. First for your own mother. Then for Minette, for Aristide, even for me for goodness sake. You've taken risks when you could have taken the easy way out — planted that gun, gone off with him. You didn't do any of those things. Instead you were willing to give it all up to try and save others."

She turned but couldn't seem to make her feet start walking away from him. He reached out and held her hand, gently pulling her around to face him.

"I'm a murderer's wife. I'm chained to

him, and he'll kill you if he gets the chance. Don't you see that?"

"I know that. I'll just have to make sure not to give him the chance." He smiled, a playful light in his eyes, but she could see the drawn lines of fatigue at the corners of his mouth.

Impulsively she took his other hand. "Don't joke, Caleb. Please. He's deadly, and I have no idea how to stop him. The worst part of it is, I'm sorry I didn't kill him myself, when I had the chance the other night. He's finally brought me down to his level."

He led her to a big flat sawn-off stump of an old oak and gently pushed her to sit down. "I can't live without you, Madeleine." He gazed, unflinching, into her eyes. "And even if I could, I don't want to. After everything, after Elias's death last night, I want to get on with my life. I don't want to waste any more time."

She made a move to rise, but he stopped her. "No. Hear me out. Don't run away. We've both seen too much death, too much hardship." He sat down next to her, hands on his knees. "I don't know how this is going to end, Madeleine. I've no idea. But after last night, I'm wondering if Le Blanc isn't running out of rope. He just seems to be taking bigger and bigger risks. That nonsense with Minette and the ransom notes a couple of nights ago. Coming back here and attacking you. Then Hardacre's death last night." At the mention of the surveyor's name his jaw tightened. "It feels like he's getting desperate."

Madeleine gazed out over the field. "Perhaps he is."

"But I don't want you anywhere near him when — if — he finally goes crazy. Promise me, Madeleine."

She took the risk of looking him full in the face. "Caleb, it's sweet what you're saying." She stepped out of his reach. "But I can't see any way we can ever be together. With all my heart I don't want anything to happen to you. So promise me you'll stay out of his way."

Caleb stroked her bruised neck with one lightly caressing finger, his face somber. "I would take any risk in the world to be with you. I'm not making any promise except that. I promise to do everything I can to be with you, to make you my wife."

She caught his hand and stilled it. "Except kill him. At least promise me that. Tempting as it may seem, I'd rather be a murderer's wife for the rest of my days than lose you. Please. Promise me."

She didn't want Caleb killing him. God forbid. And she couldn't kill him herself, much as she'd love to. She didn't have the money to pay someone else to do it, and anyway that would make her as bad as he was. But she was running out of time. She felt it in her bones.

She couldn't wait another day, especially after that talk with Caleb.

She put her hand to her waist as she was swept by a half-sick, half-excited feeling. Caleb Stewart was a crazy romantic, and her heart rejoiced that he was.

So what if it was Sunday? Thomas Halliburton would be up and about. Someone had mentioned he lived in a suite at the St. George Hotel right next door to his legal chambers. He'd surely be in one place or the other. She'd throw herself on his benevolence and beg an audience.

Aristide protested it could all wait until Monday, but under Madeleine's desperate appeals he capitulated and drove her to town.

They stood on the street together, looking up at the monolithic form of the St. George Hotel, home of the Government Land Office and the destination for the first Pony Express run. Scent from nearby market stalls — a mingling of orange, early lilacs and freshly baked bread — lingered. People intent on their normal Sunday chores bustled by, when another man was dead. She shivered.

That poor Elias Hardacre. Next time it could be Minette, or Caleb.

The St George was four floors of cement with a heavy veranda. Lined with rows of double-hung windows, it provided not just permanent accommodation for many of the city's workers, but also commercial offices for architects, lawyers, doctors, real estate and insurance agents. On a Sunday afternoon it was probably quieter than usual, and they climbed the stairs to Halliburton's suite — having extracted his suite number from the maitre'd on the front desk.

She tapped hesitantly at the suite's door. "Mr. Halliburton? Anyone there?" A harried housekeeper answered, wiping her hands on her apron. "He's next door," she said with a reproving tilt of her head. "You just can't stop the man working. On the Sabbath too."

The heavy glass door of the office

bore his name in gold script: "Thomas Halliburton, Esq. Attorney-at-law and court solicitor."

In answer to her timid knock, Halliburton peered through the heavy plate glass, his eyes unfocused behind wire-rimmed spectacles. She heard a key turning from the inside, and he opened up to let her in. "It's Sunday, young lady. I'm not officially open, for goodness sake."

"I know, Mr Halliburton, I know. But I appeal to you. It's urgent. If anyone else gets killed . . ."

She turned to Aristide. "I'll be fine now. See you back here in thirty minutes?"

Halliburton took her arm and led her inside. "Now, now, my dear. Calm down. What's all this talk of people getting killed?" He settled her in a chair in the waiting area.

"Can I get you a glass of water?"

"Oh no, thank you. I'm fine really. I just need your help. Urgently. If I don't do something that man is going to abduct Minette. He might even try and kill Caleb."

His eyes pricked into extra vigilance. "Minette? That's Sir John's niece? And Caleb Stewart? How does he come into all this?"

For the next thirty minutes the story flooded out. Of her marriage to Philippe Coubert, the murder and fraud in France, his decision to run and her refusal to accompany him. Of finding him here eight years later under another name.

Halliburton raised his hand in a calming gesture. "I've heard this part of the story already, Mademoiselle. Sir John is taking steps to get your husband deported."

Madeleine frowned. "I know. But that's going to take too long. He'll probably die of old age first."

Halliburton nodded reluctantly. "It will be a difficult case." Then his eyes brightened. "But I must say, with first-hand sworn evidence from you, it will be a lot stronger."

"Anything. Anything at all," Madeleine said. "But I'm worried about the present, especially as far as Minette is concerned. Le Blanc is ruthless, and now he's discovered her, he's obsessed with getting his daughter back. Not because he wants her — he never showed any interest before — but because he doesn't like other people having her. I don't think we have much time."

She told Halliburton of Le Blanc's attack yesterday. Of the abduction and ransom notes a few days before. "I want him out of our lives. Any way I can. I'm desperate. So I was wondering . . ."

She ran through her idea of getting Phillipe Coubert declared legally dead. "He's been missing for eight years. He hasn't used the name for about six of them — I'm not sure when he became Gérard Le Blanc — but it was years ago." She frowned. "Is it wrong to get someone declared dead when you know they're still alive?"

Halliburton gave a wry smile. "It has the advantage of freeing you to marry again, that's one benefit I can see for you, Mademoiselle. Isn't that right?"

Madeleine blushed. "Oh goodness. It's been a long time since I thought of any such thing," she lied. She blundered on. "Or if getting him declared dead isn't possible, I want a divorce. I used to worry about the Church. I can't afford an annulment, so I'd be banned forever if I sought a divorce. But I've got so desperate now, I don't care. I just want him out of our lives so he can't cause any more trouble."

There was a scuffle behind her. Halliburton glanced up and his face drained of color. She swung in her chair — and gasped.

Gérard Le Blanc stood in the dim entryway, a gun pointed at Halliburton, a strange smile on his face. "Well, I didn't expect to see my darling wife so soon after our last encounter." He leered at her. "And to learn she's planning all sorts of tricks. Getting me declared dead. Planning divorce. Frankly, my dear, the second would be far easier. But neither of them is going to get rid of me. I'm going to be hanging around like a bad smell for the rest of your life." He spoke with biting resolve. "Until I decide to kill you."

Halliburton stepped up to block Le Blanc's path. "Mr. Le Blanc, I'm not open for business today. Please come back tomorrow. I can see you then."

"That's most generous of you, old chap, but I'm afraid my business is rather urgent. It can't wait." He waved the pistol threateningly and Halliburton retreated, backing out of the waiting area and down a dim hallway, his hands held up in surrender.

Within a few feet he backed into a closed door and stopped. Le Blanc sprang forward and smashed down on his head with the butt of his gun. Halliburton fell like a big tree. As he crashed to the floor Madeleine's knees buckled under her and she too collapsed.

Gérard sprang across the small gap

that separated them, grabbed her and put the gun to her head. His hand over her mouth, he dragged her toward Halliburton. When he reached him, he kicked his body hard. The attorney groaned.

"Out cold. Good. I'll kill him before we leave. But meantime—"

Madeleine bit down on his fingers, but he just pressed harder, cupping his hand across her mouth and pinching her nostrils so she couldn't breathe. "You and I are going to have a little bit of fun before I finish you both off," he growled into her ear.

Her blood ran cold. "No! No!" Her cries were muffled by his hand, but she fought hard. "Never!"

The door to the street banged, and Gérard brought the gun down from her head to aim at the doorway. "Well, well," he said. "Look who's here. Just the man I wanted to see."

Madeleine's eyes met Caleb's across the dark room, and their conversation of yesterday felt like it had taken place a million years ago.

Le Blanc's barking laugh sent a gust of hot air down her neck. "Come and join the party."

Caleb's hand went to his hip, but he was too slow. It was hard to make out shapes in the unlit waiting room, and the precious seconds it took his eyes to adjust from the bright street gave Le Blanc the advantage.

He could make out Le Blanc, holding Madeleine in a stranglehold across her bruised throat with one arm, a Smith & Wesson revolver to her head. The office was dark — no lights had been turned on. It looked as though Halliburton had not had a chance to open up. Behind the Frenchman lay a bulky form clad in an office suit.

Noah Jones's words from a day or two ago came back to him: "I hope you are not setting any unrealistic hopes on Halliburton's brilliance and cunning, Mr. Stewart. He won't be getting you off the hook this time, of that I am quite certain."

His mind was racing, searching for the best option. Charge Le Blanc and he'd just shoot Madeleine and then him. What else was there? On a Sunday it was unlikely anyone else would be coming in. Best to let Le Blanc roll on with his little game and await an opportunity. Because he sensed the man was enjoying himself.

"Mr. Le Blanc." He steeled himself. "You're not a bad loser, by any chance?

First Elias Hardacre, and now Thomas Halliburton. They couldn't put your neck in a noose in France, more's the pity, but I'm sure our US marshals won't show the same reluctance."

Le Blanc's face flushed, his shaky fingers tightened around the gun, then cold calculation kicked in. He narrowed his eyes. "Nice try, Stewart, but you're not knocking me off my perch quite that easily."

Madeleine had stopped struggling the moment Caleb had arrived. He could only imagine she didn't want to provoke Le Blanc into shooting them both on the spot.

"You see, I've got some unfinished business with my wife."

"Your *former* wife, you mean."

Le Blanc glared. "I never divorced her. I might just enforce my right in this regard, if you get my drift. I'd enjoy a little marital pleasure before I finally kill the traitorous bitch." He spat on the floor by Halliburton's still form. "And you get to watch. The carnal embrace of her sister wasn't nearly as much fun as this will be, I promise."

19

Le Blanc pulled Madeleine closer. Strange, he thought, how after all the other women, all the rage and hatred, he still warmed inside when he held her.

He jerked his head towards the man who stood frozen in the doorway, his hand hovering uncertainly at his side. "Hands up, Stewart. Above your head. Keep them where I can see them."

He dragged Madeleine with him across to the entry. "Undo his gun belt," he growled. Madeleine flinched away from him, her eyes dark green with fear. Le Blanc pushed the gun harder into her temple. "Undo the belt."

Her eyes flicked to Caleb's face, but

his eyes were fixed on the ceiling. With trembling hands she loosened the belt, which fell with a heavy clunk to the floor.

Le Blanc kicked it away. "Now the boots. Off with them. Just in case you've got something tricky like a knife in there."

Caleb hauled off his boots, then moved his eyes to Madeleine's face as if trying to read her mind, as if they shared some secret language.

The volcano Le Blanc carried inside overflowed. "Eyes to the ceiling! I don't like other men ogling my wife. You'd understand, if you had one."

He dragged Madeleine with him to the door and clicked the inside lock with his free hand. Now what? He hadn't expected to have two extras when he came after Halliburton. Not that he exactly objected.

"You'll never get away with this, Le Blanc. You know that, don't you? You're finished." Caleb Stewart's jaw was set in a determined line. "For starters, a sheriff is going to be banging on that door anytime soon. His name's Roscoe Honeyman. I've just been with him, making arrangements for Elias Hardacre's funeral. They've found the knife you used to kill him. And it seems your sidekick Durand isn't averse to singing if it means getting himself off the hook. He's ready to testify it's your knife and you killed him."

Caleb's eyes rested on Madeleine, but she was unaware of it because Le Blanc had her head tilted towards the ceiling. "It's coming to an end, Madeleine. Just hold on a little while longer." The damn Scotsman was trying to reassure his wife.

Red hotness surged in Le Blanc, another scorching wave that hit him in the back of the throat. The rancho was lying. The bastard had to be. Roland would never rat on him. Never!

A wormy doubt wriggled out from the cauldron inside. *Except if he thought he might be headed for the scaffold himself.* That could turn any man into a snitcher.

He heard a loud boom and glass shattered all over the floor. Someone was shooting at the damn door! A second shot blew apart the lock and the unsecured door swung open. The entryway was empty, but a voice called from along the wall. "Madeleine? Are you in there? Are you all right?"

He felt Madeleine stiffen in his arms. He hissed into her ear, "Tell him you're fine. Tell him it's all okay. He can come in." He slowly dropped his hand away from her mouth.

She took a long slow breath. Then she screamed. "Run Aristide! He's got a gun! Run!"

She ducked her head low to avoid the blow from his swiping hand, and then rose and spat in his face. "You're despicable. Kill me. I'd rather die than draw the same air as you."

She was raging now, hot with fury, and a responding, scalding lust surged through him. She was his, all right. "I've got her, Laurent. Come out now with your hands up. One false move and she's dead."

After a long hesitation, Madeleine's brother stepped into the doorway, his hands raised, a gun hanging from the index finger of his right hand.

Le Blanc's pulse slowed as he watched Aristide Laurent's eyes widen to orbs.

Madeleine was pulled up satisfyingly hard against his chest. His Smith & Wesson — the one he'd bought that day she'd escaped him in the alleyway — caressed her jugular. His beard was leaving a red rash on her delicate cheek. Just like a lover's burn. His heart sped up again as he inhaled her jasmine fragrance. "Drop the gun and kick it toward the wall," he snarled. "Then get over there with him." Aristide complied without protest.

Le Blanc edged past them, watching for any move, gun ready. With Madeleine as a shield, he eased himself out of Halliburton's office into the deserted hallway. Now what? It was Sunday, sure, but someone — a visitor, a guest or a cleaner — could be along at any time. He had to disappear.

He banged on the door of Room 310, and after a few seconds' wait, it was opened by a harassed-looking housekeeper. His arm still tight around Madeleine, he pushed past her before she had a chance to object and slammed the door behind him.

It was only then that he remembered he'd forgotten to finish the job on Halliburton. He hissed through his teeth. *This devilish woman!* He always ended up in trouble when he forgot himself with her. He back-handed her across the face and she crashed down, head first, out cold.

"You!" he yelled at the cowering housekeeper. "Bring me some rope and I might let you live."

Barely a minute after Le Blanc dragged Madeleine out, Aristide and Caleb had retrieved their guns. Caleb hauled on his boots and they were kneeling one either side of Thomas Halliburton's slumped form. "Looks like he'll have a very bad headache but, if he's lucky, nothing worse than that," said Caleb. "Why don't you go and get him help — find a doctor and a sheriff — while I go after Madeleine."

Aristide covered his face in his hands for a moment, then pulled them away and stared straight at Caleb. "You're not going to let him take her, are you?"

"No, I am not." They turned and started for the door at a run.

Aristide called back over his shoulder as he sprinted downstairs, "I'll come and find you as soon as Halliburton's safe."

Caleb stared wildly down the hotel corridor, first left, then right. Where would he go? Feet rooted to the spot, he calmed himself.

Think, Caleb. Think.

The wall outside Room 310 reverberated. Through the wall he heard a loud thump, like something heavy falling. Then a woman's sharp cry, and a man's voice, raised and angry. He couldn't make out the words. Something was going on in there. He stood staring at the door, calculating the best approach. And then he heard the squeak of trolley wheels, and a maid appeared pushing a hospitality cart loaded with food trays. Room service.

A smell of beef soup and hot rolls wafted along with her. She gave him a curious look as she passed him and pulled up outside Room 310. She raised her hand to knock.

Caleb leapt forward. "Excuse me, miss, but is that delivery for Mr. Halliburton?"

"How did you know?" She raised her eyebrows in surprise. "Mr Halliburton is a regular. He always orders brunch for this time. He tips very generously, too."

"I, ah, I have a message for him, but when I knocked just now, no one answered. Maybe his maid was busy doing something. Let's see if you have better luck."

"Sure. If he's not there, the housekeeper usually takes care of it."

Caleb tipped his hat at her and flattened himself against the wall, out of view. "After you." She reached up and knocked confidently. "Lunch for Mr—" She gasped as the door swung open. "Where's Mr. Halliburton?"

The door opened wide enough for Caleb to see a man's hand, gripping a gun. He waved it in the maid's face. "Shut up and get inside."

Le Blanc turned back into the room, pushing the door closed behind him, but he was too slow. Caleb shoulder-charged in, pushing aside the maid and tipping her trolley over as momentum carried him in. The sound of crashing china and the maid's howl as hot soup splashed announced his arrival. Le Blanc stumbled backwards and fell over a woman's body sprawled on the carpet but was instantly back up on his feet again. In his right hand he held the revolver pointed straight at Caleb. In his left he clutched a handful of hair. Madeleine's hair. With a deft sidestep he took cover behind her limp form, her rag-doll legs dangling.

"Put the gun down, Stewart. You won't be needing it."

Caleb placed his gun on the carpet and raised his hands above his head. His head swam under a wave of dizziness that threatened to topple him. Close to his ear the maid whimpered in fear.

"Shut up!" Le Blanc snarled. "Sit down over there and keep quiet." She collapsed into an armchair in the corner and buried her head in her hands.

Still holding Madeleine as a shield between him and Caleb, Le Blanc reached down, scooped the gun off the carpet and thrust it down the front of his shirt. "As I said, you won't be needing it."

Caleb swallowed down hard on the knot of doubt that was choking his throat.

Funny how an emotion can feel so tangible.

Madeleine was pulled up against Le Blanc's chest. She'd come back to consciousness in the last few minutes, and was gazing at Caleb with a strange, dazed expression. It wasn't fear, it was . . . What? Admiration? He raised an eyebrow infinitesimally and she smiled. The briefest of smiles. She squeezed her eyes shut and lifted her jaw a notch. She was telling him she wasn't giving up. And that she was glad he was here.

He stared out past their two dark silhouettes, outlined against the cerulean sky visible through the open window. A lazy-winged pigeon flapped past. They were four floors up, with no fire escape and a straight fall to the ground broken only by the concrete pediment that jutted at second-floor level over the street. Built no doubt, for that very purpose — to protect pedestrians from being hit by falling objects.

Le Blanc was coming to the end of his rope, Caleb reminded himself. For the last few days his behavior had been getting wilder by the day. He was chaotic rather than calculating.

Okay, he had the gun and the upper hand right now, but all Caleb needed to do was keep him distracted until Roscoe and Aristide got here. He was really the one who held the power.

I just need to keep him talking.

"You're not going to get away with killing Halliburton, Le Blanc."

Le Blanc's head jerked involuntarily. "Kill him? I didn't kill him. What are you talking about?"

Caleb continued as if he hadn't spoken. "The others, maybe you will. Rory. Miguel. As far as the system is concerned, perhaps they don't count. But not Halliburton."

Le Blanc's face darkened. "I tell you I didn't kill him."

Caleb shook his head. "A respected

senior lawyer? A certainty for appointment as a judge any day now? Even your San Francisco buddies won't be able to get you out of this one."

"I tell you I didn't kill the guy!"

Caleb smiled. "If you say so."

"What? Did you finish him off so I'd get the blame? Is that it?"

Caleb shook his head, laughing now. The guy really was going loco. "So what's next? Even if you get out of here alive, where will you go? You'll have to change your identity again, start all over again. Where? South America?"

"Not impossible." Le Blanc was cooling down, getting himself back under control.

Caleb straightened up to his full height, brought his hands up to chest level and began cracking his knuckle joints, pressing first one bent set of fingers and then the other into the cup of his palm. "Nah. Not going to happen. Any minute now Roscoe Honeyman is going to come pounding through that door. Any minute. So why not let Madeleine go? Shoot me if you must, but let her go."

Le Blanc surveyed him coldly. "My, my, quite the hero, aren't you?" He stroked Madeleine's cheekbone with the gun barrel. She flinched. "You wouldn't be so keen to die for her if you knew what she's really like." Le Blanc's knowing smirk was pure venom.

Madeleine was staring straight ahead, her lips in a tight line, her face ashen.

"Back in France. Bet she hasn't told you about how she was my accomplice in murder."

Caleb's heart did an unhappy lurch inside his ribs. "I don't have a clue what you're talking about Le Blanc. But you're obviously dying to tell me, so go right ahead."

"Non!" Madeleine struggled to free herself. "Don't do this, Philippe. It's not necessary."

"Oh, I think it's very necessary. She didn't tell you, did she, Stewart, that she lured a man to his death, and then turned around and betrayed me to the gendarmes." Le Blanc's cruel eyes gleamed in triumph. *"C'est vrai.* As true as I stand here. Beware the black widow, Californio. She brings nothing but trouble."

"Don't listen to him! He's got it all wrong!" Madeleine's face was deathly pale.

"It's ancient history, Le Blanc," said Caleb levelly. "And if she's that bad, why hold onto her?"

Le Blanc grinned. "*Touché!* But you'll live to regret you ever knew her. She's like poison in your blood." He shoved Madeleine sideways, pushing her roughly into a wooden chair positioned under the open window. "Mind you, she does have her uses," he sneered. "How about this, for one? You arrange with Honeyman to let me get out of here, and I won't kill her." He made it sound almost magnanimous. He peered into Madeleine's stony face. "How's that for a deal? He can have me, or he can have you, but he can't have us both."

20

Don't fall for it, Caleb. He's never letting me go. Don't do it!

Madeleine moved her heels up and down, working her ankles, releasing the cramping in her legs. Even if she had a chance to run, she didn't think her legs would carry her.

She suppressed a shudder at the revulsion she felt every time Philippe Coubert touched her. She clenched her jaw tight so as not to groan, to protest, to cry. The agony of being held like this was close to intolerable.

The only thing that made it endurable was Caleb Stewart's nobility. Such an old-fashioned word. Practically medieval, straight out of the stories she'd told her pupils back in France about knights of yore. But that was what he was.

"Shoot me if you must but let her go."

What was it she had said to him only hours ago?

"Promise me you'll stay out of his way."

She allowed herself a quick glance in his direction. If Philippe caught her looking, even for a second, it would set him off. But she couldn't resist drinking in once more, maybe for the last time in her life, the clean-cut profile, the virtuous mouth, the green-flecked hazel eyes of the one man she'd give anything in the world to walk beside.

"I can't live without you, Madeleine."

Philippe's sick desire for revenge was going to get them all killed.

Caleb Stewart's face took on a thoughtful cast, as if he might be seriously considering his offer. He must really want Madeleine, if he was ready to give up on the satisfaction of taking him in, seeing him hang. Le Blanc's guts twisted inside, and he grunted as the hopelessness of his situation pierced him. All the more reason not to let it play out the way Stewart wanted. He'd rather die than see Madeleine left to some happy ever after with that man. A picture of his daughter flashed across his mind. Her alive face, framed with Francine's luxuriant curls, head thrown back, laughing, clutching Madeleine's hand. Stewart stood laughing with them. Those two? With his daughter?

Over my dead body.

If he was going, Madeleine was coming too. Alive or dead, she was coming.

He snapped back to reality. "So. What's it to be?"

"What's it to be? Well, forgive me, Le Blanc. You might have a gun in your hand right now, but you're hardly in a position to be making demands. And I've got one worrying little worm, gnawing away somewhere at the base of my brain. And that is, can you be trusted?" He opened his hands wide, as if it was a question worthy of serious consideration. "Well, Le Blanc? Can you? And I think of the cheating, double-crossing, lying scoundrel you are, the trail of destruction you've left wherever you've gone, and I have my answer. No, you can't."

There was a heavy thumping on the door, and Roscoe Honeyman's voice rang out in the small room. "Come out with your hands up, Le Blanc. It's over!"

Le Blanc's reaction to Roscoe's arrival

was instantaneous. He grabbed both sides of the chair Madeleine was seated on and lifted it like matchwood onto the window sill. The front legs sat on the sill, the back legs hovered in space. It rocked precariously. Madeleine screamed. She was facing backwards over a four-story drop, and the only thing stopping her fall was Le Blanc's hefty restraining arm.

"I told you, you can't have us both," he snarled. "But you didn't believe me."

With his gun still clutched in his right hand, he leapt onto the shelf that extended a short distance out from the window and crouched there like a monkey on the balls of his feet, holding the chair against him, his breath rasping in his throat at the exertion.

Madeleine froze, her eyes blank with terror, as he swayed back and forth, then in an act of supreme will, centered his weight. The chair steadied.

Caleb's hand had been reaching for the knife inside his boot at the first bang on the door. He whipped it free with his right hand and lunged.

His left hand latched onto Madeleine's right calf, his weight acting as a counterbalance helping hold the chair — and Le Blanc with it — in place. But then Madeleine began to slide forward off the seat. As he dropped the knife and grabbed for Madeleine's left ankle with his right hand, the equilibrium tilted. Madeleine slipped down the plane of the seat and crumpled onto the floor.

For a few seconds time stopped. The chair, and Le Blanc with it, hung poised on the edge. Caleb sprang forward again, thinking to repeat his action and grab Le Blanc's shirt, the arm of the chair, anything to stop it overbalancing into the clear blue abyss.

Le Blanc's eyes flew wide and the whites seemed to expand until his irises disappeared in a blizzard of panic. He opened his mouth to speak. The words were lost in a rush of wind as the chair tilted back, catapulting Le Blanc with it off the sill into space. The last glimpse Caleb caught of him he was squeezing his eyes shut and wrenching the gun up to his ear.

The noise of the blast that ricocheted around the room was hardly dimmed by the answering roar as someone shot out the lock, and Honeyman, Aristide and the rest of the crew trailed in.

Roscoe was congratulating the housekeeper because she'd slipped out via back stairs used only by the servants and alerted him to exactly where Le

Blanc was hiding; the maid was vomiting in the bathroom.

Caleb was bent over Madeleine, drawing her to her feet, when Aristide came to them. A moment's hesitation, and he handed her over to her brother, suddenly shy. He and Madeleine still had so much to say to one another. And after Le Blanc's recent disclosures, he didn't even really know who this woman was.

Aristide enfolded his sister in his arms and held her, stroking her hair in long soothing caresses, whispering the nonsense French a father might use to comfort a child.

And for now, there was nothing more left to say or do.

Elias Hardacre's funeral was one of the biggest Sacramento City had ever seen. Grace Protestant Episcopal Church on

Eighth Street could hold three hundred people within its brick walls, but as the choir tuned up with the opening hymn, and Caleb and the other pall bearers carried Elias down the nave to the chancel, a crowd that couldn't find pew space spilled out of the doors and onto the street.

Elias had become the hero of agriculturalists and growers as the tragedy was given wide coverage in the local papers, with Sacramento's lively Fourth Estate all searching for different angles. It was inevitable that so many people turned out to pay him tribute. The irony of it was, Caleb mused, that if he hadn't died in the furtherance of a good cause, the reclusive Hardacre would probably have been farewelled by only a handful of people who knew him. Caleb sat in the front pew, feeling strangely hollow as the rector's eulogy reminded all of the fleeting nature of life.

It was all too recent and raw, that last searing conversation before Roscoe interrupted them. Le Blanc's unpleasant insinuations, Madeleine's unwillingness to deny them. There had been no time to talk, even if she'd been willing to do so.

The one bright spot was that Thomas Halliburton sat beside him. The solicitor had suffered a nasty head wound and severe headaches after Le Blanc's attack, but he was recovering well.

The service ended and they headed out to the grave site for the committal. On a nearby plot an early narcissus was bobbing a creamy head of flowers, an early spring breeze carrying its fresh jonquil fragrance across to the dark hole yawning to receive Hardacre's remains.

Caleb's whole body felt frozen, and he

could only stare into the grave numbly, incapable of thinking or feeling anything except overwhelming loss.

The handful of cloggy cold earth slipped through his fingers and thudded on the lowered casket. He felt a weird sense of unreality as a succession of well-wishers filed past him, offering commiserations. "It was a dreadful thing, Mr. Hardacre being attacked like that."

"Yes, indeed it was."

There was an awkwardness about these conversations. Caleb wished with all his heart that he could point out that the men who were really responsible, men like Noah Jones, who'd had the gall to take a seat on one of the front pews, would never face the consequences of their corruption. Instead he murmured that Sheriff Honeyman had done a fine job and the perpetrator deserved what he got.

If the condolences were painful, the congratulations were even more so. A slow-moving file of ranchers, miners and pioneer agriculturalists, the men who were turning the Sacramento Valley into a food bowl of wheat and fruit and grapes, waited to offer their thanks to him for stopping the land scheme that would have wrecked their businesses.

Caleb was quick to remind them that another good man, Elias Hardacre, had been the one to do that and had paid for it with his life. He'd done nothing, by comparison.

In truth he was mighty relieved that his Del Oro interests — the ranch and the winery — could proceed as he'd always dreamed. His family's future was now secure. There was no specter of Consuela launching a false land claim anymore. The Land Office judge would not stand for it. If he died tomorrow, he could go knowing that his mother, the twins, and Josefa were in a good position to continue on the legacy his father had begun. He'd succeeded in what he'd spent the last fifteen years fighting for. He had security of ownership. John Russell was particularly delighted, and already talking of expanding their joint vine plantings.

So why did he feel like he did? That was the thing he asked himself, the thing he talked about with no one, but which gnawed at his guts in the middle of the night, the thing that bothered him the most.

How can a so-called triumph feel so much like defeat?

21

Madeleine wandered across the courtyard and into the cool dim cellar. Just a few days ago she'd been attacked by Philippe outside this very doorway. That was never going to happen to her again. For a moment she was hit by one of the attacks of light-headedness she'd been experiencing ever since his death. She clutched at the door jamb to steady herself and waited for it to pass. And yet for all the relief she felt, her heart had yet to sing. The best she could muster was a lukewarm flatness.

Minette was having an afternoon sleep — very unusual for her — and Graysie was happy to hang close by in case she awakened. Madeleine had been desperate to escape the house and was hoping Aristide would be in his office, twirling a pencil between his supple fingers, waiting for her to turn up for a quiet chat, as if he didn't have a business to run. She'd never felt the need of his most precious quality, his loving optimism, as much as she did right now.

They'd buried Philippe — she and Aristide were the only mourners — in a brief and completely private Catholic rite at St. Rose's, stripped of anything but the barest formalities. The priest knew he'd gone to his eternity unrepentant but was kind enough to accept he'd not committed suicide. Cause of death was recorded as "misadventure," which meant he could be buried within the church walls marked with a small brass plaque which simply recorded his name and birth and death dates:

Philippe Coubert

February 14, 1832 – January 23, 1870

Nine out of ten of the townspeople who saw it would not recognize the name and would certainly not link him to the notorious Gérard Le Blanc.

Rory Mackinnon's flower-bedecked plot was only a couple of rows away, and Madeleine hoped Coubert's presence wasn't going to stir up unhappy ghosts.

Now, the day after the funeral, she was dry-eyed and burnt out, drained of the ability to feel anything. Walking and breathing was about the limit of her capacity. She wondered how long this feeling was going to last. After seven years, she'd got rid of the label "the murderer's wife," and it hardly made any difference.

How much of this was tied up with her guilt over Caleb, her conviction without even testing it that he would never be able to understand about Bourreau's death? He was too good a man.

I can't forgive myself, so why would he?

She couldn't talk about it to anyone. It had always been her secret, and it was staying that way. Philippe had gone, but he'd covered her in slime before he slipped away. A shiver ran up her spine. That horrible business back in Bordeaux. She had been complicit. And she had betrayed her husband. Those were the facts, and no one could love her when they knew that. Talking about it wouldn't change anything.

And what about Francine? Now that the immediate danger to herself had passed, she'd had time to ponder her younger sister's last years. Her humiliation at Philippe's hands. Being seduced and abandoned, left alone in a foreign country with a baby to care for. He'd blamed her for that, too.

"Madeleine, are you wanting to see me, or just enjoying the air?" Aristide put his arm gently around her shoulders, touching her as you would a porcelain doll.

"Is it that obvious I'm feeling fragile?" She grasped his fingers and playfully pulled on them. "I'm not made of bone china, you know."

He leaned down and hugged her, gentling her head into the warm space between neck and shoulder which smelt of his soft dark hair and favorite Eau de Cologne. "I know, *ma soeur*, but that doesn't mean we shouldn't take good care of you." He drew her inside. "Did you want to see me?"

"Yes, I did." She followed him into his office and sat down with a sigh. His desk as usual was covered in papers, along with the silver tray bearing a bottle and glasses.

"Is it ever too early in the day for champagne?" Aristide asked. "I think we deserve to celebrate. Unless you consider that in bad taste?"

"Because Philippe is dead? Not at all. It's just . . . It's strange. I don't feel the sense of release or even joy that I thought I would. Sure, I'm relieved it's all over. Glad he'll never threaten any of us again or be a curse in Minette's life as she grows. But if you'd asked me before this happened how I'd feel, I would have said I'd be over the moon." She ruffled her hair distractedly. "I just feel flat. I can hardly pick myself up off the floor. And I'm asking myself all over again, what am I doing with my life?"

She stood up and paced before his desk. "Maybe I should move on. Go to San Francisco and find work. Do something. I feel I've taken too much advantage of your position here. I really need to find my own place."

She searched his face for some sign he understood. He was fingering the cork on a bottle of champagne as she spoke. "I love you to the ends of the earth, you know that, but maybe it's time I stopped relying on my big brother and made a life of my own."

Aristide stared back at her, a slight smile on his face. "That is the silliest thing I have heard anyone say in a long time." He started unwiring the cork. "Not the bit about creating a life for yourself. I entirely agree, and that's just what you're doing." He stopped fiddling with the bottle and gave her his full attention. "Here. With your family, where you belong. As for the idea that you are riding on my coat tails, or even, heaven forbid, outstaying your welcome?" He jumped up from his seat. "*Merde*, Madeleine! We adore having you here. Minette and Graysie would be bereft without you. Not to mention all your stories and games. It's natural to feel a bit let down after so much drama. You need to give yourself time to adjust. But I won't hear of you going anywhere else. And just to underline that, I insist we toast you, us, our future, in champagne. I've got some of our very own Vino d'Oro for us to try."

With a deft flick of thumb and wrist the cork flew upwards with a satisfying pop, and he poured two glasses. He passed one across the desk to her and lifted the other in salute. "To my remarkable sister Madeleine, who has come through the fire and survived — more than survived, she's triumphed — and remained as lovely as ever."

She felt the tears return. The dull, deadened place in her core was melting away like morning mist under sunshine. She laughed and lifted her glass. "Oh, Aristide. You've made me feel better already, before a drop of your amazing vintage has even touched my lips."

They sat talking into the early evening, finishing the champagne and continuing on to warming tiny glasses of port, as she chatted more freely than she ever had before of Philippe and his bitter revenge. "I think he deliberately sought Francine out to get his revenge on me for not coming here with him." She took another tiny sip, feeling warmed and mellow inside. "It makes me so sad to think of sweet Minette being conceived in that kind of hatefulness."

Aristide gestured to a narrow cigarillo he held, unlit, in one hand. He lit it and a cinnamon fragrance filled her nostrils. "You don't know that for sure, Madeleine. He'd have told you anything to hurt you. Francine was a lovely young woman, and we can never know what's really going on in someone's heart. Francine probably saw it all very differently. I'm certain from what Graysie has said she didn't regret having Minette. Not once, not ever."

"Really? Did she tell you that?"

He nodded. "When I first moved here. One of the first times we sat down and had a good chat. She told me how Minette's mother made her promise to take Minette if anything happened. Of course I didn't know then that she was talking about our Francine. But she did say how much Minette was loved and what a tragedy it was when her mother died. You should sit down and have that conversation yourself, now you've got the chance."

"What conversation?" Graysie stood in the doorway, a sleepy-eyed six-year-old hanging off one hip.

"On my goodness." Madeleine jumped up. "Caught out. We've been drinking." She laughed. "And I'm afraid I might be just a little tipsy. Come and sit down." She settled herself on the wooden stool that doubled as a make-shift side table and gestured to the chair.

Graysie sat down and snuggled Minette into her lap. "Little Miss has just woken up and she wanted to know where

Tante Maddy was. And yes, Aristide, you can pour me a glass of the very fine Vino d'Oro port, if you please."

"See?" Aristide beamed. "I think that answers your question about where you belong. Life wouldn't be the same for any of us without you."

"You're not going somewhere?" Graysie's face creased in concern. "Because Pania and I are talking about putting together another show in the spring. I'll definitely need your help here if we're going to do that. And Minette would be heartbroken without you, wouldn't you sweetheart?"

Minette stirred and took her thumb out of her mouth. "What does that feel like? When your heart breaks?"

Madeleine's heart expanded within her, filling her to overflowing. A sweet sense of loss, a needling pain in her ribs, replaced the dull nothingness she'd been feeling so recently. Caleb Stewart's resonant, resolute voice sounded in her head.

"Shoot me if you must but let her go."

Of course he wouldn't feel that way now, not after Philippe's "black widow" warning. Nevertheless, every cell in her body surged with a sudden expectancy, a singing gratitude that she was alive, and she had a future, no matter what had gone before.

"It hurts, sweet baby. It hurts a lot. But it's part of being alive, and it's good."

Epilogue

Easter Sunday, April 17 1870.

They gathered in the welcoming comfort of the Rancho Del Oro family room and watched as Doña Valentina wielded the big carving knife, slicing into the brightly festive Easter cake — *La Mona de Pascua*, Spain's traditional Holy Week dessert, the centerpiece on the big, oak lunch table.

Sir John raised a toast. "To the vines. And to our two families. To quote an ancient Greek: 'Where there is no wine, there is no love.' I think you'd all agree, we're blessed with both."

Caleb, Sir John and Aristide had

tightened their bonds, becoming closer and stronger in the lean months following the trauma of Le Blanc's deadly legacy, using the time at Vino d'Oro to strategize, to expand distribution networks and talk about selecting and planting new grape varieties.

They'd agreed to abstain from alcohol during Lent, so this Easter meal was the first celebration they'd shared in weeks. Caleb felt a sense of anticipation bubbling up from deep within him. Like champagne, he thought with a sudden quick laugh. They were entering a new season — he felt it in his bones.

Bud-burst had seen the grapes flowering into soft, downy, green shoots more than a month ago. They were fast approaching their time of most rapid growth when the main stems would grow one or two inches a day. It made his spirits rise, considering the wonders of nature, but it wasn't just that.

He broke off his musings as he sensed the anticipation around the table intensify. His mother was handing out plates of cake, urging everyone to pass them down the table. He caught Josefa watching him, a soft, loving concern in her dark eyes.

"What?" he mouthed. "Is something wrong?"

She shook her head. "Nothing that isn't easily fixed, dear brother." She leaned over and picked up a plate of chili-rubbed and roasted chicken and handed it to Santiago, who sat beside her and hadn't yet finished his first course. Caleb grinned.

Then again, some things never change.

In the days following Elias's death

he'd had plenty of time to reflect on all that had happened, and to grieve for Rory and Miguel in a way he hadn't been able to do while he was fighting for his life and land. With some nudging from Josefa and Valentina he'd acknowledged he'd been reluctant to share power. He'd been so driven to succeed, to not let his father or his mother down, that he'd carried it all alone. His shoulders were bowed down and his siblings vexed beyond measure. That couldn't, shouldn't go on.

Lying awake in the midnight hours he'd asked himself whether Rory would have died if he'd been more approachable, if they'd talked sooner, if he'd been more considerate of Josefa's talents and needs. He saw clearly that if the family was going to survive in good shape for the next generation, he had to step back and allow his siblings to share a bigger part of the deciding and directing. Only then would they appreciate how much the ranch was earning, and what was needed to steward and harvest that reward. He accepted he needed to delegate more, allow the twins and Josefa to take a bigger part in what was, after all, their inheritance too.

The twins had grabbed the opportunity with enthusiasm, and now spent their days working under Santiago's experienced hand, learning the finer points of raising cattle in this new climate where tough old beef and the occasional hide were not going to feed a family.

He'd spent a lot of his time over at Vino d'Oro, working with Aristide and learning about the art of winemaking, before sitting through long evenings with Sir John. There it was his turn to act as mentor, talking the magnate through the best strategies for wheat and sheep on the parts of his estate that were not suitable for grapes. They discussed other diversifications too, possibly into citrus or other fruit.

The only person in the wider family he'd seen practically nothing of was Madeleine. She seemed to keep herself very busy somewhere else in the house whenever he was around. He couldn't deny he was relieved at the distance they'd maintained. Every time she came into his mind, he felt such a wave of contradictory emotions he preferred to avoid confronting them. Humiliation at the idea that he'd harbored an attraction for her when she was another man's wife — and that she'd withheld that information from him. He heard the explanation — Aristide had explained how Sir John had asked her to keep it quiet — but it seemed a feeble excuse for a blatant deception. And then the accusations Le Blanc had made on that last day — awful claims that she'd never been willing to talk about. His throat contracted painfully.

A piece of the brightly decorated cake arrived at his elbow. It smiled up at him, the chunk of eggy sponge enhanced with yeast, butter and almond flour to add to its deliciousness, finished off with a chocolate glaze and dotted sugared almonds. They looked like nothing as much as pastel bird's eggs in pink and aqua, the most over-the-top confection you could imagine, with a final absurd finishing touch of a bright pink feather. It took him right back to his childhood

when his "godfather" Dougal and Aunt
Dominga had been the ones to make and
present the Easter cake.

He reached for the plate and turned in
happy anticipation to thank the person
delivering it. Madeleine stood there, her
hand trembling as she extended the
plate toward him. He jumped to his feet,
plopping the cake down on the table with
a clumsy thunk as he stood. "Madeleine!
I ..." His vocal cords locked up and he
couldn't get another word out. Even if
he'd had an idea what that word should
be.

He considered the white sponge, the
dark chocolate, the layers of glistening
apricot jam, and had the irrepressible
urge to dip into it. He wiped his index
finger across the face of the cake and it
came up dripping with jam and
chocolate. He sucked his finger, savored

the sweet sugary rush, and then grinned over his shoulder. His voice had returned. "I see you've been given the honor of distributing the cake. That's no small feat. When I was a child it was a much fought-over task!"

Madeleine's sea-green eyes widened in momentary shock, as if she'd steeled herself for rejection. The corners of her mouth crimped up. "Oh no, Caleb. I'm quite undeserving, as you know. But your family and Sir John's have shown me nothing but grace and acceptance ever since I stepped onto these shores." Her voice quavered as she stood before him, holding on, not moving.

"There is so much packed into that statement, Madeleine." Caleb shook his head in mocking disagreement. "So much we wouldn't agree on. It could take us all night to get to the bottom of it." He pushed back his chair from the table so that he was no longer standing with his back half turned to her. Her hands were empty. The cake had apparently all been shared out, and around the table family members were happily tucking in, taking no notice of them. Or purposefully avoiding them.

Aristide was calling for coffee, which Josefa was merrily dispensing. The seat next to him, which had been occupied by Mateo, was suddenly empty. The twins had disappeared outside, no doubt for a game of bochas. "Madeleine, why don't you sit down here? Share my cake. And tell me how it's been going for you. If there's one thing I'm sure of, it's that both of our families are very glad you're here. I know that's the case for Josefa, and I'm pretty sure Graysie would say the same."

Madeleine's eyes seemed to darken to a deeper blue-green as he gazed into them. She slipped into the chair beside him and gave a light silvery laugh. "It's a relief to be talking," she said. "Because I still haven't had a chance to properly say thank you for saving my life."

He caught Josefa's sparkling eyes, one ironically raised eyebrow.

This is your chance, brother. Don't stuff it up.

He raised his brow in ironic response.

I haven't got a clue what you're getting at.

And Josefa laughed, a pealing joyful laugh he hadn't heard from her in a very long time. Even before Rory reappeared in their lives.

Yes. Things are definitely changing for all of us.

Long after the rest of the family dispersed to other pursuits — the menfolk, young and old, to their bowls or port and cigars, Graysie, Pania, and Josefa to tuck in children — Caleb and Madeleine sat side by side at the oak table and talked. It was as if they'd found a safe haven where they could rest and clear the air of the doubts and unspoken accusations. Madeleine was terrified that if they moved, even into another chair, another room, her opportunity to try and explain, to at least earn some forgiveness, would slip away forever.

She had no higher hopes than that. To explain to Caleb why she had kept secrets from him for so long and hope he would understand. Then they could both move on. After the ruin Philippe had wrought, she would always be polluted, spoiled, contaminated, in Caleb's eyes. She understood that, she couldn't expect anything else. She had simply hoped, for the last three months, to find the right time to thank him for his actions on the night Philippe died. He'd been willing to risk his life for hers. He'd come to her rescue. That was monumental, and she didn't want it to go unrecognized. Finding the words to say it all was another matter.

As it was, Caleb got the jump on her. "I'm sure you'd prefer to forget about Philippe's last day, but I have to say to you, you were so brave. Being forced to witness the attack on Tom Halliburton, and then being so horribly threatened yourself. You showed remarkable courage under fire, Madeleine. If you'd been in the army, your commanding officer would have commended you."

His hands rested on the table in front of him, unusually still. She realized he usually gestured as he talked, in sweeping spontaneous movements. An endearing trait, she supposed, from his creative, Spanish soul. But not today. Today he was so Scottish, so trying to be like his father, she imagined, in his steadfastness, his serious-minded commitment to duty.

She ringed the rim of a water glass on the table in front of her, watching her finger circle the top. "I didn't do anything anyone else wouldn't have done. I was just trying to stay alive. But having you there . . . ." Her eyes flicked to his, no longer willing to stay under her control.

His face was lined and weary, and she could see the toll the last few months had taken on him. She felt a surge of hope. "Having you there made all the difference." She was suddenly anxious to get the next sentence out before she lost the courage to speak. "No one has ever, never ever, in my whole life risked their life for me. Caleb, I'm serious. I guess it's a once-in-a lifetime thing. You'd hardly want it to be happening every week." She pulled a wry face. "But now I'm jabbering. Seriously, though, I will never forget that moment as long as I live. Even if you didn't really mean it."

She started laughing, and he joined in. "Well, of course now I'm going to insist that I did mean it. And you're never going to know now, are you? Thankfully it wasn't put to the test." He teased her with his eyes and they both fell silent and serious again.

"I don't want to go all religious on you, Caleb, but I'm sure you know that verse in Romans about 'scarcely would a man die even for a just man.'" She regarded him, her eyes brimming.

"In our French translation it goes something like this: 'For scarce for a just man will one die, yet perhaps for a good man some would dare to die.'" She gave her head a vehement shake. "A good man, or woman. And we both know I am far from a good woman."

After a long, comfortable silence Madeleine said, "Caleb, that last day. Those things that Philippe said. I want to tell you the whole story if you're interested in hearing it." She searched his eyes. "It's extremely painful, but important. I kept secrets because I didn't even want to acknowledge what I'd done to myself. But I see now, I just have to stop running away."

Caleb reached out and stilled her hands, which were twisted in a linen serviette. "It's okay, Madeleine. You don't have to. "

"No, but I want to." She let go of the serviette, and let her hands fall into her lap. "But maybe you should get a coffee refill first. It's going to take a while . . ."

"And so, that's how it all happened. I'll regret it till the day I die the part I played, but you know what? I had no idea Phillipe was going to kill him. He coerced, he tortured me into setting up that meeting so he could implicate me, soil me. He thought it would put me even further under his thumb. It was a horrible thing but Philippe would have killed him whether I'd been there or not. And I did what I knew was right by telling the police everything. Well, nearly everything." She was gazing at her hands, interlocked in front of her.

Caleb reached across and placed one hand lightly on top of her interlocked fingers. His touch was warm and electric, sending a sizzle up her arm, elbow, shoulder.

She continued staring straight ahead, biting her lip to fight back tears. He squeezed her hand gently. "I admit, Madeleine, to have him make those nasty insinuations . . . It rocked me, especially as you didn't deny them. It hit me right at my core. I guess I felt a bit of a fool, too."

She risked a shocked, sidelong peek. "A fool, Caleb? No! That's not you. I never intended—"

"Let me finish. I felt a fool because I knew the strong feelings I had for you. And then the whole 'black widow' thing surfaced again. And I wondered about that old saying 'Love is blind.' Was I just a pathetic blind man, ignoring what was staring me in the face?"

They gazed at one another, their eyes devouring the other's face, not saying a word.

Madeleine released her interlocked fingers and slipped her left hand into Caleb's warmth. "You know, right at the beginning, Sir John asked me not to divulge anything about this man Le Blanc to protect Minette — and I was happy to oblige. But that was a cop-out because really, truly, Caleb? I didn't want to tell you anyway. I couldn't. Because it would mean the end of my own foolish dreams as well. I am just so, so sorry you had to learn the worst of it from Philippe. I would have avoided that at any cost, if I could."

He cupped her face in his two hands, and then ran his thumb along her bottom lip. She held her breath, too shocked by the feeling he invoked to do anything except hold tight. "I may have to say this a few more times before you believe it, but you are not responsible for what your husband chose to do, last week, last year, or last decade." He leaned into her and kissed her lightly on the lips, the briefest brush of butterfly wings. "I don't mind if I have to tell you that a dozen times, Mademoiselle, because I plan to stay close to you for a goodly time. You are not responsible for your husband's mistakes. I'll keep repeating it if need be, until I become a nuisance."

She leaned into his shoulder and breathed in the smell of fresh soap and maleness. "Oh, I think hell will freeze over before that's likely."

And they breathed in their laughter.

THE END

FREE PREVIEW

Hope Redeemed, A Spanish Novella, Book Six, Of Gold & Blood.
She's grieving her intended's death. He's loving her from afar. But will a long-kept secret spoil their chance at everlasting happiness?

Sacramento Valley, 1870. Josefa Stewart yearns to control her own destiny. Pregnant and mourning the murder of her betrothed, she's running out of time to find a suitable husband before she becomes a Californio nobility scandal. But that doesn't mean she'll settle for just any man who comes courting…

Vaquero Santiago Alvarez knows his

growing feelings for Josefa can never be requited. So when his estranged cousin makes a bid for her hand, he takes investigating the up-and-coming attorney's credentials to heart. But Santiago's probe uncovers disturbing secrets about his own family history that could destroy any prospect he ever had for love…

Convinced his cousin's intentions are not fully honorable, Santiago vows to warn Josefa even though he'll sully his own good name. And while the truth forces her to finally notice the handsome man right under her nose, Josefa's pride may doom her to a lonely existence.

Can the unlikely pair shatter boundaries and family traditions to embrace a joyful life together?

Want to read more of Hope Redeemed? The first four chapters are available for FREE Download at https://www.jennywheeler.biz/unbridled-vengeance-free-chapters/

Enjoy this book? You Can Make a Difference

Reviews are the most powerful tools in my kit when it comes to getting my books noticed. Much as I'd love it, I don't have the budget of a big publisher to buy bill board ads and other national advertising. But I have the promise of something more powerful – something publishers envy. And that's a committed and loyal bunch of readers. Honest reviews of my books help them gain the attention of others who might appreciate them too.

Post Your Reviews Here:
For Amazon: https://amzn.to/33t5qZx
For Goodreads: https://bit.ly/2MF3pCF

ACKNOWLEDGMENTS

Thanks are due to so many people for fielding my queries on weird and wonderful minutiae, and I thank you all, too many to mention individually. However, I can't overlook once again the sterling assistance I received from the New Zealand Library Service interloan facility, which enabled me to access hard-to-obtain books from specialist libraries across Australasia. In this regard, I'm especially indebted to the services of CJ Simmons, Interloan & Information Supply Librarian – Research, Heritage & Central Library, Libraries and Information - Ngā Whare Mātauranga o Tāmaki Makaurau.

At the Center for Sacramento History. archivist Kim Hayden was kind enough to direct my attention to a book which became my "Bible" when checking facts relating to daily life in 1870. History of Sacramento County, With Illustrations, by Thompson & West, 1880, is a coffee-table-sized tome filled with remarkable detail and entrancing black and white engravings which bring the period alive. It's become one of my personal treasures.

I'm so grateful for the support group who continue to act as my sounding board, giving me feedback on possible titles and covers and acting as cheer leaders for my work. Everyone needs this kind of encouragement, and I count myself especially fortunate in my readers and advocates.

I've once again been in exceptionally safe hands in the editing and proof reading process, with Stephen Stratford in charge of developmental and final edits, and fellow mystery author Nikki Crutchley of proof reading. Both of them picked up on a myriad of mistakes and inconsistencies which we have tried to amend. As ever, any that escaped our net are my fault entirely.

Formatting of this volume in the series was done once again with alacrity and wonderful attention to detail by Jason and Marina at Polgarus Studio in Tasmania. You are my author champions!

Publishing books is such a team activity, and I honestly could not have got any further than producing a raw MS without the assistance I've received. I can't thank you all enough. I'm busy working on Book Seven, so I'm not planning to go away anywhere, and I look forward to the continued opportunity to work with you all.

ABOUT THE AUTHOR

Jenny Wheeler is the author of the Of Gold & Blood Old California mystery series:

Poisoned Legacy #1.
Brother Betrayed #2.
Double Jeopardy #3.
Tangled Destiny (Christmas novella and Prequel.) #4
Unbridled Vengeance #5
Hope Redeemed, A Spanish Novella, #Six
Boxed Set/Book Bundle Of Gold & Blood, Books 1 – 3.

Jenny's online home is at jennywheeler.biz or email Jenny@jennywheeler.biz

You can connect with Jenny on:

Facebook: @JennyWheeler.Biz

Twitter: @Jenny_Biz

Instagram: @jennysbingereading

Pinterest pinterest.nz/Jennywheelerbooks

Goodreads: goodreads.com/author/show/11371547.Jenny_Wheeler

Bookbub: bookbub.com/profile/jenny-wheeler